Also by Scott Alexander

The Dracula Illusion

The Battle For Boxer

I Like You Too, Adam Strange

Wraith's Hollow

Scott Alexander

ISBNs:

Paperback: 978-1-0683255-2-6
Ebook: 978-1-0683255-3-3

Chapter One

The Island

Wraith's Hollow. A perfect place for murder.

Ever since the first inhabitants began carving out a life on the island, many have spoken of their devotion to their home. They could never imagine a life beyond the rugged yet forgiving cliffs to the west, or the golden sands of the beaches to the east. They could not conceive of a more beautifully gothic forest to the north, where the tree limbs posed by day and contorted by night. And that moorland to the south – well, they knew they were lucky to behold such rich earth.

It's not quite correct to speak of the wind as a character but it is perhaps best to think of it as being one. From the first dwellers right up to the present, the wind has accompanied them, day by day and night by night. The fishermen out at sea; the workers running the tourist shops and supermarkets, and the staff at the one and only pub; the children walking up School Lane at the beginning of the day and down it at the end; the coastguards, firemen, and police navigating through and round the island; all have their feelings about the wind. Because, though no one would admit it, the wind can be a beast at times. The wind, when it howls over the stone cottages and scrapes over the town's cobblestones, brings with it the full force of the weather's biting chill – even in the warmer months.

A peculiar thing happened last year. A stunning spring morning transformed into the most awful howling wind and storm they'd ever seen – or had seen, at least, for a very long time. The warmth of the morning sun quickly gave way to a gale that gathered speed across the ocean, ripping through the sailing boats, then drenching them in a fog so dense that one resident believed they saw the outlines not of real boats but of ghost ships. The crashing ocean could be heard by the few that were still out on the streets. All those who peered out of their windows – almost everyone with a few exceptions such as old Father Hemmingway who had seen this sort of thing before – saw their peaceful island captured by a perfect storm.

One of the reasons most thought it peculiar was that no one had felt that there was a storm coming. But those in the know, such as the small group who met in Hollowspire Church – Father Hemmingway none the wiser – on the night of the storm understood that it was caused by Veritas in a vengeful rage.

But what could be done to placate Veritas? It was as one of them stepped forward into the middle of the circle – meeting a breath of wind that caused their candle flame to snuff out – that the ideal way to remove the cancer from their beautiful island presented itself.

That night, they all slept soundly.

Chapter Two

The Inhabitants

Mrs. Appleby

A fine Saturday morning. Mrs. Appleby placed her hand on the garden gate. The wood, rough and old, swelling and rotting, both practical and strangely beautiful, and most definitely made of the tough stuff from the good old days, felt good against the skin of her palm.

Good morning, George.

She brushed her hand over the hinge – the rust and chipped, what was it, acrylic paint? – were a little rough. For some reason, though she had many other things inside the house to remember George by, it was the old gate at the end of the front garden path that was the one thing she visited when she needed to feel near to George. Of course, it still functioned as a gate, and there were times when Mrs. Appleby would stroll right through, in the way that one could only do at eighty, and only give George the slightest thought. But she never went past without thinking of him.

Today, nearly a year since George died in that horrible way – poor soul, he had years left in him – she allowed her hand to rest for a little longer than she normally would. If she was honest, standing there, as she had done so for many years – God the years fly by! – was not as easy as it used to be. But, be strong for dear George.

Mrs. Appleby looked down at the name on the gate, Hollow Crest. It really needed titivating – or replacing altogether. Perhaps Tim could do it, he was handy, had done some work on her cottage before. Trustworthy. Honest. The kind of man Wraith's Hollow needed.

The sea was seen easily from her vantage point. Hollow Crest was one of the older houses and was located high up on the island. Getting around was difficult at times, as coming home always meant the tough climb up Wraithmoore Lane. Cobblestones, when you are young, are full of character and charm, but when eighty-one is right on your doorstep, they are difficult and treacherous. But, we press on, don't we George.

The sea was calm and the light reflecting off the surface was kind to Mrs. Appleby's old yet still vibrant blue eyes. From where she stood, facing east, she could see Tide Fall Beach down the way with the sailing boats on the water that looked so tiny. It was a view of which she would never tire. She had many lovely memories of walking along High Cliff Point – unofficially renamed by the locals as Ghost Cliff Point; why and when this happened, Mrs. Appleby didn't remember. It was a silly name. She could also easily bring to mind those lovely days walking with George through Wraith Forest, spotting the bluebells that flourished there year in and year out. But, of all the delights that Wraith's Hollow had to offer, Tide Fall Beach was the place where her heart truly belonged.

Mrs. Appleby had it in mind, before coming out to George, to do something in the garden but couldn't remember what it was. Never mind – if it was important, it would come to her.

Just as she was about to turn back inside, a car rumbling slowly down the cobblestone street caught her attention. She knew the red car and driver very well. It was Martin Howler: the man who lived in that monstrosity up the hill and whom she despised. Martin Howler and that dreadful car were the reasons her George was no longer with her. Mrs. Appleby could still see in her unforgiving mind's eye, her husband dead, limbs twisted, face bloodied, across the street by the bank. He'd been run down like, like, like . . . God, she gripped the gate with her arthritic hand and snapped a chunk of rotting wood off and then crushed it between her fingers.

Martin Howler slowed enough so he could wave to Mrs. Appleby. She turned as though she didn't realise it was him.

Nathan Waters

Nathan Waters stepped to the window quickly and pressed his telescope uncomfortably against his eye, tracking Ellie Crick jogging along the promenade of Tide Fall Beach. From his converted lighthouse he'd aptly named *The Tide Watcher*, he could easily see all of his beloved beach, and – though there was no way he'd ever admit his feelings to her – he could see his beloved on the beach every morning when she went for a run. Sometimes she would be running faster than normal, other times she'd be walking. Spotting either of these states worried him. As a marine biologist, he was used to tuning into the minute changes of behaviour in the sea life he studied – so he could easily see that when Ellie wasn't jogging at her usual pace, something was wrong.

Thankfully, this Saturday morning, everything with Ellie was fine: she looked good, comfortable – must've had a good night's sleep. She looked ready for the world. She looked ready for her long climb up Wraithmoore Lane too – which she usually did, every run.

Placing his telescope down on the small, half-moon table by the window, Nathan went to the kitchen to make a coffee. He returned to sit at the table – placing his cup next to the model lighthouse. Perfectly painted, every attention to detail taken care of – though there was a very annoying chip in the red dome roof of the lantern room. It really needed attention, but not now.

Things weren't as good as they could be.

That morning, not all that long before seeing Ellie along the beach, he had had an important but unfortunately fraught conversation with Martin Howler. Nathan knew he could catch Martin early, before Martin left for work on whatever next wrecking-ball-business-venture he had planned. But speaking with him early also meant he would get an irritated Martin Howler. Nathan, though, was equally irritated by Martin's selfish attitude towards everyone and the island.

Disagreement had been a feature of their relationship

over the years, and the reason for it could be explained in the following manner: Martin Howler was a businessman whose focus was to develop anything and everything just to make a few quid whereas Nathan Waters was a preserver. Preserver of the local seas and land and all the life that inhabited them. Martin had no empathy whereas Nathan had too much. Martin didn't give a damn about the special and unique biodiversity around Wraith's Hollow whereas Nathan could not see anything more important than dedicating himself to developing an understanding of it. Especially the recent growth of the mysterious fungus which seemed to be spreading over the island. Right now, Martin didn't care. Right now, Nathan had no idea how and why it was there; but, through analysing it, he was determined to find out. He'd already begun running tests the moment he saw it.

Ignorant. Totally ignorant, Nathan thought as he took a small sip of hot coffee. We don't need people like him here. This island will be ruined because of him: he's not going to build another single bullshit luxury flat as long as I'm here. Even if it kills me.

Ellie Crick

Jogging helped. It really did. Got the brain thinking, sorting and sifting. Uphill was hard going – it fried the quads and calves but giving in was not an option. Never. Ellie had jogged most of her route round Wraith's Hollow. It was a good five miles and, although she'd been running it for most of her life – except when she moved away to study Business at university – she never tired of it. Because of the twisty nature – through different roads, alongside the beach, over the old cobblestones near the forest – it meant there were times when she felt the warmth of the spring morning sun on her face and times when she felt it across her back and shoulders.

Jogging was for the mind as much as it was for fitness. It was an act of taking control, of doing something positive, in the face of all those things you couldn't control. Business was like that. Lots of things you could take charge of but there were also many that, as an entrepreneur, you just couldn't. It came down to people – they were usually the ones you couldn't control.

It was at this point, when Ellie was both climbing up Wraithmoore Lane and thinking about people's fickleness in business, feeling the burn in her calves, that she saw Martin Howler's car creep slowly by. The sight of his smiling face was all she needed to make her dig deep and grind harder, smacking and slapping the stones with the soles of her trainers. Even the sight of Mrs. Appleby struggling slowly up the garden path did nothing to stamp out the anger she felt.

Tim Thorn

Every island needed someone who could fix anything – or, at the very least, have the right connections to pull in those who could lend a hand when the job was too big for one man. And Tim Thorn was that man. Wraith's Hollow's handyman – though he didn't like the term handyman as it reminded him of someone less professional than he was, reminded him of the useless jack-of-all-trades type. He was about as far from that as you could possibly get. Proud of his workmanship, as robust as his hammer, sharper than his saw. It didn't matter whether he was fitting a kitchen or building a whole house, he put his heart and soul into everything. As a lifelong islander, Tim had worked on most, if not all, the different properties around. He was proud to have contributed to the smooth running of Wraith's Hollow; proud to have restored houses and shops after the weather had given them its best; proud that his father had given him his skills which Tim would proudly pass on to Little Liam – not, unfortunately, his son, but a young apprentice who Tim had come to like over the last year or so.

Tim stood in the doorway of his workshop facing the morning sun. The warmth was magic on his face, and it worked wonders on his left shoulder as he rolled it towards the sky to loosen it up. Being in his late fifties with a life outside climbing onto roofs, up and down ladders, working on his knees all day fitting carpets, was taking its toll. But in that moment, before Martin Howler arrived, Tim Thorn was a man enjoying life.

He swigged his tea, wished to have a ciggy but fought hard against having one. Three months since having had his last one and soon it would be four. He never understood why he'd started smoking them years back – certainly wasn't stress related. Whilst living on Wraith's

Hollow had its issues here and there, all in all it was the best place to live. Tim had been to many different cities over the years – Europe, bit of a culture vulture – and he'd swum many seas on his hols, but coming home was always the best part. The island had its few bad apples, but most folk were golden. The old-fashioned kind of golden. It did have one rotten apple, the kind that would ruin the whole batch of cider: Martin Howler. The more work Tim did for him, like the bookcase he was putting together in the workshop now, the more he disliked the man. Tim knew the bookcase wasn't the real reason why Martin was on his way over that morning. No. Tim Thorn had seen something at Martin's house that he really shouldn't have. It had shocked the hell out of him, and he didn't know if it was true or not.

But as long as he kept his cool, he had Martin where he wanted him.

Jasper Flint

Just a fisherman. Bastard! Martin Howler hadn't changed since school. Always a stuck-up prick.

Jasper Flint, known as Jax around Wraith's Hollow, placed his pliers on the grass. He stood up and leaned against Martin Howler's boat. The morning sun felt good on his achy neck. Fixing boats wasn't the most comfortable job, but he loved it. It was a good second income alongside his main job fishing.

Jax's last exchange with Martin wasn't great. Some

home truths were dealt. Martin had made it crystal clear in the pub last night how he felt. Just a fisherman! That stung Jax a fair bit. But he'd always known Martin looked down on him. This was the last job he'd ever do for Martin – all these years and nothing to show for it. Jax even started to hate the boat he was fixing.

Martin was no friend – hadn't been for a long time. Jax didn't want friends like that. He liked people like himself: salt of the earth types. People with good hearts.

He lit a cigarette. Their argument had started because, having worked on the damaged hull of the boat earlier that day, Jax told Martin someone could've damaged his boat on purpose. The marks were unusual – not the kind you'd normally see. This sent Martin down the road of claiming no one would dare do that to him. The usual crowd in the Ram's Head got the gist of it and were especially aware of what Martin said next: you keep your ignorant ideas to yourself. In fact, why would I listen to you, you're just a fucking fisherman! Keep to your station. The next part, however, was for Jax's ears only. And so, when Martin stepped towards him – nearly spilling his pint in the process – he got so close he could whisper in Jax's ear: remember, I know what you did all those years ago and unless you want everyone here to know, I'd keep my mouth shut if I were you.

Jax puffed away for a few short minutes. Should he move away from Wraith's Hollow? He wasn't sure. It was changing, that was for certain. But that was down to Martin. He wanted the upper crust types to live on the island – they were the only ones rich enough to afford the houses and flats he kept building. Martin was obsessed with denying his background, his working-class roots – so much so that he wanted to rid the island of normal folk, Jax was convinced of it. Jax was proud of where he came from. Funny, he and Martin grew up on the same street, but unlike Jax, Martin had forgotten that.

Flicking the cigarette butt to the grass, Jax picked his pliers up. He looked at the damage to the boat; he had a morning's work to do. Cut away the damaged sections of fiberglass without screwing more of it up – something he'd love to do! – smooth it out, sort the trimming, sand, clean and prep, apply the fiberglass cloth and resin. Final inspection. And try to realign the prop shaft – Martin wasn't prepared to buy a new one. Tight bastard.

As he was making the final inspection on the outside, he noticed, towards the stern of the boat, an unusual patch of mould. Just one. Quite large. Strange and a bit slimy to the touch. It looked a bit like that weird thing growing on the island, but Jax wasn't sure if it was the same thing. He was sure, though, that it pulsed when he tried scraping it off. What was it? The colour. Like a rainbow. He couldn't think of the term. But he knew a man who could.

Sophie Marlow

Another one nearly finished. Another one dedicated to Cynthia, her sister. Not that Sophie would ever make the dedication explicit to the client buying the painting – it was more a personal honouring of Cynthia's memory. God, she missed her.

The final dabs of oil paint on the canvas are often the most tense. It's very easy to overdo things. Adding too much of one final colour can dominate the painting and change its meaning. But Sophie felt confident that adding the final flicks and flecks of sky blue across the sea and cliffs would harmonise the composition.

Yes! That was perfect.

Placing her brush down next to her cold cup of tea, she stepped back and took a satisfied breath. She felt this painting was the closest she had ever been to Cynthia. Ghost Cliff Point where she was murdered all of those years ago – it wasn't an accident like they said! – was vividly depicted. The cliff seamlessly joined the sky above and the sea below. The rocky face bloomed with yellows, blues, purples, and greens, all rendered in dots and lines that knew no bounds. They flew this way and that like a starling murmuration. The sea was calm and mirrored the calmness of the sky above and their rich blues invited, no willed, the viewer to introspection.

Sophie was delighted. The painting was big, colourful, bright. She'd managed to capture the morning sun – like that of the spring morning enveloping her in that moment. It reflected Cynthia's happy side, her bright side. The Cynthia before her addiction to drugs and alcohol – before her addiction to Rowan Black. When she was under the spell of both – she was so lost. It hurt Sophie to remember the things she did but there was nothing she could do about that. What could she do? How could she remove the memories – any memories – of her sister from her mind?

The conversation she had with Martin yesterday morning swirled into her consciousness as she swirled the brush in the jar of water. She had never seen him so aggressive. The moment she told him she didn't want his gift of an art studio up on the cliffs, he turned. It wasn't because it was too much – though an art studio built just for her was immense – it was because he wanted to build it where Cynthia had taken her last steps on Wraith's Hollow. How could she paint happily knowing that whenever she looked out of the window, she would see Cynthia's ghost walking by the cliff edge? How could she accept an art studio – even if it would be beautiful and made mostly from glass – and have yet another building on the landscape she loved to paint? The land and seas were her life – she had no one else. She painted them as though they were portraits of people – all with complicated backgrounds and lives. Sophie knew more flats were coming near the cliffs to the west and near Tide Fall Beach to the east. That she couldn't change. But she didn't want to play a part in any of it.

If you don't want it, then that's up to you! I'm trying to help you move on, Sophie. You need to get over your fucking dead sister! It's been fucking years!

No, Sophie was certain that cutting ties with a man like Martin Howler was the best thing to do. He was evil.

Martin Howler

Martin Howler woke early. A little earlier than normal: 06:25 was the time on his phone display. He squinted his eyes at the bright screen and, rather than dimming the brightness, he pushed through the sensitivity and scrolled through the news. All rubbish.

He rolled out of bed and pulled back the curtains. April mornings on Wraith's Hollow were some of Martin's favourites across the year. The idea that the sun was beating back winter, day by day, attacking the cold, was never far from his mind. It was like a competition: the weather in a continuous battle, each season triumphing over the last.

He stood there naked, smoothing his thumbs over recently manicured nails, looking over Wraith's Hollow from his position high up on Wraithmoore Lane. He sucked in a deep breath of satisfaction: he'd conquered everything life had chucked at him.

He'd met every challenge with passion and finesse – though he knew others saw him as overzealous and fussy. And argumentative – he'd allow them that. But . . . to hell with them!

Martin's business sense and achievements (and bank balance) were enough to make him impervious to any criticism. Nothing would change his views: it'd taken him forty-five years to figure things out – why would he let someone change his mind now? About anything.

Facing east, he looked directly into the rising sun as its reflection dominated the sea beneath it. A triumph of nature. Couldn't paint it better. That bitch, Sophie, could learn a thing or two from Mother Nature. But her ego wouldn't allow it. Martin had, at one time, found Sophie quite attractive. Her long dark hair, brown eyes, and cute figure used to be enough to get him going.

But she always argued with him, just like yesterday morning when he went round to her place. That and her obsession with her dead sister was a turn off. She was fiery, but she'd misunderstood his intention yesterday. All he had said was, you need to get over Cynthia, Sophie, move on – it will help you. But she just flipped. Maybe it was all that talk before about building a new studio up on the cliffs. Why wouldn't she accept his offer? Stupid bitch. No one else would be that generous. The art studio wasn't what she thought: it wasn't just about building over where Cynthia died. It was his way to commemorate her life.

But somewhere along the line, his intention got lost in translation. Now she hated him.

What the hell. Life is short. He was going to do what he liked when he liked.

He continued with his morning routine. Shower, breakfast – poached eggs on toast with avocado – then he changed into his Tom Ford suit. Slim fit, navy, one-hundred percent wool, silk lined, accompanied by a light grey shirt and a metallic silk tie. The suit was crucial to Martin's life as a businessman. It signalled his wealth and influence to everyone around him. Even these backward islanders, who wouldn't know the difference between a Tom Ford and a suit from George, understood his wealth and power.

As he was slipping into his leather shoes – midnight-blue, plain-toe Oxford, from Ferragamo – feeling like a million dollars, his phone rang. Nathan bloody Waters.

"Yes, Mr. Lighthouse," he said at the phone.

"Martin, I could do without the sarcasm. I want to talk to you quickly. I know you're a busy man–"

"That I am. Look, I already know where this conversation's going. The answer's no. I don't give a damn about how many locals you get to sign your petition. I'm building all over Wraith's Hollow and that's that, Dr. Fish."

"Can't you see the damage you're doing? We have unique marine life here, plants *and* fish – then there's that fungus. I need more time to study it, Martin. It's invasive. Growing uncontrollably. It's my duty to study it."

"And I have a duty to show off our island to the world. Do you realise the potential here? No. Of course you don't. I wouldn't expect you to!"

"Please, Martin. Just give me some more time. This fungus could be crucial. I haven't seen anything like it."

"I'm afraid the deal's done. I'm buying the land. The Island Trust's pushing the paperwork through. There's only one thing we can do with a fungus like that – remove it. Destroy it. You said yourself, it's invasive."

"But that's why I need time, Martin! We need to understand how it's going to affect our ecosystem. It could affect our waters, the soil, the plant life – we just don't know yet!"

"The sooner it's destroyed and the sooner I start building over where it lived – the better."

"That's not how it works. You know it's been spotted in other places around the island, don't you?"

"Look, I haven't got time for this. Was there anything else, Water Boy?"

"Yes, actually, there is." There was a pause. Then: "If you don't hold off until I've studied the fungus on your site, I'll let everyone know on this island what you did to Ellie, you prick. Bit of–"

Martin ended the call. He had no desire to dignify Nathan's statement with a response of his own. He slipped his wrist into his Rolex and, once again, felt like a million, maybe twenty-five million, dollars. He loved life.

*

Martin checked his phone as he sat in his BMW. A message from Jax: Your boat will be done today. Then no more.

Martin wasn't bothered. If he needed someone else to fix his boat, he could easily get someone else. He didn't have to do Jax a favour by employing him. A little cash in hand. Martin had done that for years for his old school friend. But not anymore. Jax fucking pissed him off last night in the pub. Speculating like an idiot that someone damaged his boat on purpose . . . to what purpose? There wasn't one. Even if there was, no one round here would even fucking dare.

Martin was above all of them. And he knew, even if they hated him, despised him, they still respected him. He was the one bringing Wraith's Hollow kicking and screaming into the twenty-first century. Yes, he was lining his own pockets, but some cash would trickle down.

Starting his engine, Martin smiled at the thought of reminding Jax that he knew what Jax did to Cynthia all of them years back. Shut the little prick up.

*

Reversing out of his driveway, seeing the garage door closing automatically, Martin felt wonderful. He had that feeling of . . . what was the word, insouciance. Yes, that was it. Of true peace. Carefree.

Rolling down the hill, he soon got to Mrs. Appleby's place. He could see her in the front garden. He waved but she turned, pretending not to see him. She was still angry. A year on roughly, and she was still holding him responsible. Martin had apologised, sent flowers, gifts – everything you thought necessary in situations like that. He even offered to pay for her to go on holiday. But she'd declined.

She hated him.

But what could he do? The whole episode was deemed to have been an accident, an unfortunate accident. The sun was low, obscuring his view, and George just stepped into the road without looking. But Mrs. Appleby would never see it like that.

The sight of Ellie jogging by distracted him from replaying the whole, unfortunate incident in his mind. God, she was struggling up Wraithmoore Lane. It was a bastard of a hill. Why in the hell anybody saw it necessary to go jogging about like that, Martin had no idea.

He smiled at her. It was a beautiful, condescending smile. Never would he go into business with her again. She was a mess. And, despite what Nathan thought he knew, Martin would never do that to her. He was not a prick!

*

The town of Wraith's Hollow was small, and that meant there were only a few car parks dotted around. Martin didn't bother going to any of them. He parked on double yellow lines outside of Tim's workshop on Hollowbrook Lane. He shut his car door and said to Tim, who was standing in the doorway, "Beautiful morning, wouldn't you say? Perfect for a coffee and a cigarette!"

"You know I've stopped, thank you very much. Nothing will tempt me to have another – not even a beautiful morning like this. And I'm drinking tea, not coffee."

"Well. I want a coffee," Martin said. "Send Little Liam to Diane's for me. Double espresso. Tell him he can get whatever he wants."

Tim did as requested, and so did Little Liam. Little Liam handed over Martin's drink and asked Tim if he could take a short break.

"Liam, I get the feeling you don't want to be around me," Martin said.

Liam went red.

"Go on, Liam. Go for a walk," Tim said – giving him the excuse he needed to leave.

Sipping his coffee, Martin smoothed his free hand over the bookcase Tim was fixing together. He stepped back and delayed his response. He knew Tim would be waiting for his approval.

Having squeezed the silence to an almost insufferable tension, Martin said: "On second thought, I think I do want the gothic style doors . . . but well done, Tim. Do they all rotate?"

"Of course, each tier rotates and has adjustable shelves – readymade for those compartments you want off show, so to speak."

Martin nodded. "That's between you and me. No one else. Are we clear about that?"

Tim nodded and stayed silent.

Martin stepped back to view the bookcase. If his suit was an extension of his wealth and power, the bookcase, standing eight feet tall, was an extension of his class and sophistication. Tim had really worked wonders on it. It was beautiful. Three-tiers laid out perfectly, housed by a frame of intricately carved wood, finished with a deep, lustrous wax. Full of old-world charm – not something about which Martin would ordinarily be bothered. Beautiful! It was a repository for stories as old as man and his many secrets.

"I like it. When will it be installed?"

"I have the other doors – didn't get rid of them since you changed your mind last time. I can have them on and everything else sorted by the end of the day. Install on Monday."

"I want it in my study upstairs by the end of the day.

Please ring when you're on your way."

"I'm sorry, Martin. But that's a stretch too far. Liam finishes early today – it's not fair to make him stay on, especially on Saturday."

"Well, I'm sorry but life isn't fair. He needs to be taught the ways of the world. They have too much, too soon, and we all have to bend over backwards for the little darlings. Not me. And you shouldn't either. If you want paying, you'll do what I want. It's your choice whether your apprentice helps you or not." As Martin got to the door, he turned to face Tim and said: "Oh yes. About what you think you saw at my house the other day. I don't actually think you saw anything at all, did you?"

"Don't threaten me, Martin," Tim said as he walked towards him.

Martin closed the gap, his nose nearly touched Tim's. "Tim. I could fuck you up in a second. Don't give me a reason to. And put the hammer down, you fool."

Tim looked down at the hammer in his hand. It was as if he didn't know it was there.

"I know what I saw," Tim said. "I don't understand it, but I know."

"Care to elaborate?"

"Something about brain implants – computer chips or something."

"Well, what a little Miss Marple you are. But if you can't explain what you saw – because that sounds pretty vague to me – how do you know what you saw?"

"I know what I saw!"

Martin grabbed Tim's throat, but Tim was stronger

than Martin thought. Tim threw him off, pushed him and stepped back.

Martin laughed. "I was only joking with you." He stepped to the door. "Just get my bookcase delivered and installed by the end of today."

Each called the other a prick under their breaths such that the other heard but chose not to react further.

Chapter Three

The Boat and the Body

The boat and the body, by sheer coincidence, were found at exactly the same time Thursday morning. Ellie Crick was out earlier than normal on her morning run and Nathan was out walking by the rocks, just along the coastline from her. It was remarkable that Nathan had missed the body on the sand, but he was too focused on hunting the fungus. Ellie also would have missed it had it not been for the fact that she had taken a moment to pause and catch her breath. After a few deep breaths, Ellie noticed something unusual along Tide Fall Beach, catching the low-angled rays of the rising sun. She paced quickly towards it, feeling with each step that she was about to see something awful. The same foreboding feeling struck Nathan as he advanced over the rocky terrain towards the boat wedged between the rocks.

They both, at exactly, three minutes past six, said: "Martin."

Ellie Crick

Ellie's hand flew to her mouth. There was blood was all over Martin's body. He was in a strange position – flat on his back, his arms outstretched like a cross.

People don't fall like that! Someone put him in that position!

Something was carved into his chest, but Ellie couldn't tell what it was. There was something round his neck and, as Ellie crouched, she saw something in his mouth. She grabbed a nearby stick and tried pressing it against Martin's lower lip to open his mouth, but her fingers were trembling and the stick dropped free.

It was awful. She stood up; started laughing. Her uncontrollable laughter gave way to a strange dreamlike state in which she felt oddly relieved at seeing Martin dead on the beach – the same beach she used to run along as a child. It occurred to her that, as a child, she had probably run right across that very spot where Martin had been . . . what, murdered?

Was it murder? It bloody looked like it!

She looked at the open sea and took the deepest breath she ever had; then looked at Martin again; then back to the horizon . . . it was relief she felt. Seeing him there powerless even brought a taste of satisfaction. She checked her watch and rang the police, the thought of how much she hated him running through her mind.

Nathan Waters

Nathan recognised Martin's boat straight away. Especially as Jax had taken him to see it Sunday night to inspect the fungal growth underneath. Nathan knew he was right! Martin would not listen. The fungus was invasive: surviving in submerged, saltwater conditions, clinging to the surrounding rocks, and spreading on land. It was possible it was some strange hybrid species with resilient spores. The fungus spores could be carried through the air, water, even by animals. Who knew what it could be about! Jax had told Nathan that after he touched the fungus, he had strange visions and dreams and woke up in the night feeling sick.

Nothing like this had happened to Nathan yet, though he hadn't touched it with his bare skin, and he would never test it without protecting himself. Since Sunday night's investigation, he had begun running more growth and environmental tests on the fungus at his field station not far from the coast. After Jax's experience, Nathan wanted to look at the psychoactive compounds of the fungus.

The boat was deserted, its hull battered and splintered, as if it had been abandoned for weeks, endlessly pummelled against the rocks by the tide. But the sea had been calm – every time Nathan had looked out across the ocean from his lighthouse the water was still.

Nathan swung himself over the side of the boat, his shoes sinking into the cold water as it sloshed against his legs. He scanned quickly, searching for any sign of

Martin's body – not knowing what the hell he'd do if he saw it. He peered into the cabin. Sheets of paper floating on the water. He was about to turn away but a stain on the back rest of the bench caught his attention. There wasn't just one red mark; there were lots of them.

His pulse quickened – it was blood. There were no signs of a struggle, but had Martin been injured and then left? Nathan grabbed a rag from the corner and worked hard at cleaning the blood off. It was difficult. He was petrified someone would see him – but he had to clean it off. There could be no traces left.

When he got home, he dried out the cloth and set fire to it.

Chapter Four

The Letter and Welcome back to Wraith's Hollow

Rowan Black

Thursday morning. Eight-fifteen.

Rowan had left home early to catch the ferry and visit Martin Howler on Wraith's Hollow, but a phone call from DCI Hargrave had informed him that Martin had been found dead on Tide Fall Beach. "It's definitely Martin Howler. Visual ID confirmed by local officers. Rowan, you know the island. You know the people. And you've got Martin's letter – it might be our only lead. Find out what happened."

Rowan didn't know what to make of the news. If only he'd opened the letter yesterday when he received it at the station instead of putting it down and forgetting about it, he might have been able to save Martin's life. His team had had a sudden lead in a robbery investigation, keeping him at the station on the mainland until late in the evening. By the time he'd finished the paperwork and coordinated with everyone, the last ferry was long gone. It was too late to go anywhere when he read Martin's letter at home last night.

The reported condition of the body was bizarre. Laid out in a cross position with strange symbols, something in his mouth – all pointed to a ritualistic murder. Rowan had been a detective for years, and he'd never come across a case like this before.

"It's not wise jumping to any conclusions about it being ritualistic or sacrificial just yet, Rowan. Keep me informed," DCI Hargrave had warned.

The boat cut through the water at a good pace. Rowan walked towards the cabin where Reg Harris sat at the wheel. Rowan had grown up on Wraith's Hollow and had known Reg for years – he'd been the island's ferryman for decades.

"You know who I reckon it is," Reg said. "I reckon it's Martin Howler. You remember him – arrogant prick."

Rowan had known Martin since he was child; being a few years older than him, Rowan knew what Martin was like growing up. He was arrogant – a bully, and a bit of a prick. His arrogance and aggression grew in tandem with his age.

"I'm here professionally, Reg. Can't divulge any information. You'll hear the news soon enough. Surprised you haven't already. There's no such thing as a secret on Wraith's Hollow."

"You know it! But I've been on the mainland since my first trip this morning. I only heard that someone had been murdered just before I left. I saw Martin's boat on my way out. It was up on the rocks – looked abandoned to me." Reg shook his head. "Murder! Awful."

The boat on the rocks – that was new information.

Rowan wrote it down in his notebook.

"Did you call it in, Reg?"

"No, I'd sooner tell Sergeant Jennings in person." Reg eased back on the throttle; eyes fixed on the sea ahead. "How long you been away from the island, Rowan?"

"About fifteen years."

"You been in the police since?"

"For my sins."

"What are you now? Heard you went into being a detective a number o' years back," Reg said.

"Detective Inspector."

"Tough job. I'd rather be out on the open sea, thank you very much."

Rowan agreed. "Have you seen anyone suspicious, different on the ferry? Or anyone unusual hanging about the terminal?"

"No, sir, I know everyone on my boat."

"Well, if you think of anything, come and find me," Rowan said and went to the front of the boat. The air was salty. He pulled the letter from his pocket and opened it up. His eyes scanned the lines: *Please help me, Rowan. You're the only one I can trust.* And: *My life is in danger. You've got to help me! I have to tell you in person.*

The writing was neat and even, not one letter looked as though it was written by someone in distress. And there was the obvious question of why Martin would write a letter? An email, maybe. A phone call would've been better. Would've been faster. Martin was all about progression, development, advancement. The idea that he would sit down and write a letter didn't feel right to

Rowan. But none of this did. The body, the letter . . . guilt lapped at his conscience.

Rowan shoved the letter back in his pocket and held onto the rails. He never liked Martin, but he wished he'd looked at the letter earlier yesterday. Would he have responded if he had? Would he have drawn some ridiculous conclusion like it was a joke – Martin's way of reaching out to an old pal (Martin would never have thought that Rowan didn't like him, Rowan never made it obvious to him)?

Wraith's Hollow was looming – he estimated about another three minutes and then he'd be setting foot back on Havenmoore Port. Despite the memories he had colouring his perception of the island and the current circumstances of the dead body, Wraith's Hollow looked idyllic: the church, the beach, the lighthouse with the red dome roof reflecting the sun, the faintest wisps of morning mist that seemed to disappear in the blink of an eye, Wraith Forest in the distance, and the stone cottages dotted here and there. Rowan, if only for a moment, allowed himself to indulge in that nostalgic feeling everyone has when returning to their childhood home. It was only a moment because the reality that his parents were no longer alive on the island hit him hard. The feeling sent a sharp pang of guilt through him: guilt because he hadn't been in contact with Stacey, his sister who lived in Northamptonshire, for some time. He must do better.

The island ferry began bearing towards Havenmoore Port, and more of Tide Fall Beach came into view. Local police held back the large crowd gathered around where, no doubt, the body laid. Rowan couldn't see much of anything else. SOCO weren't there yet – they'd be arriving just after him via the police boat.

As Reg continued towards the port, they passed Martin's boat on the rocks. A team from the marine unit had just arrived – pulling on dry suits, ready to inspect the wreck. Someone had already called it in then. Reg was saying something to him, while other passengers were talking around him, pointing out the obvious. But Rowan's attention stayed fixed on the wreck: he'd get SOCO on that ASAP.

Chapter Five

The News

What with Reg being away from the island since his first ferry load to the mainland, the news hadn't travelled to him in the way that it had to almost everyone else on Wraith's Hollow. By eight o'clock in the morning, those who'd been out had heard that Martin Howler had been found dead on Tide Fall Beach in, what appeared to be, the most dire circumstances. Of course, what those circumstances were changed greatly as the news passed from person to person. But the essential facts that he had died, had something weird carved on his chest, something round his neck, and something in his mouth stayed consistent throughout.

Nearly everyone was in shock – to think something like that could happen on the island! There was a consensus of opinion that Martin Howler was not a nice man, but he did not deserve that end. Some on Wraith's Hollow, however, were not as shocked by what had happened, and were not surprised either – they merely felt that justice had been served.

Mrs. Appleby

Mrs. Appleby placed the phone down slowly but firmly. She was, indeed, one of those people who felt Martin got what he deserved. Well George, it's finally happened. You can truly rest in peace. This thought brought her a sense of tranquillity; but it was soon replaced by frustration. Yes, she might be getting older, but she still held the cards – she was still in control. Someone had acted without her approval.

She had just spoken to Tim. He was as concerned as she was. Like her, he had no idea who from Hollow Kin had murdered Martin. Mrs. Appleby requested that he organised a meeting. She felt she could trust Tim; though, could she? Of course she could. He'd done the job she wanted him to do. But someone, or a few people, had acted away from the interests of the group when they decided to murder Martin. That meant they placed their interests above the group: *above* Veritas. Mrs. Appleby couldn't have that. Some from Hollow Kin were annoyed with how long Mrs. Appleby had been planning Martin's murder. A year was too long. Their argument was that Martin could do a lot of damage to Wraith's Hollow in one year – and the truth was, he did. Mrs. Appleby, however, was careful and meticulous. And someone had gone against her wishes!

She picked the phone back up but placed it down again. She was unsure of what to do. Tim had told her about his recent exchange with Martin in his workshop. Martin, therefore, knew that at least Tim understood what he was doing on the island. That was the evidence she needed to present to Veritas – their beloved God.

Veritas belongs to Wraith's Hollow. She is the keeper of the island's secrets. She is balance and order, knowledge and wisdom. She reveals hidden truths only to those who love and respect her and the island. But she is not a benevolent god. The purpose of Hollow Kin is to protect Wraith's Hollow by carrying out Veritas' desires. They serve to protect Wraith's Hollow from corruption – they are the last line of defence against forces seeking to exploit or destroy the land. Central to Hollow Kin's beliefs is sacrifice. When Veritas desires it, a life is taken to restore the harmony.

Tim had told Mrs. Appleby of the condition of Martin's body. The symbols found on him left her with no doubt that Hollow Kin were responsible. Carved into his chest was *The Mark of Veritas*, tied round his neck was *The Binding of the Kin*, and in his mouth was *The Tongue of Silence.*

She knew Detective Inspector Rowan Black was on the island sniffing around. She picked up the phone and thought briefly about making another call; but instead, she slammed it back down.

Rowan Black

Rowan was on his way to the local police station. He wanted to speak to Ellie Crick as she was the one who had discovered Martin's body. Though she'd been interviewed already, Rowan had made it clear that he wanted to speak to her as well. PC Everett was bringing her back to the station.

He could have had a lift in the car, but it was a short walk from the beach to the station – one of things he'd found when he lived on the island: nothing was ever far away. And the fresh air was nice after seeing Martin's body. Tim Thorn had walked with him a short while along the promenade before heading off to his workshop. Rowan was pleased when they parted, not least because Tim was asking more questions than a journalist, but also because he wanted time to reflect on the pathologist's take on Martin's body.

There was blunt force trauma to the side of his head – most likely the cause of his death – inflicted by a hand-sized rock. A number of rocks near Martin's body had been gathered up to be analysed. Multiple areas of trauma were visible on his face, head and neck, indicating he had been hit repeatedly. Defence wounds were found on his arms, suggesting he had been struck, knocked to the ground, and had tried to fight back against his attacker. The pathologist confirmed he was killed on the beach.

The carving on the chest was post-mortem. The tissue around the symbol showed no signs of inflammation. There was minimal bleeding around the circle, and the skin was jagged – evidence the knife had caught as it was forced through the tissue. Furthermore, the symbol was uninterrupted, indicating that Martin was still when the carving occurred.

"Have you got an estimated time of death?" Rowan asked.

"Well," Connie, the pathologist, replied, "rigor mortis has developed, lividity's mostly fixed, and with the body cooling in this environment, my best estimate is around two a.m. – until I've completed the post-mortem."

The police station on Quayside Lane looked small – even though it had been converted from two cottages once used by local fishermen. A couple of the other cottages along the lane were still used by fishermen but most had been sold off and were now occupied by locals. Rowan looked at the stone walls he'd remembered seeing the last time he was there when he was thirty-three. For some reason, he had been drawn to seeing the station one last time before he left the island to join the police. There were many places he could have gone and many people he could have seen, but visiting the station seemed to be the right thing to do.

Ivy crawled up the cottage walls and met the moss-covered tiles of the old roof. Quayside Lane was just off Pier Road, and as Rowan breathed deeply, the scent of the ocean filled the air. A breeze swept up the lane, causing the wooden sign above the station entrance – *Wraith's Hollow Police Station* – to swing back and forth. Rowan was just taking in the wooden-framed windows and weathered shutters when the door opened.

"DI Rowan Black," Sergeant Frank Jennings said. "What the hell is going on in the world!"

"Frank," Rowan walked down the small stone pathway towards the door. He noted the range of wildflowers thriving in the garden, either side of the path. "It's good to see you again." Jennings had been an officer on the island for as long as Rowan could remember.

"I wish it were under different circumstances. Honestly, I thought there was nothing else the Lord could throw at me – thought I'd seen everything. Until Martin's dead body turned up this morning."

Rowan shook his hand. "It's an unusual one. What's your take?" Rowan asked as they stepped inside.

"I'm not sure. We've never had murder on the island before – accidental deaths, sure. Mother Nature's claimed many on the ocean out there. But premeditated murder? Never."

"What about the symbols?" Rowan asked, but Jennings, who was leading the way down the short, dim corridor, didn't appear to hear. Rowan did a rough calculation: Sergeant Jennings must be nearly retirement age – if not past it already.

Humble was the first word that came to mind when Rowan walked into the main office. Exposed stonework filled the top half of the walls and wood panelling filled the bottom. There was a curious area of damage near one of the corners where it looked as though something small – like a hammer – had been used to knock a few holes in the panelling. It was as if someone had made attempts to fix it, then given up. An old nautical map of the island – crisscrossed with creases – was framed on the wall along with discoloured photographs of Havenmoore Port. Wooden chairs, the kind that creaked and groaned when used, were dotted around, and a couple more were tucked under equally creaky desks.

"This is more museum than police station, Frank,"

Rowan said. The air was dusty too. "Does the wood-burner work?"

"Absolutely – works harder than all of us put together in the winter," Frank let out a little laugh – he seemed to ignore Rowan's 'museum' comment. "Come through," he said.

Frank led Rowan to a room at the end of the station. A slightly more modern office with a desk inside that didn't look used. Wooden desk in front, wooden flooring under his feet, and wooden beams above his head – and a couple more of the same chairs lined one side, ready for the visitors the room clearly hadn't yet received.

"You've got a beautiful view from this office, Rowan."

Rowan went to the window. It overlooked the sea and the harbour. "It's really something, Frank."

"Where are you staying?"

"I'm waiting for my DCI to get back to me. I've requested to stay on the island. It will help."

"Certainly will. Will this do for your office then? I've already spoken to DCI Hargrave. She seems lovely."

She is lovely but bloody-minded, Rowan thought about offering but nodded instead. Things were moving fast. When he'd woken up that morning, he believed he was going to see Martin, have a coffee, iron out whatever troubles he had, spend some nostalgia-filled time on the island, then be home late afternoon. Now, he'd been assigned to investigate Martin's murder on Wraith's Hollow, given a temporary office, and was waiting for accommodation to be sorted. And Ellie Crick was on her way to meet him.

"You know, when I lived here years ago, the cult was never far from people's lips. What do you think about the symbols found on his body?"

Frank waved his hand, dismissively. "The cult this, the cult that. Never had any time for it. Never seen any evidence of them all the years I've been policing here."

"Never seen – or never looked, Frank?"

"Both. Look, I'll be clear with you, Rowan. People've been talking about the cult for years, but I don't give it much thought. I deal with real crime. If there ever was or is a cult, then as long as they don't break the law, that's fine by me. If they do, they'd have me to deal with. I don't let anything slip."

Rowan leaned against the desk, facing Frank, and folded his arms. He noticed Frank stepping back slightly and turning his head momentarily. "You don't think much about these symbols then? Not evidence of the cult?"

"You think they are?"

"Well, don't you?" Rowan asked. "I think we'd be foolish to dismiss anything at this stage. Someone carved that circular shape into his chest – at the risk of being seen – stuffed that stone sigil in his mouth and tied that vine-like necklace round his neck."

"Let's wait for the post-mortem, shall we?" Sergeant Jennings suggested.

"No, I want you to start looking into it."

"Okay, sir. It's up to you. I'll dig around."

"It's better if you do it than me – people know me around here, but now I'm an outsider–" Rowan paused.

He heard PC Everett calling Sergeant Jennings from the main office. It looked as though Jennings was about to say something – but after a brief pause, he headed towards the door.

"Frank," Rowan called after him. "Two things. First, talk to Reg. See if anyone unfamiliar has been on the ferry in the last week or so. I did ask, but something might've come to mind. Let me know if anything looks off. Second, make a visit to Martin's house – anything relevant: documents, bills, correspondence, letters, condition of the home, anything – let me know straight away."

Sophie Marlow

Saltmere Way had the reputation of being a place for those who preferred listening to the sea rather than their neighbours. It was a quiet road which curved around the outskirts of the town – branching off Wraithmoore Lane and tapering into narrow footsteps leading up to Ghost Cliff Point. There were a few cottages along the road but no more than that. It was perfect for development – as Martin had expressed to Sophie many times.

Sophie loved the quiet. She had stayed in her cottage – Drift Edge – all morning to avoid hearing anything about Martin.

She had made coffee in the morning, which she drank peacefully scrolling through the news on her phone, occasionally reflecting not on the news but on how well she had slept. Cynthia often featured in her dreams and last night was no exception. It was a beautiful, relaxing dream. Even though Sophie could not remember the details, she remembered the feeling it gave her when she woke up. Most of the time, unfortunately, she would have nightmares about Cynthia, usually of her failure to save her, to stop her from being murdered.

Sometime before ten Sophie walked towards the town with it in mind to buy a coffee from Diane's Coffee Pot. She could then stroll along the seafront and watch the commotion. Passing Mrs. Fender's cottage, she brushed her palm over the lavender that grew alongside the wooden fence and breathed the refreshing fragrance deeply.

"Lovely morning," Mrs. Fender called out from her kitchen window.

"Beautiful," Sophie replied, realising that Mrs. Fender had obviously not heard about Martin yet. She wasn't going to spoil Mrs. Fender's apparent happy mood.

Sophie strolled onwards. She entered Diane's and immediately heard everyone talking about the news. When Sophie ordered her takeout, she made all the right noises about how shocking it was, and how she couldn't believe what had happened.

Sipping her drink, walking towards Tide Fall Beach, Sophie saw the place was overrun with locals. People everywhere! She edged her way through and eventually got to where the police had barricaded the scene. She couldn't believe it had happened – Martin was actually dead. God that felt good.

Looking over the shoulder of a police officer she

didn't recognise, she spotted Rowan Black crouched near Martin's body. Anger surged through her – heating her cheeks. She hated him for killing her sister, Cynthia.

She left the scene quickly, shoving her way through the crowd – someone called her name asking if she was okay. But Sophie didn't look back. She was going to break her rule: she had to make a phone call.

Ellie Crick

Ellie shifted her weight in the wooden chair. She was so uncomfortable. Why was she being interviewed again? She'd told Sergeant Jennings everything she knew.

"Can you tell me exactly how you came to find the body?" DI Black asked.

"I've told Sergeant Jennings this already."

"I understand, but I'm trying to establish for myself what you saw."

Ellie sighed. She looked momentarily out of the window in DI Black's office. Shit it felt claustrophobic, and the room smelled of dusty, old books even though there weren't any lying around.

"I was running as normal in the morning – my usual route. I stopped along the seafront as I sometimes do to catch my breath. Then something on the beach caught my eye. I went straight over and saw Martin, dead."

Ellie watched DI Black writing in his notebook before he asked: "It was your normal route – was this your normal time, too?"

Ellie nodded. She was out earlier than normal but chose not to say so – it really didn't seem important.

"Good. Thank you. What time would you say it was when you found Martin's body?"

"I remember exactly as I checked my watch after a minute or so of being there. It was five past six."

Another scribble in his notebook. "What made you check the time?" he asked.

Ellie shrugged her shoulders. "Not sure. It was just before I phoned the police. Habit, I suppose. You often look at the time before you call someone. I do anyway."

"Let's go back to when you were on the promenade. How did you see the body from there?"

"It's an odd angle, but I could see it sort of catching, no not catching, but, well, it was the low light of the sun. It was rising but it was still low in the sky. I guess it was something to do with the light on his body. Though I had no idea what it was at the time."

"Would you normally interrupt your workout to check something out – I, myself, would've been tempted to carry on with my run. Wouldn't want to cool down too much."

"I wouldn't normally, I guess. This was more intuition. I just felt I should go see what it was."

"When you discovered the body, what did you notice?"

Ellie said: "I really have told Sergeant Jennings all of this. Going over it again is making me feel terrible."

"Please, I need to ask you these questions. There's no pressure. Have a drink of water."

Water won't do! Ellie really wanted a bottle of red followed by another one. Before PC Everett had arrived to collect her, she had intended to drink herself into oblivion to try and forget the sight of Martin – even if a tiny part of her still felt good for seeing him dead.

"There was blood all over him. He was in a weird cross position. I saw the carving on his chest, and that other thing round his neck," Ellie breathed. "I crouched, I could see something in his mouth, so I got a stick and tried to get it out. But my fingers were trembling, and I dropped it."

Looking up from his notebook, DI Black asked: "What made you want to see what was in his mouth?"

"I wasn't thinking straight. Maybe I thought if I removed it, he'd start breathing. I really don't know!" Ellie raised her voice. Was she under suspicion? And why the fuck was he writing down everything she said?

"What do you make of those symbols on his body? Have you seen them before?" DI Black asked.

Ellie shook her head. "Not sure what I saw, but I haven't seen anything like them."

"Just a few more questions, Ellie, and then you're free to go."

"Thank you."

"How well did you know Martin Howler? How would you describe your relationship with him?"

Ellie shrugged. "I knew of him – but only in the way that everyone knows everyone around here . . . Well, we were acquaintances a few years ago – only through the necessity of the small business I was setting up."

"I'd argue being business partners is more involved than the everyday familiarity people have with each other on the island."

"Would you? I know you used to live here. You won't remember me, but I remember you," Ellie said, lightly; then with more force: "Perhaps you've forgotten what it's like to live here."

"Maybe so. But anyway, did you notice a change in Martin's behaviour in the time leading up to his murder?"

Ellie shook her head. "Like I say, other than the business we thought about a number of years ago, I've had nothing to do with him. Barely spoke to him."

"I thought it was impossible to avoid people on Wraith's Hollow. How did you manage not to speak to him from time to time?"

Ellie was confused by DI Black's questioning. One minute he was kind the next it was like he was accusing her.

"Am I under suspicion here?"

"No, no, of course not. I'm just trying to understand what happened to Martin. I need to understand him and his situation from the people that knew him on the island. That's all . . . Just out of interest, what was your business venture?"

Ellie looked down at the wooden flooring before meeting DI Black's eyes. "It was nothing. Just an idea for eco-friendly real estate development. I thought green housing could be the island's USP. Nothing came of it. Shame."

"That is a shame," he said without looking up from

his notebook. "I want to go back to the symbols on Martin's body. Are you sure you haven't seen them before? Anywhere on the island?"

Ellie knew what he was getting at but chose not to bite. "Never seen them before."

"Thank you, Ellie. One more question. How did you feel when you saw Martin on the beach? You've obviously got some kind of history, albeit short-lived – as you say."

"It was awful. Look, if that's everything. Can I go now?" Ellie stood.

DI Black stood behind his desk. "Of course. Thank you, you've been very helpful. I may need to catch up with you in the future."

"Why? I've told you everything I know."

"Sometimes things come up in these cases – if I think you can help me, I'll be in touch."

Ellie relaxed her expression into a brief smile. "If I can help you, I'm sure I will." She headed for the door.

"Just one last thing, Ellie. Do you know if Martin had any enemies on the island – whether someone would want to hurt him?"

Ellie turned to face Rowan. "Not to my knowledge, DI Black."

Rowan Black

Ellie walked out of his office. It was coming up for eleven o'clock. He sat back down and reviewed his notes from their conversation. This first interview he'd conducted on the island felt like the first interview of his police career. Awkward. Difficult. Ellie was peculiar in places. What was she hiding? She was evasive about her relationship with Martin, and when she claimed to have no knowledge of the symbols, it was obvious she was lying.

"Danny," Rowan called and waited for PC Everett to enter his office. "Look into Ellie Crick's dealings with Martin Howler. They had some kind of business idea, plan, that didn't work out. Be discreet. I'm not sure what she's hiding, but we need to find out." Rowan observed PC Everett's face. "Don't look so worried, Danny."

"I'm sorry, sir. I'm just, I haven't dealt with this sort of thing before."

"You're not alone, okay, Danny. I'm here to help. What's the CCTV like on the island? I take it there isn't much of a network?"

"No, sir. It's mostly tied to private businesses. We've got council ones around Havenmoore Port, the school, and other council buildings."

"Okay. When you've looked into Ellie and Martin's relationship – start piecing together Martin's movements leading up to his murder from CCTV footage. Let's see if we can figure out where he was before he was killed, and whether anyone was with him. Remember, time of death is around two in the morning. Thank you."

PC Everett left the room. Rowan checked his phone. DCI Hargrave had just messaged: *Accommodation sorted. You're six doors down from the station. You need to meet Margaret Warren at 18:00.*

This gave Rowan plenty of time to log on to DEMS – the Digital Evidence Management System – to pull up the beach-scene photos of Martin's body and start building a timeline on the whiteboard in the main office. He was hoping the post-mortem would be done that evening. He'd worked with Connie Smith, a senior pathologist with over fifteen years' experience, before. She was flexible and always helpful. What he wasn't holding out for was fingerprints to be discovered on any of the rocks found near Martin's body. Their surfaces were too irregular and rough. But evidence on Martin's body? Hopefully.

Rowan's phone rang. It was Sandra Mead, the senior CSI overseeing the forensic sweep of Martin's boat. After brief pleasantries, Sandra didn't really do small talk, she said: "We've got a potential blood sample on the boat – inside the cabin near the bench."

"Much blood?" DI Black asked.

"Not much. Someone's tampered with it. Looks like they've tried to clean it, but they won't get anything past me. I'll let you know more once we're done."

Rowan made a note: potential blood – reason for boat on the rocks? Was Martin attacked on the boat?

He was taping photos of the crime scene to the whiteboard when Sergeant Jennings burst through the door with the energy of a man half his age, saying:

"Martin's house has been broken into and completely wrecked."

Nathan Waters

"I've been trying to get hold of you for hours – it's ten-thirty. Where the hell have you been!" Nathan said over the phone. He was at home, sat at his table, looking out of the window.

"We agreed that we wouldn't phone each other – so get off the–"

"Wait, wait, wait a minute. I know what we said. But we didn't agree on the boat being abandoned or blood being left all over the bloody place."

"Stop talking! Look, calm down. Losing your fucking mind isn't going to help us. Did you clean the blood?"

"As best as I could. Why didn't you tell me about the boat?" Nathan asked.

"What, really? At that time of night. You think I should've called or text?"

"Something would've been nice! I only found it because I was out early. I thought we agreed it would be his home."

"Well, if your concoction wasn't as strong as it bloody was then maybe we could've stuck to plan A. Anyway, why the hell were you out?"

"I had to get out. Sitting around was driving me crazy," Nathan said.

"Okay, okay, fine! Let's just be cool. Let's think for a minute. Look – I'm hanging up. We'll meet soon. Just shut up, talk to no one. If you go out, go out normally, study some birds or something. But no more calls – or messages."

The phone call was ended.

Nathan threw his phone onto the sofa. It bounced off the cushion and fell onto the floor.

Tim Thorn

Tim was sanding a new chair he'd made for Father Hemmingway. It was a simple farmhouse with a plain back rest and smooth, nondescript spindles. That was what Father Hemmingway requested. Despite the simplicity and general ease of making it, Tim was sanding it too hard in places. He was agitated. And even though he wore a facemask, tiny particles got through, causing him to cough.

He cleared his throat, decided to stop for a minute and tossed the sandpaper to one side. It had just gone eleven. He kept thinking about the paperwork he'd hidden in the office cabinet at the back of his workshop. It wasn't best to leave it there – it needed to be secure and well out of the way. He told Little Liam to go home early for the day as he had things to do. Little Liam, of course, wasn't going to argue, but his surprised expression told Tim that he needed to reassure him that everything was okay.

No need to raise extra suspicion.

Little Liam left and Tim went to the cabinet near the desk in his office, grabbed the paperwork, shoved it in his overall pocket, and left the workshop. He needed to see Mrs. Appleby.

Chapter Six

Post-Mortem

Rowan Black

Sergeant Jennings was driving Rowan from the station to Martin's home, Nexus House. They were rumbling slowly up the cobblestone street, approaching the top of Wraithmoore Lane. Passing Mrs. Appleby's home, Rowan remembered that, as a teenager, he used to do some gardening for her for extra cash. It was a nightmare pushing his wheelbarrow up Wraithmoore Lane full of gardening tools – and back down again full of garden waste. Mrs. Appleby had always seemed peculiar. Even now, Rowan couldn't say why – but he'd picked up on something all those years ago. She would watch him weeding, cutting the grass, strimming the edges from her window, but when he'd look back, she would move away and pretend to fix the curtain in place.

That was over thirty years ago now. It was a shock when Rowan heard that Martin had killed George with his car – it must have knocked Mrs. Appleby for six. Perhaps Rowan should call in, reminisce about the old days, and tell her how he was, in fact, really quite fond of George.

George was a nice man. He would always talk to Rowan when he worked in the garden. It didn't matter what their conversations started with; they inevitably ended up talking about the magnificence of space. George loved space. The stars always reminded Rowan of George.

They drove from the quaint cobblestone road onto the smooth tarmac driveway leading to Martin's home. Rather than mirroring the curvature of the cliff, the driveway cut through the land, in a straight line.

"That is one ugly place," Rowan said.

"You're not the first to say it, and for as long as it's there, you won't be the last."

First impressions are everything. Even though Rowan had not lived on the island for years, nor had plans to move back, he knew Nexus House didn't belong on Wraith's Hollow. It sucked in the island's historic, rugged charm and its sharp, angular lines of glass and steel cut through everything that Wraith's Hollow stood for. It was perfectly polished. It didn't seem to matter where Rowan looked, the sunlight bounced off its metallic surfaces, causing him to squint. As they followed the driveway to the front of the house, floor-to-ceiling glass ran along its façade. Even the reflected sky, normally so beautiful and warming to the eye, looked gloomy. Black stone columns divided the east-facing windows into neat sections.

"How many floors?"

"Three," Jennings said.

"Was the garden worth having?" Rowan remarked. There was a small, highly manicured garden, clinging to the edge of the cliff. The wind was fairly strong, but it blew straight through the trimmed hedges without rustling a leaf, and around the metallic abstract feature, without a sound.

"Any idea?" Sergeant Jennings asked, nodding at the sculpture.

"None whatsoever."

"Cost?"

"More than we'll ever earn, Frank. Tell you that for nothing," Rowan said. He made a mental note: Martin must have a gardener, and he needed to track them down.

"The door was open when I arrived," Jennings said. "No signs of a forced entry. No windows smashed. This keypad's intact."

Rowan looked at the keypad to the right of the glass door. "Whoever broke in must've known the code. Any alarm system that you saw?"

"None." Jennings led the way through the door. "No CCTV either."

"Doesn't that strike you as odd? No alarm? No CCTV."

"Not really. Martin Howler was as arrogant as they come. He would never think himself vulnerable to being robbed. Come on, you know what he was like – you grew up with him."

"I did. And he wasn't the easiest to deal with even back then."

"Come on, sir, he was an arsehole. I'm sorry, not professional. But he was. Believed he was above everyone – including the law."

"Really. What makes you say that?"

"There's the lounge," Sergeant Jennings said, without qualifying his previous statement.

"Keep your eye out for his mobile. It wasn't with him at the beach, so I'm guessing it's here somewhere."

They walked through a short corridor into a room that was utterly trashed. The glass windows to Rowan's right showed the view of the sea. The open-plan living room was in utter chaos – everything seemed to be upturned, knocked over, smashed. The flatscreen, once mounted to the wall, now lay face down on the dark wooden floor. The cream leather sofa – once positioned to get the best view of the television – was overturned, its underside ripped as if someone had been trying to access something hidden inside. Seascape paintings still hung on the walls, their canvases torn and slashed.

"You remember, Sophie Marlow. She's our local artist."

"I do, yes," Rowan said. He and Sophie had fallen out years ago over Cynthia's death. Rowan had nothing to do with her dying. It was an accident – Sophie could never accept that.

The kitchen was no better than the living room. The oversized island in the centre had papers scattered all over the surface, the oranges from the smashed fruit bowl contrasted with the black granite top. Rowan accidentally kicked one across the floor – amazingly, it found a clear path, rolling past the plates, cutlery, and glassware that had been thrown from the cupboards.

"What's the motive, revenge?" Rowan asked.

"Can't be sure. Nothing seems to be missing. It's such

a mess!"

"It's definitely not robbery. If it was, that money over there would've been snapped up. The TV in the other room," Rowan gestured back toward the living room, "would've been taken – not smashed. Who hated Martin this much to come and destroy his house?"

"Three-quarters, if not all, of the island," Jennings said.

Rowan was about to ask who'd be on top of that list but instead said, "What the hell is that?"

Sophie Marlow

Sophie hurried home from the beach, paying no attention to Mrs. Fender's attempts to continue their earlier conversation as she passed her house. One thing was on her mind: making that call. Once inside, she locked the front door, tossed her bag onto the sofa, and headed to the kitchen for a swig of single malt. Her hands were shaking as she scrolled through her phone and pressed it to her ear, the dial tone ringing. "Hello, it's me."

"We said no calls."

"I know. I'm just so pissed. He's here. Rowan Black."

"I know, I saw him earlier. Don't worry. Everything's fine. Be calm."

"Don't tell me to be calm."

"Am I the only one who isn't fucking losing their shit?"

"What do you mean?" Sophie asked.

"I spoke to Nathan earlier – told him to keep his shit together."

"What did he phone you for?"

"Because our plan didn't go as *planned*. I told him I'd see him later and to get off the damn phone – which is what I'm telling you now."

"No phone calls. I know. This is going to be harder than I thought." Sophie sighed: what the fuck have we done? "Why's Rowan here?"

"Because he's a detective. He's obviously been assigned to investigate. Don't know why – might be his connections here. Something like that."

"Will he find us out? Will they track these calls?" Sophie asked.

"Not unless we give them a reason to. Look, take a deep breath. Pick up your brushes and paint the sea or something. Be in touch later – we need to discuss what Nathan found on the boat."

"What do you mean?" she asked. "What the fuck do you me–"

The call had been ended. She tried calling back but got no reply.

Sophie slammed her phone down on the kitchen side. Another shot of whisky. Cynthia, have we done the right thing?

Hanging on one of the charcoal grey bar stools was a necklace. Rowan went over to it and, not wanting to disturb it, leant down to inspect it.

Jennings said: "What is it? Looks like–"

"The necklace found on Martin's body. Same pattern – same vine-like style," Rowan said and shook his head. It was difficult to ascertain what it meant, why it was there. Amongst all the chaos – someone had gone to the trouble of leaving it there; specifically in that place so no one would miss it.

"Leave that where it is for SOCO. Let's head upstairs," Rowan said.

This time Rowan took the lead back through to the living room. Somehow in all the damage and destruction he had missed the grandeur of the floating staircase to the left of the room. The polished marble steps looked both delicate and impossibly strong, and the silver and gold veining told Rowan that his shoes were no way near expensive enough to be using the staircase. He dared not touch – even with gloves on – the glass panels which were framed in a fine, brushed gold metal.

DI Black and Sergeant Jennings met the same level of destruction upstairs. There was the addition of a few holes smashed into the corridor, bedroom and office walls. Something like a hammer rather than a fist because the holes were small. And, as Jennings pointed out, someone would've broken their hand hitting that much plaster in one go. Someone had gone crazy, had destroyed everything in sight.

"This laptop will never work again," Jennings said. On the desk, the laptop was smashed to pieces.

"They've left no stone unturned!"

"I'm trying to put myself into the mind of a man who'd go to this level."

"Assuming it is a man, Frank. I'm going upstairs. The main bedroom must be up there."

"I'll check out the bathroom on this floor."

Clothes from the wardrobes were scattered across the carpet and bed. The bed linen, a shimmering blue, was pulled halfway down and the pillows were thrown on the floor. Rowan went into the ensuite and made a quick scan: it was pretty much untouched apart from the smashed mirror. Rowan shook his head and left.

Across from Martin's bedroom was another office – more of a reading room. It was completely untouched. Nothing broken, nothing destroyed. Everything in place: sofa, desk, bookcase, impressionist painting on the wall, mahogany side table, plush armchair – all left untouched. Why destroy everything else and suddenly stop here? Rowan walked towards the bookcase at the side of the room. The rich, dark wax sat cosily with the green wallpaper and wood panelling décor.

"One, two, three," he counted the bookshelves and then smoothed his hand over one of them. The style, the look, didn't match what he knew about Martin Howler. The gothic doors and carved wood seemed too old, out of keeping with the rest of the house.

As Rowan smoothed his hand over another shelf, he felt it give – like it wanted to move. Removing the books first, he then rotated the middle shelf in the direction that had the least resistance. As it turned on a central axis, it clicked under his touch with a faint whisper of wood on wood. Making the full turn, a small alcove came into view. It was the perfect size to hide something that needed to be kept out of sight.

The compartment was dark, the wood appearing darker due to the lack of light being able to reach into this secret world. Rowan smoothed his hand over the velvet-lined base and felt something. He pulled it free carefully and held the small stone sigil between his fingers. The shape was unmistakable – a familiar eye-shape, eerily like the one found in Martin's mouth on the beach. There was a sealed, crescent-like shape at the centre, reminding Rowan of a mouth – and lattice lines covered it, indicating silence? The rest of the surface was smooth, polished. Finding a safe place for the sigil on Martin's desk, he called for Jennings.

"I think you want to look at the bathroom downstairs," Sergeant Jennings said as he entered the room, his voice urgent but steady.

"Yes, but first – what do you make of this? It's the same as the one found in Martin's mouth. And this room. The bookcase – everything's untouched. What's special about it?"

"Did this come out of there?" Sergeant Jennings saw the books from the shelf on the floor and the symbol on the table and put two and two together.

"Yes. Inside a secret compartment."

Jennings went over to the bookcase. "Not much of a secret – you found it straight away."

"Only because this room was left untouched. I might've missed it had it been destroyed like everything else."

"Well, one thing's for certain. Whoever broke in knew about that compartment. We should pay Tim Thorn a visit."

"Why, this one of his?" Rowan asked. He remembered that Tim had a workshop in town and was considered one of the finest cabinetmakers around. Years ago, Rowan had been to see Tim about an apprenticeship after he'd finished school, but Tim turned him down. A decision that still left a bitter taste in Rowan's mouth.

"I reckon this is one of his. If not, he could probably tell us where it came from."

"Great. I'll call DCI Hargrave, get more uniformed officers from the mainland. I'll need Sandra Mead to arrange a forensic sweep here, too. She'll love me for that."

"Yes, but first," Jennings pointed towards the hallway. "The bathroom."

Downstairs on the first floor, Rowan stood in front of the bathroom mirror. There, sprayed in black across the glass, was the same eerie, circular pattern that had been carved into Martin's chest. There was more detail than in the one on Martin's skin. At the centre, a small circle filled with paint, appeared like a dark void. Spreading outwards from this core, was a rippling pattern, like waves – creating a strange, cyclical, hypnotic effect.

"Getting all that detail on Martin's body would've been impossible," Jennings said. "But there's no doubt in my mind, that's the same thing."

"Definitely. Do they look different because they were done by two different people? Or is it just that glass is easier to draw on than hacking through someone's skin?"

Sergeant Jennings shook his head. "I don't know."

Rowan looked at him. "The fact we've found the same three symbols here that were on his body points to a working cult. Wouldn't you say?"

"Possibly. Or it could be someone who knows the cult myth and is using it to send us down the wrong path."

Rowan hesitated. There was something slightly off in Jennings' tone when he spoke about the cult. Was he hiding something? He seemed against the idea that it could even exist.

"Rowan. I can see it in your eyes. I'll do as you ask and dig into it. But I've had nothing to do with any cult over the years. I don't get involved with hearsay and childish whispers."

"It's not hearsay and whispers if they're responsible for murder, Frank. It's not going to be the only avenue we explore, but we must keep an open mind. Someone's planted these symbols for a reason," Rowan said and stopped. He glanced at the tap. It was a single spout with a polished chrome finish. It looked barely used. But from above the black sensor panel, a couple of spots of dried blood glared at him.

Tim Thorn

It was coming up for one o'clock. Tim hated the climb up Wraithmoore Lane at the best of times, but in the sunshine and still in his work overalls, he was sweating something rotten. Quitting smoking hadn't done anything for his physical fitness! He desperately wanted a cigarette.

He looked down at the view of Tide Fall Beach before pushing open the gate to Mrs. Appleby's cottage – Hollow Crest. Tim had always been fond of that name.

"Your sign needs replacing," he said to Mrs. Appleby when she opened her door. She was smiling. "Almost falling off the gate. Rotten as hell."

"I know. I was going to ask you to make me a new one. Now George isn't here, I've only got you to rely on for the DIY jobs that life throws at me."

"Lucky for you, I'm at your service."

Mrs. Appleby smiled warmly. "Come in, dear. I'll put the kettle on."

"Coffee for me, please. I need something to get me over climbing up that hill."

Tim stood by the open door in the kitchen, looking out into the back garden. "Your tulips and rhododendrons are looking beautiful, Mrs. Appleby."

"Thank you, dear. They are. Shall we sit?" Mrs. Appleby placed the cups of coffee on the table. They stayed in the kitchen, but she gestured for Tim to shut the door. "You never know who could be listening."

"Absolutely true . . . That's lovely coffee."

"It's just instant – but I like it, too. Hurt your hand,

dear? Your knuckles are swollen."

"I did. Smashing up Martin's place. Had thick gloves on as well. I really went to work on his place."

"Good. Get some ice on it when you get home. Take some of that swelling down."

"Thank you, Mrs. Appleby. It's not too bad. It looks worse than it is. When I'm working, I don't even notice it."

"Make sure you've got a cover story . . . Now, tell me you placed the symbols around his house."

"Certainly did."

"Good. He got everything he deserved. I'm just sorry he didn't get to see your handiwork before someone else killed him."

"I was surprised, Mrs. Appleby, by two things that night. First, that he hadn't changed the pin number on the door like he said he would. It was still the same one from when me and Little Liam delivered his bookcase last Saturday. He only gave it to me because he had to dash out somewhere for the evening. I did ask him where, but he told me to mind my own business. And the other thing that surprised me was I really thought he'd be home, that I'd need to knock him about a bit."

"It was part of the plan."

"I know. But someone beat us to it. When I was there, he was out being murdered. Have you thought any more about who it could be from Hollow Kin?"

Mrs. Appleby shook her head. "Not yet. Did you arrange the meeting?"

"I did. It's tonight."

"Well, I'm sure we'll find out then. Have you got the document?"

Tim nodded and told Mrs. Appleby that he'd got it from the compartment in the bookcase he'd made. He pulled it out of his overall pocket and slid it across the table to Mrs. Appleby.

"Project Genesis," she read aloud. "Project Genesis will revolutionise human potential across every discipline and industry – from business to military applications. Genesis uses cutting-edge technology to enhance the intellectual and physical capabilities of each and every recipient. Our goal: to develop a bio-augmented human who is not only intellectually superior but also physically enhanced, offering superior mental acuity and physical endurance." Mrs. Appleby put the papers on the table. "How does that even work?"

"I read it all and still don't understand. But it's something to do with a neural chip, surgically implanted into the brain. Some sort of bio-compatible technology that connects to the brain's neurons. Boosts memory, thinking speed, improves learning. Like I said, I read it all and don't get it."

Mrs. Appleby huffed. "And he wanted to do this on Wraith's Hollow. Our home. Bring people over to *our* island to be operated on?"

"It's as we suspected, Mrs. Appleby."

"I know. Bastard!"

It always surprised Tim when Mrs. Appleby swore, even though he'd heard her do it many times over the years. "Well. The game's over for him and this," Tim said.

"Our island will be protected. Veritas will be at peace once more."

"At peace once more . . . Who is Dr. Naomi Bennett?" Mrs. Appleby asked.

Tim shrugged his shoulders. "According to that, some kind of MIT whizz researcher."

"Let's look her up – find out everything you can about her, Tim."

"I will. Did you see that Martin was seeking investment for this Genesis project?"

"Yes. Twenty-five million," Mrs. Appleby said.

"If this proposal's already been sent out, we could be in trouble. The type of people who invest in this sort of thing don't exactly abide by the law. If they've already put up cash, they'll want to protect their investment . . . Mrs. Appleby, are we sure it was Hollow Kin who killed Martin? It could've been this Bennett woman. Or someone she knows."

"The symbols, Tim. Clearly, it was someone from Hollow Kin."

"I was meaning it could still be Hollow Kin, but if Bennett's involved, who knows who she's reached out to on the island. People like her or these investors – well, all I'm saying is if they had a reason to get rid of him, these people can."

"Would anyone else know about Project Genesis on the island – assuming Dr. Bennett hasn't communicated with anyone?"

"I don't think so. Can't be certain. I first saw this," he motioned to the document, "a week ago – Thursday. At his house."

"Why were you there?"

"Measuring up for the bookcase."

"Fine. We need to keep this quiet. We have the benefit that Martin would've done his best to keep it from everyone – so let's use that to our advantage. What do we know about the boat?" Mrs. Appleby asked.

"I haven't heard. But I couldn't see it near the beach. I checked before knocking your door. Might've been moved – probably to Havenmoore Port."

"Keep an ear to the ground, Tim. One of Hollow Kin must've been with Martin on that boat, then on the beach."

Tim finished his coffee and said he'd be in touch.

"Also," Mrs. Appleby said to Tim before she closed the front door. "Watch out for Rowan Black. I've never trusted him – even way back when he did my gardening. Be careful around him."

Jasper Flint

Jax had been waiting for DI Rowan Black for some time. He was in the small reception of the police station on Quayside Lane, sitting on a hard, wooden chair. Shifting about did nothing to reduce the pressure against his coccyx. He'd missed his lunch, it was coming up for one-thirty, and he was starving.

He really wanted a cigarette, too.

Where the hell was he? He was thinking he'd call it a day when Rowan Black walked through the door – followed by Sergeant Jennings. They were saying something about Martin's boat.

"Jax, how are you?" Jennings said. It was as if Rowan hadn't noticed him there.

"I'm fine. Just wanted a quick word with Rowan, if that's okay?"

"Of course. Come through, Jax."

They walked through the main office – which now doubled up as the incident room – following a temporary corridor made of fabric screens and metal frames. Jax heard voices he didn't recognise, phones ringing, and someone laughing – which seemed odd, given the circumstances they were working in. Approaching DI Black's office, Jax accidentally kicked one of the screens.

"Sorry about that," he said.

"Not a problem. It's probably those massive steel-toe boots you're wearing!"

Jax gave a short laugh as he entered DI Black's warm, airless office.

"Still into boats and fishing?" Rowan asked as he gestured for Jax to sit at the desk. Rowan sat opposite.

"I do both. More fishing than fixing boats but, well, actually–"

"You hot, Jax?" Rowan asked.

"I am. A bit of air wouldn't go a miss." Jax watched DI Black open the window.

"Better?"

"Yes."

"When did we last see each other?"

"God, I really can't be sure. Years, Rowan. Years."

"It's been a long time," Rowan said. "Perhaps we should leave what happened between us in the past. Bringing it up now could be counterproductive to my investigation. Besides, a lot of water's run under that bridge."

"I agree," Jax said, smoothing his eyebrow with his finger.

"So, what's on your mind? Why have you come to see me?"

"Well, it's just, I've obviously heard about Martin – it's all over the island already."

"Nothing changes."

"It doesn't," Jax smiled – mirroring Rowan's. "I wanted to give you some info. It might be nothing, but I felt I had to tell you."

DI Black opened his notebook.

"Before he died–"

"Before he was murdered."

"Yes, sorry, murdered." Jax paused. He anticipated Rowan would be like this, so he wasn't going to let it affect him. Rowan's speciality was making him feel small, stupid. "Before he was murdered, I did some work on his boat and, well, having heard about it being found on the rocks near the beach – I just thought maybe the two were related."

"Related how?"

"I told Martin last week that someone might've damaged his boat on purpose. I was fixing his boat, you see."

"What day was this? When you told him?"

"Last Friday evening, in the pub."

"Nearly a week ago, then."

Jax nodded. "I'd been out to his boat earlier that day to take a look, start working on it. I phoned him as I thought he should come down to the marina–"

"Is that Silver Cove Marina?"

"Yes. The marina wasn't built when you lived here. But it's down the coast a bit from Tide Fall Beach. It's in a secluded inlet – from the sea, you can easily miss it. The rocks shelter it."

"Do you have access to the marina? Any staff looking after the place?"

"I have my own key. I'm the only boat mechanic on the island so it's just easier if I can get in and crack on when it's best for me. I need to have access after Roger's gone. That's Roger Stone – part timer, mostly retired, not sure if you know him. He may've arrived on the island after you'd left. He keeps an eye on the place in the mornings before he finishes for the day. Keeps things tidy. Meets new clients, rich clients, when they come in."

"Sounds like an expensive place," Rowan said.

"You're damn right it is. None of us normal people can afford it. Martin hadn't a bloody clue about the people on this island."

"Meaning?"

"Meaning he was so rich. Building houses, luxury flats – that marina. He was ruining our home – wanted others like himself here. These people takeover everything."

"Would you like a glass of water, Jax?

"No, I'm fine," Jax said, watching DI Black scribbling away.

"Is there any CCTV at Silver Cove?"

"Yes, there are a couple of blind spots, but the entrances are covered."

"So, if someone damaged his boat on purpose, they would most likely be aware of the CCTV, would you say?" Rowan said.

"I guess."

"I don't suppose you can access the CCTV?"

"Above my paygrade. Not sure about Roger. Martin liked control over everything. There's a laptop down there, but my guess is Martin accessed the cameras remotely."

"Okay, thank you. Let's get back to your phone call with Martin. You invited him down to look at his boat and then what?"

"I didn't get the chance to tell him about his boat on the phone in the morning – as I say, I told him that later in the pub."

"Why didn't you get the chance?"

"He was angry. He didn't tell me the ins and outs of it all. Something about arguing with Sophie Marlow. I know we said we wouldn't bring up the past . . . mentioning her."

"It's fine, Jax. This is different. That's all in the past. Totally different context. Are you sure Martin didn't say anything at all that could point towards what their argument was about?" Rowan asked.

"No. Nothing. It was a quick call."

"When do you think they argued. Was it on the phone or in person?"

"I really couldn't say," Jax said.

"When did you phone him – roughly?"

"Midmorning – roughly."

Jax waited for DI Black to finish writing in his note-book.

"Can you describe the damage to the boat – why did it make you suspicious that someone had done it on pur-pose?"

Jax leaned back in the chair – another awful, wooden seat. "I've fixed a lot of boats, Rowan. Seen natural dam-age, collisions with rocks, scraping the ground, general corrosion, wear and tear – that sort of thing. But this damage was different. Holes, smashed in with a hammer or something like that. There was a distinct pattern, like someone thought about what they were doing."

"Where on the boat?"

"Just below the waterline."

"How many times had the boat been hit, damaged, would you say?"

"I patched up about six holes. I noticed the propeller shaft was out of alignment too. Not a lot, but enough to potentially cause trouble."

"Why would that have been the case?"

"Could've been struck or forced while she was moored. Or collided with a rock. The prop shaft is strong, but it can be knocked out of alignment. I tried to tell Mar-tin that and about the holes in the pub, but he didn't be-lieve someone would damage his boat. I recommended he just bought a new prop shaft, for safety, but he didn't want that. Told me to just sort it."

"For people like me who know nothing about boats – what would a damaged propeller shaft do?"

"A misaligned shaft could cause you all sorts of propulsion and, because of that, steering problems. Martin's wasn't too bad, but the potential for it to shear or pull free out on the water was high. The shaft takes loads of pressure. Rotational torque, propeller forces."

After scribbling away, DI Black said: "Do you think it ended up on the rocks because he lost control? The propeller shaft snapped?"

"Likely, yeah – especially if it sheared or worked free."

"You seem fairly certain, Jax."

"I just know my boats, Rowan."

"Was there anything else about the boat that you noticed?"

"There was. A fungus, a growth, like mould. I found it at the stern: strange and slimy, coloured like a rainbow, iridescent and," Jax stopped, thinking about how best to describe it.

"And," Rowan prompted.

"And, sorry, I was trying to think about how it smelled. Strange smell. I can't really describe it."

"Interesting you found it on the boat – I've seen it around the island. What do you know about it?"

"Not much at all. It hasn't been around long but it's spreading quickly. Nathan Waters is your man. He knows a lot about that sort of thing. Studies the land and seas around Wraith's Hollow. He's a good man. You might remember him."

DI Black wrote the name in his notebook, shaking his head slowly. "Not sure, it might be ringing a bell somewhere."

A moment of silence.

"We're almost done, Jax. First, tell me, how would you describe your relationship with Martin?"

"How do you mean?"

"Well, if I think back to my youth on the island, you two were as thick as thieves. Always kicking about together."

"We were close when we were young. As kids like. But after his dad died and left him all that money – he changed."

"How so?" Rowan asked.

"In the way that money changes everyone. It turned him into an arsehole. He was always arrogant – but the money made him ten times worse. We drifted apart ages ago – especially after he started making more cash."

"His mum died in childbirth, didn't she?" DI Black asked.

"Yes. He's been alone for years. Was alone, I should say."

"You weren't friends at all? Were you friendly when you bumped into one another?"

Jax shook his head slowly. "Not really."

"But you were fixing his boat."

"Yeah, but not because of friendship – it was business. Nothing more."

"Cash in hand stuff," Rowan smiled.

"You could say that. We all have to get by."

"We do. And I've got bigger fish to fry than worry about a little cash in hand, Jax . . . Would anyone want to hurt Martin? That you know of?"

"Most of the island," Jax grinned.

"That's interesting. It's just when I asked Ellie Crick the same question – you know Ellie Crick, don't you? Thought so – she didn't know of anyone who'd want to hurt Martin."

"I was speaking hypothetically. Is it hypothetically? If that's the right word. I just meant that he rubbed everyone up the wrong way. Most of the island could have a reason for murdering him, I'm sure."

"Oh really? What would yours be?" DI Black asked.

"Sorry, dark humour, Rowan. Disliking the man and murdering him are two different things."

"Not as different as you might think – one can sometimes lead to the other. Anyway, as I've mentioned Ellie. Do you know anything about their business venture years ago?"

Jax said no.

"Thank you, Jax. To recap, you say Martin and Sophie had an argument last," Rowan looked at his notebook, "Friday morning?" Jax nodded. "Also, that Nathan's my man if I want to learn more about this fungus?"

"Yes. He's a good man. Bit soppy, bit nature happy – you know the type."

"Great. And in your professional opinion, the damage to Martin's boat that you looked at last Friday could've been done by someone with the purpose of causing him harm?"

"I believe so."

DI Black stood. Jax did the same and shook his hand.

"Thank you, Jax. I appreciate you coming in. Before you go, would you say Martin and Sophie got on – was this argument a one off?"

"I really wouldn't know, Rowan. You'd have to ask her."

Jax held Rowan's stare for as long as he could before smiling and looking away. He turned and left the police station.

PC Danny Everett

PC Everett had DI Black's words in his mind as he left the station: you're not alone, okay, Danny. I'm here to help. This relaxed him. Danny had been a police officer on Wraith's Hollow for two years now, and at twenty-four years old, he felt ready. That's what he told himself when he caught up with Ellie Crick. She'd just left the station having been interviewed by Rowan.

"Ellie," he said by her side.

"Really, Danny, I'm not up for this. Leave me alone."

"I won't take all your time, Ellie. DI Black's asked me to do this – I don't want to let him down. I need to ask you a few questions about your business thing with Martin."

"Great. Another interview," Ellie said.

"Why are you smiling?" Danny asked. He had always

loved her smile.

"Are you interviewing me just to sit and talk to me?"

"No. This is police business." Danny knew he'd never get bored of saying that.

"Well, if you want to interview me, I need coffee. You can buy me one."

Diane's Coffee Pot was unusually quiet. Danny paid and carried their drinks over to one of the tables near the window. Lowering the tray to the table, Ellie's tall latte glass slid almost to the edge of the tray, nearly toppling over. Danny's hands were trembling. She'd think him a right idiot. Get a grip, he said to himself as he carried the empty tray back to the counter.

Taking a seat opposite Ellie, he said: "How are you? That must've been awful finding Martin's body."

"It wasn't great, Danny," she replied.

Ellie's green eyes and blonde hair were mesmerising. It was hard for him to concentrate.

"Well?" Ellie prompted.

"How would you characterise your relationship with Martin?"

"Danny, stop talking like that! You forget I know you inside out. And, besides, I already told Rowan everything. About my relationship with Martin, how I found the body. It's been really stressful," she said, reaching her hand out and momentarily resting it on Danny's.

"I know. Poor thing. But I need *something*, Ellie. What was your business about? Did it get off the ground?"

"It was real estate. An eco-friendly project. But Martin was an arsehole to me, Danny, a real shit," Ellie looked away.

Danny handed her a napkin. "Ellie, I'm here for you. It's okay."

"Thank you." She held his hand again. "It's nice to know that I can rely on you. I can trust you, can't I?"

"You can," Danny's heart leapt with love and joy. An image of himself and Ellie walking along the beach came to mind – he was holding her hand, and she was gazing at him, lovingly.

"Basically, Martin screwed me out of the deal," Ellie said, removing her hand and taking a sip of her latte. "We'd planned to build eco-conscious housing, ones that blended with nature, that used green technology. That was my dream. You know the development at Beech Heights?"

"Of course, the gated place near Wraith Forest."

"Yes. That's what he ended up with. Nothing like my original vision. Just more luxury housing. He wanted seclusion, status, swimming pools, state-of-the-art kitchens, bathrooms, glass balconies, stone façades etc – and the profit margins were huge. He was driven by money; obsessed with making more of it."

"You said he was a shit to you. What did he do?" PC Everett asked.

"Promise you won't get angry with me, Danny?"

"I promise."

"Promise me you won't tell Rowan, either?"

"I can't do that, Ellie, you know that. He's my boss."

"Well, I'll let you be the judge as to whether you think he needs to know." Ellie gazed at him with her green eyes, and she curled a strand of hair behind her ear. "Because it's my business – but I know I can trust you . . . Danny, Martin raped me."

"Bastard!"

"I told you not to get cross – there's nothing to be done about it now."

"Sorry. That kills me to hear that. When was this?"

"When our deal went sour. About six years ago. He was such an arsehole. Evil."

"Bastard," Danny said again, leaning back in his chair. He looked around Diane's. No one was close enough to hear their conversation. He sat back up and leaned against the table. "Why didn't you tell me this sooner – before he died? We could've nailed him for it."

Ellie laughed. "Danny, despite being a police officer, you clearly have no idea how the law works. People like Martin, with his wealth, get away with what the hell they like. They do what they like – nothing happens to them. You really think Jennings would've pulled him in? Don't answer that! I know he wouldn't. Look, there's no point in dragging it all up. Martin got what he deserved."

Danny took Ellie's hand again. "What do you mean by that?"

"Don't look so scared, Danny. I didn't kill him. I just meant that life has interesting ways of bringing about justice. The island can be at peace once more."

"I need to tell Rowan about what Martin did to you."

Ellie pulled her hand back. "Why?"

"It's important!"

"It will look bad on me, Danny. Think about it. I was

raped and now Martin's dead."

"What happened to you was a long time ago. Rowan wouldn't treat you as a suspect, I'm sure of it."

"You're sure of it are you? You don't know him. Look, trust me. Don't tell him. It has nothing to do with DI Black."

"Okay, but did you tell him about what happened between you and Martin with Beech Heights?"

"Of course not, Danny. For the same reasons. I don't want Rowan thinking I'm suspect number one. In his eyes, I'd have motive. Martin royally screwed me out of millions. Just tell him that we had a deal, and it fell through – that's what I told him. You do the same. Please."

"Alright," PC Everett said. "Did you think about what I said to you the other day?"

"I did. Maybe tomorrow night you can come round – not tonight. I'm not up for it. I need to drink wine and be by myself."

As soon as Ellie had said this, as soon as he looked into her eyes, Danny had all but forgotten most of what Ellie said.

*

Fuck Martin Howler.

Danny Everett tried to get Ellie out of his mind. He hated Martin for what he'd done to her. How could he rape her and screw her over like that? It was no use thinking about it, he couldn't concentrate. He was trying his best to focus on DI Black's request to track down Martin's last movements on the evening he was murdered.

CCTV wasn't great around Wraith's Hollow, but Danny had a brainwave. He decided the place with the most cameras – therefore offering the most coverage – was the local council offices, located at Hollow Cliff House. Sitting at the edge of the town centre, Hollow Cliff House had a good view of the sea to the east. Built of dark stone, it looked at odds with the lighter stonework of the cottages and other buildings dotted around Wraith's Hollow. PC Everett walked through the small garden, which surrounded the building, not bothered at all by the colourful display of wildflowers and neatly trimmed grass at the edge of the gravel path. The steps leading up to the large wooden door with its bronze fittings were wide and worn, and the thought of how slippery they could be in the winter entered Danny's mind. He read the name of the building which was etched into stone as he went inside.

"Officer Everett," Jenny Briggs said with her hand extended. "I'm ready to help."

"Danny, please, Jenny. Danny's fine." Although he'd met the community safety officer many times when dealing with minor complaints – mostly of kids causing too much noise in one form or another – she always addressed him formally in the first instance.

Jenny blushed a little. "Okay. You still need to look at the CCTV?"

"Absolutely," Danny said.

"Great. I have the room ready. I've made you coffee, too."

"That's nice of you, Jenny."

Jenny led the way through dimly lit rooms and wood-floored corridors that seemed to creak with every step. They went to the second floor and headed through the main chamber room where thick, dark red curtains hung, preventing the warm spring sun from entering. If Danny had to ever describe what a traditional place looked like, he would base it on Hollow Cliff House.

They went into the archive room at the back of the building. With the door pushed to, it was quiet, and Danny could smell the dusty atmosphere of the windowless room.

"Good thing I double up as the IT queen of Wraith's Hollow, isn't it?" Jenny said as though she had never said this before to Danny.

And obsessive data protection queen, Danny resisted saying out loud. "You do know your computers."

She accessed the security system's login page and then entered her username and password. After a moment the portal opened, displaying a series of folders organised by camera location and date.

"Thank you," Danny said and sat at the computer. Jenny placed his coffee down next to him and stood back. He began looking at the footage feeling daunted. Suddenly, the challenge, the necessity to get it right, to not miss anything, to review all footage possible, weighed on him heavily. It would take him a while to look through all the potential places so he started with the town centre and the main intersections where traffic and pedestrians moved as this would cover good ground from the off. He was hoping to catch a glimpse of Martin either walking through or driving near the time of his murder. But there was nothing. Wraith's Hollow was dead.

PC Everett approached the rest of the task systematically: examining all the footage as close as possible to the site of Martin's murder – Tide Fall Beach was not covered – and then moving outward from there. He was on his second coffee – he found it difficult to say no to Jenny's offerings of coffee as she was very enthusiastic about helping in any way she could – when he opened the folder named Pier Road. He navigated to one in the morning and began scanning through. Just as he was about to give up and take a break, he saw a hooded figure heading in the direction of the seafront – facing away from the camera. Danny wasn't sure how he knew, but he believed the person they were looking for was this hooded figure walking to the beach at one thirty-five in the morning.

PC Everett, staring silently and intensely at the video footage, jumped at the sound of DI Black's voice over the radio.

"Sir, over," Danny said.

"I need you to get over to Silver Cove Marina. You need to check the CCTV on the night of Martin's murder. I also want you to check if there's any footage of his boat being damaged at night. Start with last week. Jax Flint told me he worked on his boat on Friday, and he suspected someone might've damaged it on purpose. See what comes to the surface."

PC Danny Everett agreed enthusiastically and then told DI Black what he found at Pier Road: "It's not clear footage, but I think it's our killer," he said with pride.

*

PC Everett was headed for the marina – feeling great. He was doing proper police work on a proper investigation. The fact that his current happiness depended on someone else having been killed totally escaped him.

Danny passed Nathan's lighthouse and continued the short drive to the marina. As he drove through the iron gates, his eyes caught the gleam of a golden sign: *Silver Cove Marina.* It shone brightly in the sunlight, as if freshly polished. He parked his car and climbed out, spotting the type of boats he wished he could own someday. PC Everett loved being a police officer, but it wasn't the road to travel down if you wanted to be rich. Danny was going to make his money as a fitness influencer. There was nothing that he loved more than working out and spreading that knowledge. You could make loads of money online. At the back of his mind, if it didn't work out, he could stay in the police. Work his way up – maybe become a detective like DI Black. He wondered for a moment which Ellie would prefer: detective or influencer?

Luxury boats, gleaming white, shiny railings, beautiful decking – perfect for parties – enticed him. Right. Focus. DI Black wants me to look at the CCTV. He said Martin's boat was damaged. Probably last week.

The marina office was spectacular. Made of glass and

steel, it was sleek and modern. There were windows all around, giving PC Everett a great view of the boats below and the ocean beyond. Silver Cove Marina was the complete opposite of Havenmoore Port. The former was wealth and posturing; the latter was functionality and history.

"Hello," he called out. It didn't seem as though anyone was around, but Roger Stone must be, Danny concluded, as the doors and gates would be locked if he wasn't there.

A door opened to Danny's left. It was Roger Stone. "Young, Danny Everett. Good to see you. You've saved me a job," he said.

"Hi, Roger. What do you mean?"

"Well, I wondered about coming down to the station – and here you are."

"Pleased to have saved you a job. How're you doing?"

"A little shaken if I'm honest, Danny, what with all this Martin business."

"I know. It's not what usually happens around here. How long you been working here now?"

"Couple of years . . . It's sad news. Terrible." Roger placed his hands on his hips and looked out of the glass windows at the sea for a moment. "Anyway, what can I do for you?"

"DI Black wants me to check your CCTV footage."

"I heard about him. How he used to live here then he moved away. Bit before my time. It's funny, he left Wraith's Hollow to work on the mainland, and I left the mainland to retire here. I'd never have thought that something like what happened to Martin could happen here. Unthinkable."

"It is. That's why we need to find whoever did this. Make sure it doesn't happen again."

"I'm afraid you're going to struggle with the CCTV. That's what I was coming to the station about."

"How come?"

"It's been playing up. It went down last night again. It was working during the day. I checked before I left. I usually leave by lunch time. But that's flexible depending on what jobs I have on. In fact, you're lucky to catch me here this afternoon. I was at a loose end, didn't really know what to do after I heard about Martin. Coming here seemed like the right thing to do."

"What happened with the CCTV?" Danny asked.

"Come through," Roger said, leading them through the door he had come out of earlier. "It's been playing up as I say," he said, pointing to the laptop on the desk in the office, "for a while now."

"How long we talking?"

"What, that it's been playing up? Couple of months."

"Did Martin know about this?"

"Wouldn't be doing my job properly if he didn't."

"What's gone wrong with it?" PC Everett asked.

"Coming up with messages like system failure, unauthorised access warnings, missing footage from the data log – I told Martin about all of these."

"What did he say?"

"Nothing much. He didn't seem bothered – which struck me as really odd or really stupid. Odd because of the amount of money kicking about here and stupid because if there was an actual problem – i.e. someone playing silly buggers – it meant they could cause a lot of damage."

"So, you had no footage last night?"

Roger shook his head. "Nor on the night his boat was damaged."

"So, nothing last night when he was murdered, and nothing when his boat was damaged?"

"That's correct. I told Martin the next day after his boat got done over. That was a week ago, Thursday, well, Wednesday night."

"What did he say?"

"He wasn't bothered at all. You see, Danny, people like him, with loads of cash, don't think they're vulnerable to anything . . . What's odd is that on the night his boat was wrecked and when he was murdered, the cameras went down at midnight and came back on at six in the morning."

"Shit," Danny said.

Roger nodded. "I think the person who shut the cameras down both nights, is the person you're looking for."

"Whoever it is must've known that last night, Martin was going to get his boat and take it out on the water. Someone else must've been with him. Otherwise, there was no need to shut the cameras down. Martin getting his boat alone wouldn't have been an issue," Danny stopped, that was as far as his thinking took him.

"My thoughts exactly," Roger said.

"Okay. Just so I'm clear, ready for when I tell DI Black

about this. On both nights, the cameras went down at midnight and came back on at six?"

Roger nodded.

"Okay. And they've been playing up over the last couple of months. Got it. Who else has access to the marina? Do any of the owners have a key?"

"They can access certain areas. They can get in and out of the marina at any time of the day or night – but they can't get in this building. The only other person who has a key besides me and Martin – to my knowledge – is Jax. He's a good man, salt of the earth. He fixes the boats as you probably know. In fact, I was the one to call him last Thursday to see if he could come look at Martin's boat. Jax came out Friday morning for a bit and then finished Saturday."

"Does Jax's key allow him to access this room?"

"It does – the alarm keypad is there," Roger pointed to the system on the wall. "You need to punch in the code to stop the building singing and dancing."

"Is the alarm linked to the CCTV?"

"Damn, sorry. I should've said. When the CCTV stops, the alarm won't work. They're both hooked up. CCTV catches motion, the alarm goes. So, without the CCTV eyes, the alarm's blind."

"Even if the alarm was active, because the cameras went down, it stayed off?"

"Correct. It's a stupid system."

"Is it only you and Martin who can access the CCTV?"

"I believe so. Martin does it remotely – how often, I don't really know. He wasn't security conscious at all. I can check it. Don't need to that much but since his boat was damaged and now since he was murdered, I did."

"Okay. When did you last see Martin, and how did he seem?"

"Saw him Tuesday morning – briefly. He seemed himself. Made a joke about us being ships in the night. Then he left."

"Any idea what he was doing here? What time was it, by the way?"

"Must've been after nine but not as late as ten. As to what he was doing here – haven't a clue."

"Thanks, Roger. I appreciate it."

"Not sure how much help I've been."

"A great help, actually. Whoever damaged his boat knew the security system you have inside out. And they knew that Martin was taking his boat out on the night he was murdered."

Rowan Black

Cramming in a wholemeal tuna sandwich from the local shop at two-thirty in the afternoon wasn't Rowan's idea of lunch. He could've bought some fish and chips – or probably just the chips – from Wraith's Hook, but the idea of fighting through a load of carb stodge wasn't appealing.

He'd spoken to DCI Hargrave about contacting Martin's next of kin on the mainland – seeing as there was no one on Wraith's Hollow – before deciding to visit Tim

Thorn, find out all he could about the bookcase and its secret compartment. Afterwards, he'd arranged to meet Sergeant Jennings. They were going to speak to Sophie Marlow – something he was dreading. Having Jennings there was Rowan's idea. He couldn't tell how Sophie would be towards him. At least with Jennings around she might show a bit of restraint.

Tim's workshop had a sign which read: Be back in five – if not, I may be ten. And a smiley face underneath. Rowan held his notebook and scanned up and down the road. Hollowbrook Lane looked just as it did when he was growing up. It was a couple of streets away from the heart of the town centre, so it had a quiet, calm feel. Three locals strolled by, smiling warmly. They didn't have a care in the world. For a second, Rowan forgot he was the lead investigator in a murder enquiry: he was back on Wraith's Hollow, as a young man, holding Cynthia's hand, wandering slowly up and down Hollowbrook Lane.

The air was sweet, warm and fresh. The sound of seagulls above relaxed him. He entertained the idea of moving back to Wraith's Hollow for the first time in years.

There were a couple of shops along the road, looking like Tim's: each made from stone, now weathered, with strong oak doors. One of the charity shops used to be Jan's Sweetshop. Going there as a kid with 50p in your pocket was one of the best feelings in the world. Rowan remembered stepping inside and being hit by the smell of sugar. Seeing bright colourful jars all lined up on the shelves, and boxes of sweets all around filled with fizzy, sweet, sour, cola, cherry, boiled and soft.

There was something about Hollowbrook Lane that caused, almost urged, him to reflect on the past, on how things could've been different with Cynthia. If she hadn't killed herself, would they have been together now? Would they have had a family? Rowan had loved Cynthia – but Sophie would never understand this.

She blamed him.

"Rowan Black."

Rowan turned and shielded his eyes from the sun with his arm. Tim was heading his way carrying a bag of shopping. "Late lunch," Rowan said, putting out his hand.

"Indeed." Tim shook his hand. "And not that exciting either. Only had tuna left at the shop."

"For what it's worth, mine wasn't too bad," Rowan smiled.

"What can I do for you, Detective? You want to come inside?"

"Please."

"I'm snowed under, so it's a working lunch, I'm afraid."

"No problems at all." Rowan stepped to one side whilst Tim dug his keys out of his overalls. It took Tim a couple of tries to put the key in the lock. There was something strange about the way in which he was struggling to coordinate holding his shopping in one hand and trying to fit the key in the lock with the other.

"Bloody hand," Tim said. "Hold this." He handed Rowan the shopping bag and then swapped the keys into his left hand and unlocked the door in one smooth action.

"How'd you injure the hand?" Rowan asked as they

stepped inside the workshop. Wood and varnish fra-granced the air – it was a wonderful smell.

"Oh, one of those really silly, stupid work injuries. I was, now, what was I doing, ah, yes!" he said, taking the bag back and placing it on the worktable. He grabbed his tuna sandwich with his left hand. "I was tightening that bench vice there, slipped, and smashed my knuckles on the underside, right there," Tim leaned towards the clamp and pointed to the corner.

"You're lucky you didn't break anything. Looks nasty. Is that your dominant hand? Your right?"

"It is. Luckily, I don't notice it when I'm working," Tim said. He took a bite out of the sandwich, then left it on the table amongst wood shavings and sawdust, and announced he was putting the kettle on. He headed over to the corner of the workshop.

Rowan made a note in his book: Tim Thorn, right hand hurts, winced when taking bag but stated injury doesn't bother him.

"You want tea?" Tim asked.

"Please. Half a sugar and a splash of milk."

"I'm the same. Too much milk makes me want to vomit!" Tim laughed.

"Lovely chair I see you're making."

"Thank you. It's for Father Hemmingway," he said, raising his voice over the boiling kettle.

"Father Hemmingway! I can't believe he's still alive. How old is he now?"

"Not sure. But put it this way, he's been the local vicar all my life. He must be in his eighties."

"Yeah, he must be. I thought maybe a little older than that. Mind you, he can't be far off Mrs. Appleby's age. How is she, by the way? I thought I must pop in and see her."

There was a brief silence, broken only by the sound of Tim pouring water into two cups and stirring the tea bags. Rowan waited for Tim to speak first.

"Yes. She would like that, Rowan, I'm sure. She's doing well. I popped up earlier to say hi."

"That was kind of you – especially as you said you're snowed under."

DI Black was quiet. He watched Tim finish the tea, adding a couple of splashes of milk to each cup. From Rowan's perspective, it looked as though even holding the carton of milk was enough to cause Tim's injured hand to tremble.

"Well, I like to check on her, Rowan. Friendship's worth more than work."

Rowan took his tea from Tim. "I agree. It's the one thing I miss about the place. Proper community, proper friendships. You don't get that so much on the mainland."

"Agreed," Tim said and leaned against the worktable.

Rowan mirrored his position.

"So," Tim began. "What can I do for you? You haven't come here just to ask me why I didn't give you a job all those years ago have you?" Tim smiled.

"Seeing as you've mentioned it . . . Actually, let's not go there!" Rowan sipped some tea. "What was your relationship with Martin Howler?"

"Purely professional."

"Did you know him socially at all?"

"Not at all. He was an arsehole – you know that. I wouldn't give him the time of day unless he was paying me to."

"Paying you for a bookcase," DI Black said. He wasn't sure if Tim had made Martin's bookcase, but Jennings seemed quite sure.

"Right."

"Did you make that beautiful one in Martin's house?"

"I did – with Little Liam's help. Mustn't take all the credit. He's my young apprentice. Great kid."

"And where's Little Liam now?" Rowan asked as he noted the name down.

"I sent him home earlier. A treat."

"Very nice of you. My boss wouldn't be that generous. Anyway, what can you tell me about the bookcase?" DI Black knew this was an obvious leading question, given that Tim had made it and would know about the secret compartment, but he wanted to see if Tim would take the bait.

"I can tell you that Martin was a bloody nightmare. Constantly changing his mind about the style, size, just about anything I did, he wanted something altering. He was difficult."

"Difficult on purpose?"

"Absolutely. To what end – I don't know."

"Anything else you can tell me?" Rowan asked.

"He was a cagey bastard . . . Look, you seem to know about the bookcase I made at Martin's. I imagine you needed to look round – procedure and all that. Martin wanted a secret compartment built inside the bookcase. No idea why."

"Did you ask why?"

"Of course. It would've helped me design it if I knew what he wanted to store in it. But he was cagey, as I say. How come you found it?" Tim finished his sandwich and swigged some tea. "Christ that's hot!"

"Between us, Tim. His place has been trashed. Someone broke in. Just wrecked everything. Everything destroyed apart from your lovely bookcase. I was curious about that, so I looked it over more closely than I would've done. I can't figure out why it wasn't trashed like everything else."

"Beats me, Detective. That's your job, I'm afraid."

"Tell me about it," Rowan said. "Did you ever need to access Martin's house for any reason when he wasn't there?"

"I did. A few times. More recently to measure up and then a few days later to deliver the bookcase."

"What day did you deliver it?"

"Saturday just gone."

"Oh, really new then – only just built and delivered."

"Sure was."

"When you delivered the bookcase on Saturday – what time was it?"

"I can't be sure."

"Try," Rowan said, holding his notebook open, ready to write.

"I suppose it was around eight in the evening.

Actually, it must've been about then."

"How can you be so sure?"

"Little Liam was with me. I remember he said he should've been in the pub. That's it. We'd just got it upstairs – two flights! – what a bastard job that was. The bookcase was originally going on the ground floor. Something else he changed his mind about. Anyway, Little Liam checked his watch and told me it was eight. He should've been drinking a pint – not in Martin's house. That was it."

"I'm amazed you got it up there. Was the hand injured at this point? Or after?"

"After, thank God. No, I did this Tuesday."

"That's lucky," Rowan said, making a note. "It wouldn't have been fun lifting that bookcase with that hand of yours."

Tim smiled and sipped some tea.

"Can you just confirm for me, Tim. When you delivered the bookcase, Martin wasn't there, and you knew the code to get in."

"That's correct. He told me he'd change it. I guess he did."

"How so?"

"I just meant that he probably did what he said. Not that it bothers me whether I know his code or not. Like I said, I only associate with him – sorry, associated – on professional grounds."

"Did Martin tell you who he was going to meet last Saturday evening?"

"No. I didn't ask. He wouldn't have told me anyway, Rowan. But I'm glad he wasn't there – he would've been a pain in the arse. Better off with him out the way."

DI Black made a mental note of Tim's tone when he said that.

"By better off, I meant then – that evening, not altogether."

"I know what you meant, Tim. If you don't mind, pop down to the station so we can take your prints. And we'll do Little Liam's while we're at it. Both your prints will be all over Martin's place."

"Well, we didn't wear gloves, that's for sure. But yes. I'll explain the situation and bring Little Liam with me."

"Good. Tell him it's just procedure. We need to eliminate you both. It's highly likely that Martin's murder and the wrecking of his house are related."

"You think so?"

"Absolutely. Can you give me an idea of where you went in Martin's house? Do your best to remember."

"Sure. Main living room, stairs obviously, and the office on the second floor."

"Did you use the kitchen for anything? Bathroom?"

Tim shook his head. "Nope. Our objective was to get in and get out. No need to use the kitchen or bathroom."

"Thank you. You're absolutely sure you and Little Liam didn't go into any of the other rooms?"

"Certain."

"Great. I appreciate your time. I know you're busy."

"I am. Father Hemmingway's chair won't wax itself."

"Did Martin have any enemies or ongoing arguments with anyone on the island that you know of?"

"If you're asking me whether I know if someone had a proper reason for murdering him, I would say plenty of people."

"Oh really. Who?"

"Most of the island."

"Yes, Jax said something similar."

"I think most people who came across Martin Howler ended up hating him for one reason or another. He wasn't right for Wraith's Hollow. He upset the balance here, the peace. Building left, right, and centre. Monopolising, ruining the landscape . . . He had ambitions beyond what most normal folk like me could take."

"Meaning?"

"It's our Wraith's Hollow, you see. It's not his. Take that bloody house of his. Nexus House isn't Wraith's Hollow. Come on, you're from here. You know exactly what I'm talking about!"

"I do. Wraith's Hollow is tradition; good people; solid community; trust. Martin was too progressive."

"That he bloody well was. Had no values. Didn't care about anyone but himself. That's not good enough, Rowan, we don't need people like that here."

Rowan took a moment and made a show of jotting some things down in his notebook. He was, really, observing Tim, allowing him to take a deep breath, calm down. Tim's face had reddened and one of his fists was clenched.

"Is there anything else, Rowan? I'm very busy," Tim

said, exhaling heavily.

"Yes, perhaps you might be able to help. I keep running into the idea that there might be a cult on the island. As a lifelong, Wraith's Hollow inhabitant, have you ever heard about it? This cult?"

Tim brushed the idea away with his good hand and then said: "Load of rubbish. Hearsay. No more truth in it than any number of the ghost stories about Wraith's Hollow that surface from time to time."

"So, you didn't see a strange Celt-like symbol, say, with intricate patterns when you delivered the bookcase, or on any other occasion when you've been to his house?"

Tim shook his head slowly. "No, no. I'd remember them. I like that sort of thing."

"Thanks, Tim. You've been a great help," Rowan said and sipped some more tea. It was too hot to finish. He headed for the door but turned back to face Tim, looking in his eyes, and said: "To help move our enquiries along, can you tell me where you were last night, after midnight, when Martin was murdered?"

"Of course: in bed. Early to bed and early to rise, makes a man healthy, wealthy, and wise."

DI Black eyed Tim, offered a smile, and then left.

Nathan Waters

Nathan had to get out. Staying at home in his lighthouse was suffocating. Walking along the promenade, heading towards town, he couldn't face looking at the beach or the sea.

What they did, what had happened, was already too much to bear. He thought he'd be able to live with it – go about life as normal, but now, he didn't know if he could.

Despite the seagulls squawking overhead and people's conversations filling the air, Nathan was unable to escape the sound of the ocean. It was loud, drowning his eardrums. The ocean's voice taunted him. It knew the truth and was going to make everyone aware of what had happened! He couldn't bear to look at his reflection in the windows nor could he look at the people walking by.

Did they know? They can't know! But when he tuned into their conversations, Martin's death was on all their lips.

He wanted nothing to do with any one of them. They could all just fuck off.

Head down, he paced towards Saltmere Way. Away from the shops, the ocean was louder than before: Martin, Martin, Martin. He felt sick. There was nobody else around as he approached Sophie Marlow's cottage, but the feeling that people were staring at him, digging into his conscience, was inescapable.

Knock, knock – he hammered the door.

"Jesus, Nathan," Sophie said. "What the hell're you doing?"

Nathan pushed past her and went inside. "What have we done, what have *we* done, Sophie!"

Sophie slapped him. "Calm down!"

"Fuck, Sophie!"

"Shut up and sit down," Sophie said and went to the kitchen.

Nathan did as he was told and sat on the sofa, gripping his hair.

"Drink this."

He drank his double shot of whisky in one and coughed afterwards. "Another."

Sophie got him another and one for herself, and when Nathan settled, she said: "You've got to hold your shit together. If you don't, we're all fucked."

"He said he'd arrange to meet me, but he hasn't."

"I know. Me too. But don't panic – we're all in this together. We made our decision."

"Sophie, there was blood in the boat! When did we decide that?"

"What do you mean?"

"I found blood for fuck's sake! Was it yours or Martin's?"

"Jesus. Mine. Look." Sophie pulled up her dress to reveal a nasty looking cut across her shin on her left leg. It was clearly healing, but also clearly recent.

"Shit, Sophie."

"Did you clean the boat? Did you get all the blood off?"

"Yes, calm down," Nathan said – the fact that he was now the calmer one was completely lost on him.

"Oh my God. I'm done for. We're all done for!"

"Look, I'm not going to slap you, but calm the fuck down . . . we need to think."

There was a moment of silence, broken only by the sound of their empty whisky glasses being placed heavily on the coffee table, then Sophie said: "This is your fault, Nathan. I wouldn't have fallen over if Martin hadn't crashed his boat. He only crashed his boat because you fucked up the poison – you made it too strong."

"Give me a fucking break. I only had a few days to work it out. You probably did it wrong!"

"I did exactly as you said. Slip it in his drink and he won't have a clue – that's what you said. And you know what – he didn't. He had no fucking clue! He went nuts, Nathan. Within twenty minutes, he was completely nuts. Hallucinating, the lot. I was so scared on that fucking boat. I thought he was going to kill *me*."

"How did you get to the beach from the boat?" Nathan asked, trying to process what had happened.

"With great fucking difficulty. It was horrible. I used my phone torch to help – but the rocks were treacherous. The wind was loud, howling against the cliff. Honestly, it was terrible. Martin didn't stop laughing. He was wrecked. I thought he'd slip in and drown but he managed to follow me onto the beach."

Nathan exhaled. "What happened then?"

"The plan changed. I couldn't get Martin back to his house. I sent a message. We adapted."

"You shouldn't have changed the fucking plan! Stayed on the beach. Shit. We also said no messages. Are you stupid! The police will pick that up if they get your phone. Sophie, we worked all this out!"

Sophie sighed. "I had to adapt. The plan went

fucked."

"What the hell happened then?"

"Look, we got on the beach. I told Martin to stand still which seemed crazy as he was high as a kite; but he did. I told him I was going for a wee and when I came back, I was going to suck his cock. Is that enough detail for you?"

"Fine. Fine. Right."

"You can guess the rest. You need to leave, Nathan. You never usually visit me – if someone sees, it'll look suspicious."

"I don't know if I can handle this."

"You're going to have to. You're either part of the solution, Nathan, or part of the problem. Which one are you going to be?"

Nathan looked at Sophie. It was almost like he didn't recognise her. The anger in her eyes had transformed the rest of her face, and the implicit message in her last words became explicitly clear.

Rowan Black

Back at Wraith's Hollow police station, DI Black had just told Sergeant Jennings about the letter that Martin Howler had sent to him. Jennings agreed that under normal circumstances, the letter was totally out of Martin's character.

Understanding what had – or who had – spooked Martin into writing it, would move their investigation forwards. Rowan also caught Jennings up with his conversations with Tim and Jax. Both names had been written on the whiteboard in the incident room – beside the photos of Martin's body. Rowan had listed under Tim's name:

- Suspicious behaviour: would remember 'them' responding to my question about one symbol – i.e. implied he knew there was more than one at Martin's home. There were three.
- Right hand injury (dominant hand) consistent with damage at Martin's house – holes in walls. And with trauma to Martin's left side of skull.
- Visibly angry when talking about Martin.
- Knew about secret compartment – designed the bookcase.

- Access to Martin's house – knew code to deliver bookcase. Claimed that he and Little Liam didn't go anywhere in house, other than main route to study upstairs.
- Motive?
- Alibi: was in bed at time of murder – no one to confirm this.

Under Jasper Flint's name he listed:

- Suspicious behaviour: agitated/uncomfortable talking about Martin.
- Disliked Martin and his wealth.

- Believes/has theory that damage to boat and murder are linked; damage to hull done on purpose.
- Worked on boat: noted propeller shaft misaligned.

- Access to marina – has own key; knew CCTV blind spots; stated no access to CCTV.
- Noticed fungus on boat – relating to?
- Motive?
- Alibi: need to confirm.

"Are these our top suspects then?" Sergeant Jennings asked, having scanned the information.

"Everyone's a suspect, Frank, until we find the killer."

"What's this symbol reference?"

"When I spoke to Tim in his workshop earlier, I specifically asked whether he had seen a symbol lying around Martin's house – as in one. He stated he hadn't and that he would remember them – i.e. more than one – if he did because he's into that sort of thing."

"Hardly concrete evidence, Rowan. Probably a mistake on his part."

"Possibly. Possibly not. But it's crucial we take note of everything, no matter how small or inconsequential. Once we have it all before us – what's irrelevant will become obvious."

"And just like that, we'll have our man," Sergeant Jennings said with a wry smile.

"Might not be a man, Frank."

PC Everett made his way into the incident room.

"Hi, Danny," Sergeant Jennings said.

"DI Black–"

"Rowan is fine, Danny. Or sir," he said smiling.

"Sorry, Rowan, uh, sir. I've got some information." Danny relayed his conversation with Roger Stone to Rowan and Jennings.

"CCTV stopped working on both occasions? Off at midnight, back on at six?"

Danny nodded. "Roger said he told Martin about it, but Martin didn't care. They've been having problems with it for a couple of months."

"Good work, Danny."

"I think, too, sir, that whoever killed Martin knew he was coming for his boat last night, and that he'd be with someone – otherwise, why turn the cameras off? He must've been with someone. I was thinking about this on the way over. I think that other person is the one on the council's CCTV at Pier Road."

DI Black made a note in his notebook. "Right. We need a warrant for that laptop. Danny, sort the details for the application and I'll get it signed off. We'll need one as it's not a crime scene, and that computer will hold client data. Once it's back, we'll have digital forensics take a look. If someone's been able to shut off the marina's cameras, we need to find out who. Second, head back to the council and request the footage of Pier Road for the relevant time period. Let's see if we can identify the person you saw . . . Frank, let's go speak to Sophie Marlow," Rowan said, feeling his stomach turn.

"Oh, sir, sorry," PC Everett said, stopping by the door. He'd already begun to make his way out of the room. "I just remembered. I spoke to Ellie Crick like you asked. I didn't get much out of her. All she said was that her deal – something about Beech Heights, she was really vague – just that it fell through about six years ago. She didn't have much to do with Martin after that."

"Okay. Was there anything else, Danny?" DI Black asked.

PC Danny Everett shook his head.

*

There was something odd about the way in which Danny had looked at Rowan when he asked him whether there was something else. But Rowan didn't have time to think about what. He was too preoccupied with seeing Sophie Marlow again, too preoccupied with seeming like he wasn't preoccupied whenever Jennings spoke to him.

They pulled up outside Sophie's cottage. Rowan checked the time: nearly four p.m. The day had flown by. He really needed the forensic results from the boat, body, and house – but he knew he'd have to wait. He was hoping the sweep of the house would locate Martin's phone, too. Once he had it all, he could start building a picture of what really happened last night. Though the combined evidence would only tell him what happened, not necessarily why. The why usually came after he'd interviewed everyone involved and understood the gritty, neurotic details threading through their lives and relationships.

"Okay, Rowan?"

"Sure," he said, shutting the car door. "Drift Edge. Beautiful little place."

"It sure is nice along here. Quiet mind. Too quiet if you ask me," Sergeant Jennings said.

"Yes, Frank, it is compared with the other outrageously loud places on the island."

"No need for that, sir." Jennings knocked the door, smiling.

Rowan was about to speak but Sophie opening the door, faster than necessary, stopped him.

"Yes," she said, looking Rowan in the eyes. "What do you want, Rowan?"

"Sophie, I think you should–" Jennings began but Rowan raised his hand to stop him.

"Hi, Sophie. I'm here officially, investigating the murder of Martin Howler."

"Am I a suspect?"

"He didn't say that, Sophie – what's gotten into you?" Sergeant Jennings asked.

"Why don't you ask, Rowan Black?"

"Sophie, we're here to discuss Martin Howler, nothing more. Don't make this hard. What happened in the past stays in the past."

"Strangely enough, I can't leave the past in the past."

"Well, you're going to have to. Please, let us in. We can talk and then be on our way as soon as."

Sophie stepped aside, allowing DI Black and Sergeant Jennings into her home.

"Sit there," she said, pointing to the sofa. "I'll make

tea."

"What the hell is wrong with her?" Jennings asked. "I presume this is about Cynthia?"

"Not now, Frank."

"Well, maybe not now, but I need to know if this problem with Sophie is going to get in the way of this investigation," Jennings said.

"Of course it won't."

"How can you be so sure? It's clearly got in the way up to this point – and you've only said hello!"

"Shhh, she'll hear you. Look, leave it to me. Just be on guard as to what she says."

"What the hell does that mean?"

"What the hell does what mean?" Sophie said leaning into the living room.

"Nothing – we were just talking about your painting on the easel there. Beautiful. Is it finished?" DI Black tried his best to sound as sincere as he could.

"Rowan, you never liked my paintings way back when. Why start now! And yes, it is finished. Do you both take milk and sugar?"

"Splash of milk and two sugars, please," Jennings said.

"Same but with half a sugar."

"You've changed your tune, Rowan, over the years. There was a time when you had three sugars – I remember," Sophie said going back to the kitchen. Soon she was back with three cups of tea. She placed them on seaside coasters and then sat on her artist's stool opposite Rowan and Jennings.

"You've been painting all this time?" Rowan asked.

"You didn't come here to ask me about my art. So, ask the questions you need to and then please leave."

"Sophie, I'm not going to sit here and listen to you talk to my colleague like that."

"Stay or go, Frank. It's up to you."

Rowan put his hand up again as a cue for Jennings to settle down. Rowan could hear him breathing heavier. "Please, be civil, Sophie."

"Okay. I'll tell you about my painting. This one," Sophie pointed to the easel to her left at the end of the living room, "is of the sea. You've no doubt guessed that already. I know how bright and intelligent you are. This one's going to a client of mine on the mainland. You'll no doubt recognise the cliffs – Ghost Cliff Point. I've captured it well. You know Ghost Cliff Point, don't you?"

"That's enough, Sophie," DI Black said.

"No, no, why stop? You want to talk about painting. Ghost Cliff Point is where Cynthia, my sister, your ex, was killed! If you look closely, you can see the exact spot on the canvas," Sophie stood up and went to the painting. "Right fucking there was where she was murdered."

DI Rowan Black stood and shouted: "Enough, Sophie!"

"Ahhh, there's the Rowan Black I remember. You were hiding, weren't you."

"Just sit down," Jennings said. "What the hell's wrong with you, Sophie? We're not here to talk about Cynthia."

"Okay, fine. I'll sit and listen like a good girl."

This was unbearable. Rowan said: "Just a few questions. Then we'll be on our way."

Sophie nodded. She'd changed; she looked relaxed despite the previous exchange.

"What was your relationship with Martin Howler like?"

"You knew him as much as I did, Rowan. The man was an arsehole."

"You're not the only one to have said that to me today."

"And I won't be the last. Everyone you ask will say the same."

"That aside – did you get along?"

"Yes and no. He tried it on with me many times, told me he loved me, promised me the world."

"In what way?"

"That he tried it on with me or promised me the world?"

"Which do you think?" Rowan said.

"Just male, egotistical crap. Take me on holidays, treat me like a queen. Promised me an art studio up on the cliffs. Near the edge of Ghost Cliff Point."

"Doesn't sound such a bad thing, Sophie," Jennings said.

"No, I suppose it doesn't."

"Wouldn't an art studio be nice? Wouldn't have to be so crammed in here then," Jennings said.

"It would. But not built in the place where Cynthia took her last steps. I hated the idea, but Martin kept going on and on about it."

"Would you say this studio idea caused friction between you?" Rowan asked.

"What do you think? Yes! He didn't understand that I couldn't paint up on the cliffs looking out at the place where she was killed."

"All of that was cleared up years ago, Sophie," Jennings offered.

"Let's focus back on Martin, Sophie. I know it's hard for you," Rowan said.

"I'm fine. I don't need your sympathy, thank you. I've never asked for it, and I won't start now." Sophie sipped some tea, but it was clearly too hot for her. She saved face by simply putting the mug back down on the table without acknowledging it.

"Would you say you argued a lot?"

"Not always. Sometimes."

"Did you have any feelings towards him – affection or otherwise?"

"I didn't love him, if that's what you're asking; but I didn't kill him either, if that's what you're implying."

DI Black held up his hand. "Not implying anything, Sophie. I'm just trying to get to the truth about Martin's death. How was your last exchange?"

"You mean conversation?"

Rowan nodded. He was ready to write Sophie's response in his notebook.

"Fine."

"What did you speak about?" he asked.

"The studio, I think. I don't recollect much about it."

"Was this an occasion when you argued about the studio?"

"Not really. I was tired."

"Did you speak in person or was it on the phone?"

Sophie paused for a moment before answering. "In person. He came to my house."

"What day was this?"

"Last Friday morning."

Rowan checked his notes from his conversation with Jax before asking: "What time?"

"I don't know."

"Give me a clue."

Sophie exhaled forcefully. "Earlyish."

"Earlyish as in midmorning or around breakfast time?"

"About nine, I suppose."

"Was Martin in the habit of coming round early to see you?" Jennings asked.

"I don't think he even considered the fact that other people might be operating on a different time schedule to him. I think he thought the whole world catered to whatever whim he had."

"Did he visit you often?" Rowan asked.

"Not really."

"You said he loved you. When did he say this?"

"Why are you asking me that? I can't see what relevance it has to his death."

"You mean murder," DI Black corrected. "I need to understand what your relationship with Martin Howler was like, nothing more."

"I can't honestly remember when he told me the first time. It was years ago. But I never took him seriously. He just said stuff like that so he could try to sleep with me. I know for a fact that he tried the same trick with Ellie Crick. Plus whoever else took his fancy."

"Were you ever intimate?" Rowan asked.

"That's my business."

"What do you know about Martin and Ellie's relationship?"

"Nothing much. He was a sleaze to her. Didn't treat her well at all."

"Yes, I did hear something about that," Rowan said. "What do you know about the business deal they had? Beech Heights, wasn't it? Just fell through, didn't it?" Rowan prompted.

"It did. But only because he cut her out of it. He stole her ideas, used her basically, then changed direction."

"In what way?"

"Ellie wants to save the planet. Loves all that. It's not a bad thing of course but eco-housing or whatever you call it, isn't as desirable as luxury. From what Ellie told me – this is going back a few years now – Martin wanted to make as much profit as possible. Which doesn't allow any room for saving the planet. Besides, luxury housing is what attracts people to buy on the island – not energy-saving, grass-covered roofing."

"Sounds like you haven't got much time for it either, Sophie," Jennings said.

"I do as it happens. I would die for this island."

Jennings raised his eyebrows. "Seems a funny way to put it."

"I love Wraith's Hollow," she eyed Jennings for a moment. Then: "Wouldn't leave it for the world. If Martin had his way, he would've built so much, changed it so much – it wouldn't be Wraith's Hollow anymore. We can't have that. This is our home."

DI Black was writing in his notebook. "He really screwed Ellie over."

"He did. She lost a lot of money – profit."

"It's funny, you know. When I asked her about it, she didn't seem too bothered by it – the fact that it fell through was neither here nor there." Rowan looked through his notes from his interview with Ellie earlier that day. "She said it was a small business idea. Nothing came of it. From what you're saying, I wouldn't describe it like that – would you?"

"I wouldn't, no."

"Why do you think Ellie described it like that?"

Sophie shrugged and had another try of her tea. Rowan watched her. "You'd have to ask her, Rowan. Really, it's none of my business." Rowan didn't respond – he waited. Silence. Followed by more silence. Each of them had some tea. Sophie said: "Perhaps she didn't want to seem suspicious in any way."

"I don't know why her telling me that Martin cut her out of a deal six years ago would make her suspicious."

"Then maybe you shouldn't be a detective."

"Meaning?"

"I don't know. Perhaps she thought you'd think she wanted revenge or something."

"Okay . . . So, to clarify, you last saw and spoke to Martin last Friday morning?"

Sophie nodded and glanced at her painting momentarily.

"It is a lovely painting," Rowan said. "And when you last spoke, you didn't argue – you said you were tired. It was about nine in the morning." Rowan waited for Sophie to agree. "You're sure you didn't argue? You said you spoke about the studio – something that causes friction between you. But this time, it didn't?"

"As I said, I was tired. I don't tend to have much enthusiasm for anything when I'm tired – least of all, arguing with Martin bloody Howler."

Rowan double-checked his notes. "If you're certain that you and Martin didn't argue, I wonder why Jax said you did."

"No idea."

"When I spoke to Jax earlier today, he mentioned something about Martin being angry on the phone because he'd been arguing with you. This was the Friday we've been talking about. According to Jax, Martin would've been to you first and then they spoke on the phone after."

"So," Sophie said.

Rowan continued: "He was telling me his theory about Martin's boat and about the work he'd done on it."

"What business is it of Jax's whether I argued or not with Martin?"

"He didn't claim it was his business. But, you see, now I have two different accounts of the same event that need clearing up."

"What are you getting at, DI Black?"

"I need you to have a think–"

"Don't patronise me."

"Sophie, I suggest you listen to Detective Inspector Black."

Sophie was quiet.

"I'll ask again. Did you or did you not have an argument with Martin Howler last Friday morning – despite saying just now that you didn't because you were tired?"

"No. I did not have an argument with him. Like I said: I was *tired*."

Rowan made a note. "That's settled then, thank you."

"Are you finished?"

"Almost." Rowan finished his tea. "Do you know anything about there being a cult on the island?"

"What are we teenagers again, Rowan?"

"It's a genuine question, Sophie."

"Oh, come on. It's a load of twaddle!"

"Funnily enough, you're not the only one to have said that."

"Well, funnily enough, I won't be the last either if you keep asking the question."

DI Black watched Sophie's eyes as he asked: "I want to be sure about this. You've never seen any evidence of a cult on the island?"

Sophie shook her head and said nothing.

"Now I feel silly for asking . . . Okay, do you know of anyone who'd fallen out with Martin? Anyone he's argued with? Especially leading up to his murder?"

"No, I don't think so . . . No wait, actually. I know he and Nathan – Nathan Waters – had fallen out a few times

– especially recently. You might remember him. He's younger than us but he grew up on the island. He's nice. Nature happy. A marine biologist, I think."

"Yes, Jax mentioned him earlier. But I can't place the name. Probably when we catch up, I'll remember him straight away."

Sophie cracked two of her knuckles and attempted to crack a third, but the joint wouldn't give. She stayed silent.

"Do you know what they fell out about – a few times, as you say?"

"Wraith's Hollow. The landscape. The oceans. He was always arguing with Martin about preserving the land we have rather than building on it. Every development Martin's built, Nathan's challenged him."

"Sounds like you and him are pretty similar – you both want Wraith's Hollow to remain Wraith's Hollow."

"All I wish is that we can be at peace once more."

Rowan nodded. "I agree. I'll speak with Nathan soon. Can you tell me where you were last night, Sophie?"

"I was by myself – here. In bed. Alone."

"Thank you very much," Rowan said as he and Jennings stood and walked to the door. "I wish we were catching up under better circumstances, Sophie. I really do."

"So do I, Rowan. But we can't change or forget about the past."

Climbing back into the car, Sergeant Jennings asked: "Why's she still going on about Cynthia like that?"

"Not now, Frank. I need to get back to the mainland, meet with Hargrave, and attend the post-mortem. I was going to meet Margaret Warren at six, but I need to cancel. I'm supposed to be staying near the station. It's not likely that I'll make the last ferry back, so we'll start again when I'm back in the morning. Briefing first thing."

"I'll be ready," Sergeant Jennings said.

Nathan Waters

Seeing Sophie did absolutely nothing to calm Nathan's nerves. And he was now so pissed off – her telling him that it was his fault because he made the poison too strong.

Poison!

Just as he thought it, he remembered the email chain with Lena Rook on his Mac. Lena was both an academic acquaintance and a friend. They met at university years ago where he studied marine biology and she mycology, and had kept in touch ever since. At one time, Nathan had believed she was the one for him – especially after they collaborated on a research project in which they explored marine fungi as a source of bioactive compounds for pharmaceutical use. During that time, he grew close to her, a connection he often reflected on in hindsight as one of the key reasons behind their publication success.

But now, he had no time for nostalgia; he was loading up his emails ready to delete the chain about *fungi.* He opened the first email in which he requested her help:

Hi Lena,

I hope you're doing well. I'm working on a new, but sensitive project, involving marine fungi. I find myself, once again, needing your expertise! I'm looking into the psychoactive compounds of a species that has appeared on the island. I need to extract them efficiently – and quickly – into a liquid form for testing.

I don't have much time, I'm afraid as I'm rather rushed here – you know me! I was hoping you could share your insights into the most reliable and quickest methods for extracting the active compounds. I'll be honest – I've got a few days at best. I'm really interested in the species growing all over the island and whether it produces hallucinogenic alkaloids like psilocybin. Also, what solvents would work best for this extraction? One that retains potency while ensuring the extract is viable for rapid administration.

This is all part of a larger, time-sensitive project. I'm working against the clock here. Any advice you can provide would be invaluable.

Thank you – I owe you a coffee!

Nathan

He scanned the email – and a couple more – and then deleted them. God, it made him feel guilty; made him look guilty! He couldn't believe that he had sent the first email four days ago on Sunday. So much had happened. All that hatred towards Martin for what he did to Ellie, and what he was doing to the island, had been killing him. But now – after what they did – Nathan wasn't so sure.

His lighthouse was incredibly lonely. But if he went to see Ellie, she would know that something wasn't right. It wouldn't take much, and Nathan would be confessing to her what he'd done.

Even though they'd discussed everything over and over, Nathan hadn't believed they would really go through with it.

But they had. And now Martin Howler was dead.

Dead!

What was he going to do? Could he bear to live with this? What kind of future was waiting for him? Life was about ecosystems and marine life; it wasn't about murder. Nathan Waters wanted to hide from the world – could have curled up and died.

He felt sick. It was sickening what he'd done – oh, God! This is terrible! He would go to prison – for life. He stood and breathed deeply, went to the window, looked out at the sea. It wasn't blue: it was black. Nathan had to sit down at the table. He smashed his hand into his model lighthouse and smashed it again. His heart was sinking; he was breathing faster and faster! It hadn't even been a day yet and he was losing all sense of himself. What was this? It was the guilt. A terrible force, driving into him from everywhere he looked.

Nothing was helping. It wasn't his fucking fault the poison was too strong. Sophie fucked it up. She can't have given Martin the correct amount. To hell with her – we're all going to hell.

He found his phone – it was on the floor, half under the sofa. He unlocked it, scrolled through, and hit call.

"We need to talk. I'm losing my mind here," Nathan said.

"I told you not to ring. Sort your shit out."

"No, no, I'm not having it. You need to meet me or I'm going to the police! We've screwed up! I can't believe this has happened."

"Shut the fuck up. You won't go to anyone. Do you understand me? You go to the police, I'll make sure Ellie ends up the same way Martin did!"

"You wouldn't!"

"Try me."

"You said we'd meet!" Nathan said.

"I know. I'm thinking . . . Tomorrow. You've got to keep it together. If you crumble – we're all fucked."

"I know, I know, I know. But I'm losing it, here."

"Look, we agreed. What happened was for the best. Think about what that fucker did to Ellie."

"Yes," Nathan replied quickly.

"Good. Be calm. Focus on what he did to the woman you love. Any moment you feel yourself cracking the fuck up, think about that. You got that?"

Nathan nodded.

"I said, have you got that?"

"Yes. Sorry. When can we meet tomorrow?"

"I'll contact you. I can't give you a time. We need to test the water – see what's happening out and about."

"I won't ring again. I'll wait for you."

"Nathan, that's good. But remember what I said: I'll kill Ellie if you go to the police."

Rowan Black

Back on the mainland, Rowan had brought DCI Hargrave up to speed with the investigation so far and requested an Underwater Search Unit to sweep the marina where Martin's boat was moored. If the boat had been damaged deliberately, there was a possibility that evidence had been discarded underwater. SOCO had recovered Martin's phone from his house, collected blood swabs from the bathroom tap, and lifted latent fingerprints in the bathroom. He told DCI Hargrave that the laptop at Silver Cove Marina would have to wait until tomorrow – they hadn't yet received the warrant. But as soon as they did, they would send that – along with Martin's phone – to digital forensics. DCI Hargrave told Rowan that she had ordered an investigation into Martin Howler's bank records and that the Press Office had met with the media, sharing the most basic details of the case so far.

Rowan had also requested that DS Carl Hocking, a stocky, bruiser of a man whom he liked and had worked with before, and DC Mike Mann join his team to support the investigation into Martin's murder. DC Mann was the opposite of Hocking – of smaller build, more reserved, and less comfortable with confrontation. DI Black had worked with him too and liked him.

It was into the evening, and Rowan was dead tired. He and DS Hocking were in the post-mortem room on the mainland. It was cold and clinical. Its bright, overhead lights highlighted Martin's injuries. The stainless-steel table where he lay, cast shadows over the tiled floor. Rowan blinked against the brightness.

He sniffed the air. It was thick with the tang of that harsh, antiseptic smell. It was strong, overpowering. The refrigeration units hummed in the background – their steel doors lined up like futuristic tombs. The scalpels, bone saw, and rib shears lay in perfect order, ready to be used against flesh and bone. The sinks and disinfection stations were cold and functional.

Rowan exhaled. Everything in the room served one purpose – to unearth the truth of Martin's bloody end.

Connie Smith, the senior pathologist, looked at Rowan and said, "I can confirm that the circular symbol you saw at the scene was carved post-mortem. The tissue showed no signs of inflammation. Furthermore, the actual carving through the tissue was uninterrupted which suggests the victim was still when it happened."

"Can you confirm the time of death? You estimated about two a.m. at the scene."

"Yes. About two a.m., give or take, was consistent with rigor and lividity."

"Stomach contents?" Rowan asked and glanced at Alex Williams, the coroner's officer.

"Nothing in his stomach. Digestion was well underway by the time he died. I did find partially digested steak fibres and fats in the small intestine, suggesting his last meal was around eight p.m."

Rowan made a note. He turned to DS Hocking and said: "Let's get Mike to check the pub, the Ram's Head, and other restaurants on Wraith's Hollow – see if Martin had his steak out. More importantly whether anyone else ate with him." Then back to Connie he asked: "Cause of death?"

"The primary cause is blunt force trauma to the left temporal region inflicted by a rock. The impact caused a depressed skull fracture, leading to subdural haemorrhaging and cerebral contusions."

"Enough to kill him in one blow?"

"Absolutely. Rapid loss of consciousness and death. There's no evidence of prolonged survival."

"What about the trauma to the face and neck?" DS Hocking asked.

"Multiple contusions and lacerations to the face. The pattern here," Connie pointed a gloved finger at Martin's face, "suggests rapid blows. The lack of haemorrhaging in some indicates the injuries were carried out post-mortem."

"Okay. We've got defensive wounds here, right?" DI Black wanted to confirm.

"Yes. Injuries to both forearms and hands. Abrasions, contusions, and fractures. The fracture to the left ulna suggests the victim raised his arms in self-defence. Probably the last thing he did before he died."

"Considering the primary injury to the left side of the skull – can we assume the attacker was right-handed?"

"Most people use their dominant side – especially when attempting to hit hard. It's not a hard and fast rule but it's likely," Connie said.

Tim Thorn's injured hand flashed through Rowan's mind.

"Any evidence to suggest the body was moved to the beach?" DS Hocking asked.

Connie shook her head. "I've found traces of sand and organic matter in the wounds, hair, and respiratory tract. Meaning he was killed on the beach – and the post-mortem lividity matches the body's position."

"Did you find any tissue damage inside Martin's mouth where the stone sigil was found at the scene?" Rowan asked as he watched Kelly Franks, the young pathology technician, carrying away a sealed container with vials of Martin Howler's blood, each one labelled for toxicology testing.

Connie saw Rowan had spotted the samples. "Toxicology pickup is set for the morning. You won't get your results back for a few days. Don't expect miracles, Rowan. Monday's going to be the earliest."

Rowan nodded, conveying that he knew the score.

"As for the mouth, no. There were no signs of inflammation. My guess is that the stone sigil was placed carefully after Martin was killed. We've sent it and the vine necklace off to the lab for testing."

"Great. We found identical ones at Martin's house. We've sent them off for testing, too. The circular pattern was sprayed onto a bathroom mirror."

"A ritualistic Banksy," Connie said. "Whoever placed them on Martin's body wanted them to be seen. The one carved in his chest was done neatly, purposefully. They were in control. Which also suggests that whoever beat him to death was in full control."

"What are the symbols made of? The sigil is stone – but what about the vine necklace?"

"Let me focus on the stone for a moment. I haven't had it in front of me, but from the initial forensic findings at the scene and the photos taken, I'm guessing it's stone local to Wraith's Hollow. It's hand-carved, shaped. I could see from the photos that it has some salt residue. That might help us trace where it came from. Forensics are running tests on the composition but again we won't know until Monday."

"I suspected it was local to Wraith's Hollow. What about the necklace?" Rowan asked.

"There were no pressure marks around the neck, so it was most likely placed post-mortem. It is handwoven, intricate – made from natural fibres, but I can't say for sure from what. You'll have some answers when we have the results from the lab."

"Yes. Was Martin in good health?"

"I found nothing to suggest otherwise. No underlying disease. Looking at his physique – he exercised, looked strong. There isn't an immediate explanation to suggest that he would've been vulnerable."

"The initial attack must've been from behind. Martin didn't see it coming," DS Hocking said.

"My thoughts exactly," Connie said.

"Was there anything else?" Rowan asked.

"There was. I found a fibre, synthetic, that didn't match the materials of Martin's clothing. It's from a different source, different texture. But we'll need to wait for the results to identify its origin."

"Our killer's clothing?" DS Hocking asked.

"I wouldn't like to confirm one way or another," Connie said. "But like I say, it's not from Martin's clothing."

At that moment, flashing through Rowan's mind was a bloody and violent scene of Martin Howler being beaten to death.

Sophie Marlow

Sophie had been on the phone since DI Black and Sergeant Jennings left. She had to phone – everything was piling on top of her.

". . . so have we cleared that up?"

Sophie nodded, wiped her eyes and said: "Yes. Thank you. I was being stupid. But I'm fine, honestly."

"Good. Look, everything is going to plan. Don't worry."

"It's hard not to when Nathan's running about the place stressing his head off. One interview with Rowan and he's done for. Honestly, babe, he's freaking out. I told him he's either part of the solution or part of the problem."

"Don't say too much to him. If he gets wind of the actual plan, we – as in you and me – are truly fucked. Just reassure him if he turns up again. I said I'd meet him tomorrow."

"Is that wise?" Sophie asked.

"Yes. We've got nothing to worry about. Everything's planted. Besides, it doesn't matter if Rowan sees us together or not. Long as Nathan isn't being a dick, we'll be fine. I promise. I know we've been over this, but you're sure you didn't give anything away to Rowan?"

"No. I did what you said. I steered the conversation onto Nathan. Told him Nathan and Martin argued many times."

"Good. That's all we needed to do at the moment. Were you subtle?"

"I think so. I did a good job of making it look organic. Like I just thought of it there and then."

"Okay. Hopefully that was enough. Rowan Black's sharp. He'll see through it if you weren't."

"Do you think Nathan will be a problem?" Sophie asked.

"He made a vague threat of going to the police if I didn't meet him."

"Fucking idiot."

"It's okay. I told him if he did, I'd kill Ellie."

"Won't that just make him angry?"

"No."

"Would you?"

"Would I kill Ellie? You can bet your life on it. If it's

a choice between him and us, I would. But the threat will be enough to shut him up."

"Jesus, this getting out of control."

"No, it isn't. Everything's fine."

"We're going to get caught!" Sophie said.

"Just breathe, Sophie. In the first instance, Rowan will think Hollow Kin's responsible when he figures them out – the symbols I planted on his body will ensure that. Then, once that falls through, which it will, Nathan's ready for the taking. Just hold steady. We'll be fine."

"I should tell you there's been a meeting arranged for tonight at the church, in the crypt."

"As we've planned, give nothing away. I must go."

Hollow Kin

Hollowspire Church sits on the peak of the Wraith's Hollow landscape. Its watchful eye observing everything that has happened on the island since its construction in the ninth century.

Home to Christian worship, Hollowspire Church had long been a linchpin in the community. Much to the chagrin of the older generation, its influence over the community, like most traditions, was waning, but the weathered stone and towering spire stood strong, a testament to the church's resilience against the passage of time.

However, deep within the Christian theology and aesthetic of the church lay the actual truth, known only to those whom Veritas chose. Hollow Kin's origins hid within the church walls like secrets buried within a tomb. It is believed that Father Elias Thomas was the first disciple that Veritas took. Over five hundred years ago, Father Thomas was a strict reformer who tried to purge Wraith's Hollow of its old, non-Christian traditions. Following an exhausting period of sleepless, angst filled nights worrying about the future of Wraith's Hollow, Father Thomas was seen entering the church at night. He is believed to have descended into the crypt. He was never seen again.

In the days that followed, the last events of his life passed into lore. And strange symbols began appearing in blood – blood that many whispered belonged to Father Thomas. Parishioners tried to scrub the markings from the stone walls – some drawing their own blood in their frenzy to clean – but the stains remained. Veritas then chose six to bear her truth, her teachings, and so it was that Hollow Kin was born. Those first six washed the walls clean and dedicated their lives to keeping Veritas sacred and protected.

"Veritas, we devote our lives to you. Father Elias Thomas, we honour your memory. To the six, we listen, we hear you still, within these walls, within this crypt. Veritas have mercy on us who walk your path. Protect those who serve you. And destroy those who deny your truth."

The last words of Hollow Kin's prayer, spoken by twenty voices, echoed softly against the crypt walls – drifting upward through the narrow, spiralling staircase they had all descended earlier. In the central chamber, candles burned in iron sconces, barely illuminating the low, vaulted ceiling. When the flames flickered, the small, arched alcoves around the edge came alive with the shadows of the robed bodies that stood in two circles – one smaller and one, slightly larger, outer. Moisture dripped from the cracks, forming pools of water in the uneven stone and the scent of wax and damp permeated the darkness around the Hollow Kin.

"We have much to discuss," Mrs. Appleby said.

"Yes," Sophie Marlow agreed. She was standing in the inner circle, opposite Mrs. Appleby.

"I'm afraid we have one, or maybe more, of you who think you're above the guidance and wishes of Veritas herself," Tim Thorn said. He was at Mrs. Appleby's side, in his usual place.

"I don't like your tone, Tim," Ellie Crick said. She was standing next to Sophie. Other members within the inner circle agreed, in unison, with a short *hmm.*

"Well, Ellie, I don't like the fact that some among us have chosen to act against the interests of Hollow Kin. A rift has occurred. And here, tonight, we will discover who they are," Tim said.

"*Well*, it's nothing to do with me," Ellie said.

Mrs. Appleby interrupted Tim: "I'm curious, Ellie, as to what you think it is we are referring?"

Ellie didn't reply.

"Because we haven't yet disclosed to you what we are concerned about."

"Isn't it obvious?" Sophie began. "You're talking about the death of Martin Howler."

"Sophie," Mrs. Appleby said. "My bright little girl. Always the perceptive one. You are quite correct. Martin Howler has been murdered. Murdered without my consent."

"Oh, come on! You've been planning it for a year," Ellie said.

"Veritas acts only when she's ready," Tim said, slipping away into the shadows. He returned momentarily carrying an iron brazier with thick gloves on – his arms trembling from the heat. He placed it into the centre of the circle – the iron legs ringing loudly against the stone floor. The smouldering charcoal glowed red and hissed its presence to them all. The branding iron waited.

"Veritas sees all," Mrs. Appleby said. "She has demanded that we show her the strength of our faith, our submission, our loyalty to her. One or some among you have polluted our ways. You have brought Hollow Kin into question. The true and faithful will be spared – you will feel and show no pain; the liars will scream and burn!"

"One of you step forward," Tim said.

And without hesitation, Sophie Marlow stepped towards the brazier.

"Lift your robe," Mrs. Appleby said. She slipped on a glove and took the branding iron from Tim. She closed her eyes as she whispered: "Veritas will love the faithful; she will curse the guilty. The honest will be silent; the liar will scream!" Mrs. Appleby opened her eyes and stabbed *The Mark of Veritas* into Sophie's inner thigh on her left leg. Flesh sizzled and instantly scented the room. Not one of Hollow Kin winced: their faces were controlled. Even

Sophie, whose flesh was on fire, just closed her eyes and gritted her teeth.

Mrs. Appleby pulled *The Mark of Veritas* away. "Veritas has spoken. She sees your truth."

Tim took Sophie by the arm, escorting her through the gap the members had made for her, and led her to a large metal bowl on the floor. "Veritas will note your courage today in going first, Sophie."

"I am, I, I am faithful," she trembled – the pain raging through her.

"Here," Tim said as he lifted a flannel out of the ice water. Only the faintest candle flicker of light reached to where Sophie stood, but it was enough to see the blistering, angry, red skin. She dared not touch the wound with the flannel, so Tim did it for her. She leaned against a column to prevent herself from falling. She kept her balance as she took the cold flannel from Tim, pressing it against her skin. Her leg trembled violently.

Another member, followed by another and another – all demonstrated the strength of their faith, their submission. Not one of them winced, though all gritted their teeth and breathed furiously when *The Mark of Veritas* touched their bare skin. The inner thigh is particularly sensitive – as Mrs. Appleby knew. Though she would never admit to gaining a little pleasure when carrying out Veritas' wishes, she did. She looked deeply into the eyes of those she branded. The eyes reveal all. They truly are windows into a person's soul.

"Ellie," Mrs. Appleby said. "Come forward." She handed the branding iron back to Tim. He plunged it back into the embers.

"No! I'm not doing this. This is insane."

"You'll anger Veritas!" Tim said, grabbing Ellie by the shoulders.

Veritas has spoken, Mrs. Appleby thought. "Come, my dear. Show us your strength. Omission will be treated as admission that you're the one responsible for murdering Martin Howler."

"This is insane!" Ellie tried to fight Tim's grip. "The fuck! Let me fucking go!"

"Disrobe her," Mrs. Appleby said over Ellie's shouting.

Other members gathered around her, took Ellie to the floor, seized her legs and arms while Tim cut her robe right down the centre of her body.

She's wriggling like a worm, a disgusting, lying worm. "Look at you," Mrs. Appleby said. "You've angered Veritas. She has spoken: your beautiful body is now hers. For as long as you live your scar will remind you of how you acted outside the counsel of Veritas."

Mrs. Appleby smiled inside. She picked up the red-hot branding iron. She jabbed *The Mark of Veritas* at Ellie's youthful, beautiful body, catching her once or twice before lingering on her inner thigh.

Ellie screamed, frantically pushing and pulling her limbs against those who imprisoned her on the floor. Tears ran down her face.

"Enough!" Mrs. Appleby said. "Veritas has revealed you to be the one who murdered Martin Howler. *You* are the one who acted against us – acted against Veritas."

"You crazy bitch," Ellie shouted, crawling across the stones, desperate to get to the ice water. Burned legs scraped; her nails dug; her body snagged as she pulled herself forwards. Other members looked at her as though she was vermin. Ellie screamed for the water. Sophie moved towards the metal bowl – her own wound, excruciatingly painful – and was about to get a flannel for Ellie, but Mrs. Appleby stopped her.

"She's disgraced Hollow Kin and dishonoured Veritas. She does not have our mercy. Leave her!" The members gathered into the same circle formations as before, this time excluding Ellie. She remained on the floor, on the outside, dipping the flannel in and out of the water and pressing it gently against her leg. She looked at the robed backs of the other members and made a vow to kill them all – especially Mrs. Appleby.

"Now we move on. As you all know, Martin's body was discovered with our symbols – Ellie carved *The Mark of Veritas* on his chest, tied *The binding of the Kin* around his neck, and placed *The Tongue of Silence* in his mouth. Despite what she has done, we do not give Ellie up to the police. Rowan Black's sniffing around – no one give anything away. We are to unite against him. Ellie is still one of us, and when this is over, we shall all hear what Veritas has to say about her fate. Tim placed the symbols around Martin's house – Rowan asked Tim about them, so we know they've been found. These were meant for Martin; however, we did not know at the time that Ellie had taken it upon herself to kill Martin on that same night. I have no doubt in my mind that Martin would have recognised our threat. The fact that the police found them will inspire Rowan to look for us; but I am certain that Veritas is looking out for us and guiding us through this time. We have done what she has asked: rid the island of Martin Howler. We can rest in the knowledge that we have done everything in our power to please her."

"Do we still have Jennings under control?" Sophie Marlow asked.

Tim said: "Yes. Jennings is where we want him."

"Then the question that needs asking is, how much control over Rowan does Jennings have?" Sophie said. "Because the way I see it, he doesn't have any. Rowan Black does what he wants and gets what he wants. He's already been to interview me."

"Sophie, I think your past with him is influencing your perception of him. Rowan's not above the law – he must act in accordance with it . . . I trust you were discreet when you spoke to him."

"Of course. But how's Sergeant Jennings going to have any chance of protecting us if, as I know, he won't be able to manipulate Rowan."

"Not directly, no," Mrs. Appleby said. "But that wouldn't be clever either."

"Jennings is our puppet," Tim said. "He will do what we ask him to. Jennings can pull the strings from behind the scenes."

"Tim, say what you mean, stop talking in riddles."

"I mean he can lose evidence, manipulate reports, fabricate interviews."

"Well," Sophie said. "I can't see how that will help. You've never known Rowan like I have. He's determined – he'll rip Jennings apart if he has to."

Ellie started shouting but two members left the circle, went over to her, held her to the ground and covered her mouth until she was quiet.

"The point I wish to make clear, Sophie, and everyone else, is that Frank Jennings is for me and Tim to worry about. Put your faith in us and we will guide you just as Veritas guides me: we will all be at peace once more."

"At peace once more," voices chorused.

"We need to," Tim began, "remain strong in our conviction. Martin's been removed from our island. We need to make sure that we are united against Rowan and his team. Put our trust in Veritas . . . Now, I've been doing some research on one of Martin's business associates, Dr. Naomi Bennett. I can't prove it yet, but I'm sure she's invested in Martin's Project Genesis. You'll remember Martin wanted to turn our island into a science lab that performed genetic enhancing operations."

Evidently a few of the Hollow Kin members hadn't yet been aware of this and gasped in unison.

"Indeed," Mrs. Appleby said. "He was determined to ruin Wraith's Hollow. It's unthinkable. And just in case some of you are wondering why we didn't hand this information over to the police and have him arrested – or at least shutdown – it's because I wanted him dead. Not only for the sake of my George but for the sake of everyone here, too. Even you, Ellie. For the sake of even you!"

"Yes . . . Dr. Bennett was a researcher at MIT – now based in the UK. Studied genetics. Has a PhD in Biomedical Engineering. Recognised as a student-wonder – especially for her work in neuroplasticity. She's published papers on it."

"Tim, why're you telling us this?" Sophie interrupted.

"Because you need to know who we're up against. If she has, as I've already said, invested in Martin's project, she, and possibly others, will want to know what the hell is going on. Twenty-five million – that's the sum Martin needed. If he got it, we're about to have some visitors!"

"Okay, point taken," Sophie said.

Tim made a sharp *hmmm* then said: "It wasn't hard for me to discover online that a number of Dr. Bennett's projects raised serious ethical concerns with review boards. She had trouble in the US – some kind of research scandal, controversial testing on animals and humans – probably the reason she's now based here. I started down a bit of rabbit hole looking into private investors in her work on genetic enhancement, but it was already past midnight, so I turned in."

"I think, the point is," Mrs. Appleby said, cutting in. "Dr. Bennett is someone who isn't afraid to push boundaries and, if Tim is correct, doesn't care about where her funding is coming from. She's the kind of character that I don't want to know – and I certainly don't want her on my island."

"Agreed," Sophie said.

"If anyone hears about or sees Dr. Bennett," Tim said and pulled out a picture, and although it was dark in the crypt, Naomi Bennett's image was registered by all of Hollow Kin, "you need to inform us straight away."

"Agreed," Sophie said again. "Now what are we going to do with Ellie?"

Mrs. Appleby said: "We are going to do nothing with her. I am waiting for a sign from Veritas: she will guide us through. For now, Ellie is going to do all in her power to behave as she normally would – so not to raise suspicion. She is going to tell no one about what's happened . . . but Ellie knows this, don't you, my darling. She knows what will happen to her if she talks to anyone not associated with Hollow Kin say, someone like DI Black. I will look after her tonight."

Ellie, on the floor, couldn't see that bitch Mrs. Appleby, but she swore again that she would kill her.

Chapter Seven

Rowan Returns to the Island

Rowan Black

Friday morning. Eight-thirty.

DC Mann and DS Hocking had accompanied DI Black on the ferry from the mainland to Wraith's Hollow. Rowan spent the journey reflecting on the current investigation, while Hocking and Mann discussed the robbery they'd been working on, weighing whether there was enough evidence to send the file to the CPS.

At Havenmoore Port, DS Hocking and DC Mann jumped off the boat first and Rowan, taking the time to say goodbye to Reg, followed. He stepped back onto Wraith's Hollow with a large suitcase and a smaller cabin-sized one. He didn't know how long he would be staying, so he packed generously. His colleagues would be making the journey to and from the mainland each day.

Rowan breathed in the warm morning air. Spring mornings on the island!

Despite the murder he was investigating, Sophie's anger towards him, and memories of Cynthia pushing hard to be at the forefront of his mind – it was good to be back home.

Home. Never did he think he would refer to Wraith's Hollow as home again. Its charms were obvious to him; it still held wonderful memories of his time growing up there without any real-world problems. Those carefree days and nights on the beach were some of the most delightful times of his life. Cynthia was a huge part of them. When he really thought about her and their past, he realised how much he had loved her. God, it was an awful time when she died. His whole world, at twenty-one, had fallen apart.

Walking along the promenade in the direction of the police station on Quayside Lane – the suitcase's wheels grumbling along the pavement – Rowan reflected that Martin was someone he'd grown up with, even laughed with at times. It wasn't always easy remaining as objective as possible. There were times yesterday when Martin's death affected Rowan more than he'd thought it would.

Turning onto Quayside Lane, he remembered that he had to see Margaret Warren. She was going to show him around the cottage he was staying in whilst he was on the island. Begrudgingly, because he'd let her down once already, he pushed the visit back until after the morning briefing. He messaged her that he would meet her before ten.

He walked the path to the station door preoccupied with thoughts about how policing on the island had remained mostly unchanged over the decades. Yes, he had an office and a computer, which he could use to access DEMS, check the latest updates from HOLMES logged by the MIR, and access any other information he needed from the internet; but there was something, some feeling that made him think, as he took each step forward, that he was stepping back in time. It wasn't an unpleasant feeling: it was as if Wraith's Hollow itself hadn't been tainted by the ills of mainland life – which was an odd thought, considering he was there investigating a murder.

Standing by the board in the incident room, Rowan made the necessary introductions and watched as PC Everett and Sergeant Jennings shook hands with DS Hocking and DC Mann. There was a detectable air of suspicion and bluntness about the way Everett and Jennings greeted their new colleagues, which Rowan decided to let play out on its own without interfering. It was only the minor hostility that strangers often faced.

On the whiteboard, he pointed out the photos and the timeline of events that they knew so far about Martin's murder. "Found at six in the morning. Time of death, confirmed at the post-mortem, is approximately two a.m." He then informed them of the pathologist's findings relating to Martin's stomach contents, trauma to the skull, and injuries to the face. He added that they were waiting for toxicology results and that forensic analysis of the symbols and fibre Connie discovered were also in the pipeline.

"There were symbols at the house, too?" DC Mann asked.

"Yes. We're waiting for the results on those," Rowan confirmed.

"Do we take it whoever's responsible for the symbols on Martin's body is responsible for the ones at the house?" DS Hocking asked.

"I don't think we can assume anything yet," Sergeant Jennings said.

Rowan cut in before Jennings said any more in that tone. "Sergeant Jennings is correct. We don't know yet. We need to understand the significance of the symbols at either location in the context of all the evidence. Next. Martin's boat. Sandra Mead found traces of blood in the boat, inside the cabin. Evidence of someone having tried to clean it as well."

"There was blood in the boat and blood found at the house – on the," DC Mann was trying to remember so Rowan took the opportunity to remind him.

"Bathroom tap. SOCO discovered latent fingerprints also. And his phone was found – we'll be waiting for digital to get back to us on that one."

"Thank you," Mann said.

"Speaking of fingerprints," Sergeant Jennings began, standing tall, crossing his arms, and stepping slightly closer to Rowan. "Aren't Tim Thorn and Little Liam coming in this morning to provide a set of their fingerprints?"

"Yes. I'll need you on that, Frank," Rowan said, turning to him. And to everyone else: "I'm afraid we're playing the waiting game on the results from forensics. Monday is looking like the earliest we'll hear. Let's hope it's sooner, but don't hold your breath." DI Black paused before adding: "As of this moment, we don't have any significant leads–"

DS Hocking interrupted: "What about this cult, sir –

the symbols?"

"Most likely meaningless," Sergeant Jennings said.

Hocking shook his head. "All due respect, meaningless doesn't work for me."

"Oh, you know all about it, do you?" Jennings asked.

"Sir," PC Everett said to Jennings. "Let's hear him out. An outsider's opinion could be useful."

"I'm not claiming to know anything. But three symbols found at both locations isn't meaningless. You must know something about this, Frank," Hocking said. "From my understanding, you've lived here years, and you claim the cult is a load of rubbish. If they're not alive and kicking, where did these symbols come from and who put them there?"

"As I said to DI Black, I deal with real crime – not hearsay. I don't care much for mythical stories about some underground, mysterious cult on the island. My job is to keep people safe."

"Had to do a lot of that have you? Keep people safe on the island?"

DI Black interrupted before the obvious outcome of DS Hocking and Sergeant Jennings' dialogue was reached. "Enough. Hocking, your views about the cult have been noted. I believe looking into it is valid and necessary. Sergeant Jennings, as discussed previously, I need you to develop this line of enquiry. Maybe someone on the island knows about these symbols – it's highly likely they've been made from stone on the island. They represent something to someone – so much so, they thought it necessary to deposit them in Martin's house and on his dead body."

"Sir, what can I do?" PC Everett asked.

"As soon as the warrant comes through for the laptop, go and pick it up. Take DS Hocking with you to Silver Cove Marina, show him where Martin's boat was usually moored." Then directing himself at Hocking: "Coordinate with Sandra Mead and the Underwater Unit. Brief them and tell me if they find anything that links back to the time Martin's boat was damaged. A tool, hammer, wrench, a glove, anything that shouldn't be down there."

"Sir," DS Hocking said. PC Everett did the same.

"DC Mann, I want you checking with the local restaurants and the Ram's Head as to whether Martin had his steak out. If he did – where and who was he with? After that, dig into his business investments on the island and elsewhere. DCI Hargrave is having his financial records investigated, but I want to know what he's been up to. People like Martin are always looking for financial gain – see if you find anything. Who has he screwed over recently? PC Everett's already interviewed Ellie Crick about her dealings with Martin some six years ago, Beech Heights housing estate – that's right isn't, Danny?"

"Yes, sir, Beech Heights," Danny said. "I don't think there's any need to talk to her again. I got all I could from her."

"Was never in doubt about that, Danny. But let's see if Mike can get anything else out of her." Rowan eyed Danny for a moment, remembering his conversation with

Sophie. "Also, we need to discover who was out on the night of Martin's murder, walking down Pier Road."

"I went back to Hollow Cliff House yesterday, sir, and got the footage."

"Good. We'll review it – but if it's as unclear as you say, Danny, I'll get it analysed, and images enhanced. Good work . . . Let's get going." Rowan then turned to Sergeant Jennings and said: "When Tim comes in, have a chat with him. Make it casual. Ask about his hand and report back to me what he said. Currently, we know our attacker was potentially right-handed from the pattern of wounds on Martin's head and face. We know Tim is right-handed. Did he hurt his hand trashing Martin's house? Did he do it when he killed Martin? I'm not saying it's him, just keep these things in mind when you speak to him. He knows you way better than me – it's possible, if he's involved, he might slip up talking to you."

"Sounds like you're putting all your eggs in Tim's basket, sir," Jennings said.

Seemed like an odd response – but Rowan didn't draw attention to it. He shook his head. "What I'm struggling with regarding Tim, is motive. What reason would he have? Everyone hated Martin on the island – and nobody was backwards in coming forwards about that. Tim's not unique in that respect. So, if it was him, was it simply that he hated him or was there more to it?"

"I'll take his and Little Liam's prints and go from there, sir. See what I can find out."

Ellie Crick

Guilt. Shame. It was all her fault. She fell asleep – if you could call it sleep – feeling like that and woke up just the same. It was as if all the emotions from the time Martin raped her six years ago hadn't really been processed as she thought. They'd just been lying dormant, ready to rise again and choke her. It was hard to know which was worse: being physically overpowered and then invaded by Martin's cock or being overpowered and having her flesh burned by that bitch. Strangely, the audience last night wasn't bothering her at all. They were all hooded. By the time Mrs. Appleby had poked that thing against her skin, Ellie couldn't distinguish a single member of the Hollow Kin.

Mrs. Appleby was all of them: she controlled them all, led them all to inflict pain on Ellie.

Mrs. Appleby had locked the bedroom door last night after Tim had thrown Ellie in there. Mind, she hadn't put up much of a fight – her leg raged as her flesh continued to cook, draining her ability to do anything.

The inner thigh of her left leg was blistered now, raw, and as painful as if someone was scraping glass over her skin. *The Mark of Veritas* would be there forever – a reminder of not only the brutality in the crypt but also of the time Martin raped her.

There was a knock at the door.

Ellie, having been sat, leaning against the door, shuffled away on her bottom. The key turning in the lock caused her to stand in the centre of the room.

Mrs. Appleby opened the door slowly, saying, "Morning, dear. I've brought you some tea." She walked in, smiling at Ellie as if she was her own granddaughter.

"I don't want your fucking tea," Ellie said.

"Now, now, dear," she said as she placed a delicate, bone china cup of tea on the bedside cabinet. "Don't be like that. You need to have something to drink. I'll cook you some breakfast soon. But first," she said, leaving the room and quickly returning with a green first-aid box. "Let's take a look at your leg, shall we?"

"Don't touch my fucking leg," Ellie said. But her words were ineffectual.

"Sit down on the bed and lift your robe, please."

Once again, Ellie felt as though she had no autonomy. It felt like, as Mrs. Appleby put her hand on her thigh, she was being raped again. She looked away.

"Veritas' work has been done. And done well. You will never again forget your allegiance and loyalty to Veritas and Hollow Kin. This," Mrs. Appleby paused. She was about to run her arthritic thumb over Ellie's wound – did, in fact, just above it. Ellie looked into her wrinkly eyes and saw lust. She was lusting, desiring to touch Ellie's burn. Mrs. Appleby slowly moved her thumb downwards; Ellie winced and moved back but Mrs. Appleby gripped her leg. She gently dragged the blistered skin with her thumb and through her smile, let out into the awful silence, a soft moan.

"Please, leave me. It hurts," Ellie said in no more than a whisper.

"Shhhh. Shhhh. Let's get you bandaged up. I'll be gentle. Wouldn't want to pop that blister now, would we?"

Ellie shook her head. Mrs. Appleby was true to her word and gently applied a sterile dressing and bandage. Whilst she was doing it, Ellie thought over and over how easy it would be to smash her fist into Mrs. Appleby's face, but she just couldn't.

"Let's get you changed."

"But I haven't got any clothes," Ellie said.

"You have. Tim took the liberty, my dear, of taking your keys and popping home for you. I'll bring them up. You change, and I'll make you breakfast. How about some smoked salmon and scrambled eggs? That was George's favourite." Mrs. Appleby winked. "I'll make you George's favourite."

"Did Tim pick up my phone?" Ellie asked.

"No. I didn't ask him to. So, he wouldn't have done. You can look at it when you get home. This is why I won't have phones at our meetings – you youngsters are totally dependent on them."

*

She never liked smoked salmon, but she began to eat it. The toast was fine, and the eggs were cooked exactly how she liked them.

"Let's just give you a little seasoning," Mrs. Appleby said as she sprinkled some ground salt and pepper over Ellie's breakfast. "I am curious, Ellie," she said, sitting at the kitchen table opposite her. "How did you manage to get Martin to the beach and kill him? If only you had kept me informed, it could have been so much better for us all. He could have been such a wonderful sacrifice to Veritas."

"Mrs. Appleby, I didn't kill him. I'm sorry you think I did, but I didn't."

"Veritas has spoken. Are you really suggesting that I take your mortal word over Veritas' – who's omnipotent, omniscient, and omnipresent?"

Ellie shook her head. Arguing and disagreeing with Mrs. Appleby would only lead to more pain and suffering.

"Would you believe me," Ellie said in a soft voice. "If I can somehow prove it to you that it was someone else, would you believe me?"

"And how are you going to do that, my dear?"

"I don't know. Danny Everett's in my pocket. He'll help."

"Maybe . . . or maybe he can keep you informed of Rowan Black's coming and goings. Yes, I like that better. Keep Danny in your pocket for that reason. But we haven't yet talked about the fact that you might well be caught. Have you considered this? Considered that going against the wishes of Hollow Kin and Veritas has left you quite vulnerable?"

Ellie placed her cutlery down. "Thank you. I'm stuffed." It sounded so strange being pleasant and thankful to Mrs. Appleby when all she wanted to do was slit her throat. "I will make this right, Mrs. Appleby. I promise. Veritas will love me again."

Mrs. Appleby didn't respond to Ellie's statement. Instead, she said: "Finish what's on your plate, dear."

"No really. I'm stuffed. It was so lovely–"

"Eat it. Eat it now. Eat it and I will do everything in my power to see that you don't spend the rest of your life in prison."

Ellie looked down at the remaining salmon, cold toast, and eggs. Mrs. Appleby picked up the fork and stabbed some egg and salmon before raising it to Ellie's mouth.

As Mrs. Appleby pushed the fork into her mouth, Ellie fought hard against the instinct to retch – she didn't want to be sick all over Mrs. Appleby's table.

Rowan Black

DI Rowan Black had reviewed the footage of the man walking down Pier Road at one thirty-five in the morning. Unfortunately, and frustratingly, the person in question – Rowan was sure they were male – was walking away from the camera. The footage wasn't clear, so he flagged it for digital forensics to enhance it – focusing on the clothing. The jacket appeared to be . . . Rowan wasn't sure. There was just something about it. It clearly wasn't an evening jacket. It looked thick, the hood built to withstand all weathers. It was an outdoor jacket – that much he could see but the image was too poor to make out specific details.

Feeling frustrated, Rowan left the station and went to meet Margaret Warren at number twelve, Quayside Lane.

She opened the door with a beaming smile.

"Detective Inspector," she said and put out her hand. "Lovely to meet you."

They shook hands. "And you, Margaret. I'd like to thank you for putting me up at such short notice."

"It's a real pleasure. Come in. Come in!"

Margaret Warren's quaintness went hand in hand with that of the cottage. As she was showing Rowan from room to room, he saw the interior mirrored that of the police station. Although the station had been adapted for purpose, the same low ceilings with oak beams darkened by years of soot; creaky floorboards, aged and uneven; and dim corners – despite the spring sunshine outside – were present.

He sat in the living room on the small sofa whilst Margaret made them a pot of tea. The wood-burner opposite was heavy and sat proudly on the stone flooring. He wondered whether he should've taken his shoes off as he sat with his legs crossed, one shoe resting on the thick, flowered-patterned rug. It was thick! Perfect for winter. In fact, looking at the curtains, he wasn't sure which was thicker. They hung, nearly devoid of colour, bleached by the sun, draping heavily over the floor. There was a painting of a cottage on the wall with an ornate – a little too ornate! – golden frame. It was the kind of frame you would see in the National Gallery. The painting itself was charming. Despite what Sophie had said about him not liking her paintings, Rowan did in fact enjoy art, though would never claim to have extensive knowledge. Still, he could tell his Monets from his Manets.

"Here we are," Margaret said walking in with a tray and placing it on a small collapsable table she had erected previously. "Will you take a bickie?"

"Thank you," Rowan took a custard cream.

"I'll pour some tea. We don't want it stewed." Margaret handed him the cup and said as she sat in the chair in the corner: "I knew your mum. We were pretty close at one time."

"Were you?" Rowan said taking a bite of his biscuit, conscious of not getting any crumbs on the sofa.

"Oh yes. We used to run about this place. We had such fun."

"I'm sorry to say, but I didn't know you were close. Mum never said. I remember seeing you around the island, but we've never had cause to talk before, have we."

"Not really. Thinking about your mum, it sounds odd to say, because the island's so small, but we lost touch with one another. We hadn't spoken for such a long time – other than the usual pleasantries, you know the kind. I was so sorry when she died, Rowan."

"Me too. She wasn't the same after dad, Margaret. When I think back now, I lost both of them when he took his life."

"Tragedy does that to people. Then drink on top of that – well, that changes a person, Rowan. Your mother had plenty of support. I tried to help her, but she didn't want to know."

"It wasn't just you. She didn't want help from anyone. It was a tough time, back then."

"Stupid me! I'm sorry, Rowan. I shouldn't have said anything."

"It's fine. I'm surprised it hasn't come up before now. I thought someone would've mentioned my parents yesterday. Perhaps people have forgotten."

"Oh no," Margaret said, her tone darkening. "People round here don't forget anything."

"Yes," he said and then sipped some tea.

"You enjoy being a detective?"

"I love it, Margaret. Can't think of doing anything else."

"What is it about it? You know, I do love an Agatha Christie novel. Poirot. Wonderful stories. I've always thought it would be most satisfying hunting down the killer. So satisfying."

Bloodied bodies, vicious killers, and distraught families flashed through his mind. "You know, it is. Agatha Christie got it right." He didn't need to disabuse Margaret of her innocent conception of what it was to hunt down and come face to face with a murderer.

"Scary, I imagine."

"Indeed," Rowan nodded. "How well did you know Martin? Did your paths cross at all?"

"Well, as you know, having come from the island, you can't help but bump into people all the time. And you can bet every penny you own that you'll see the very people you don't want to the most!"

"That's the way life works, Margaret."

"It is . . . God it's a strange thing. Awful isn't it. Murder on Wraith's Hollow. I never, really, I never thought something like that would happen. Good God."

"Margaret, did you know Martin at all?"

Margaret breathed deeply and took a bite of her biscuit, but she didn't appear to enjoy it. After a moment, she said quietly: "Not really. I never had any trouble from him. But you could tell a lot of people didn't like him. Really didn't like him."

"Why do you think that was?"

"I keep myself to myself, but I do know he caused a lot of trouble. Building everywhere. Trying to purchase more land to build even more. He was changing the face of Wraith's Hollow – that kind of thing upsets people. Especially people who've lived here for generations. He even tried to buy the couple of cottages I own on this road."

"Really," Rowan said and thought about Ellie's business relationship with Martin. "How'd that go?"

"Fine. I told him no and that was that. I was warned by a few people that he wouldn't stop until he got what he wanted. They said he'd try all sorts to get my properties – but one word from me was enough. He never bothered me after that."

"He seemed to annoy lots of people."

"Oh, I know. More tea?"

"Not for me, thank you. I'll need the toilet every five minutes if I do."

"That doesn't bode well! You're still a young'un."

"I'll take the latter and ignore the former," Rowan smiled. "Considering most people had some kind of grudge against Martin, is there anyone you can think of who stands out as having something against him?"

"I think most who claim not to like him are following the crowd – uniting against him, so to speak. But Nathan Waters comes to mind straight away."

"Ah yes Nathan. I learned that he's a marine biologist. Why does he come to mind?" Rowan remembered what Sophie had said about Nathan and Martin arguing over the land.

"Ongoing arguments about Wraith's Hollow. He loves the land, well, we all do. Nathan studies the marine life as you know, so he has a special interest in it. And I do sympathise with him. We'll lose so much of what makes Wraith's Hollow special if we build too much. A few houses and developments don't matter. That brings new blood – some people even worry about that. I'm not concerned about that sort of thing. But too many houses – well, that ruins things. Martin didn't have an off switch. Just saw money. Nathan tried his best to stop some of his projects – he's got a petition to stop Martin building more. I signed it."

"Did many people?"

"Oh yes. But I don't think it did much good. Martin has the right people in his pockets. It's not hard to butter folks up when you have his kind of money available."

"Did you ever see them argue in public – is there a time you can think of?"

Margaret shook her head. "Not that I saw, but I don't doubt that they did. I've been to a couple of meetings that Nathan held at the community centre over the years. He didn't hold back when referring to Martin. He wasn't bothered about what people thought . . . What kind of meetings? Well, they were local flora and fauna stuff. Interesting actually. Nathan does presentations. Good speaker."

DI Black made some notes in his book. "Okay–"

"Actually, sorry to interrupt. Talking of arguments. I did see Martin arguing with someone, oh God, when was that? Yes, that's right. In the pub. You'll remember the Ram's Head. It was there. Last Friday. A week ago, today. It was with Jax. Jasper Flint. I like Jax. A good man."

"Yes, I've spoken with Jax recently." But he failed to mention arguing with Martin, Rowan thought. "I remembered him from when we grew up together. What can you tell me about their argument?"

"It looked unpleasant, heated. Martin squared up to Jax. That's what it looked like to me. I was at the bar, by the corner, and they were standing near-ish to me."

"What was it about?"

"Not sure. Jax said something to him – I'm sorry, I didn't hear it, the pub's quite loud – but it was about Martin's boat. What I did hear, though, was Martin telling Jax he was just a, and I quote, 'a fucking fisherman. Keep to your station'."

"Were those the exact words?"

"Yes. Definitely. I remember because I thought it was a, excuse my French, a shitty thing to say. Jax didn't deserve that embarrassment. He looked so mad afterwards. And even madder when Martin leaned in and said something only he could hear. Jax looked so angry."

"Thank you, Margaret. That's been useful. I want to ask you one more thing. Sorry to take up so much of your time – you must be busy."

"Not really, Rowan. I plan to carry on reading Christie's *And Then There Were None*. That's the plan for my day."

DI Black smiled. "Good choice," he said. "What do you know about a cult on the island?"

"I'm aware we have one – have had for years."

"You're the first one to have confirmed that."

"I imagine you've been told all sorts from it's a load of rubbish to just myth."

"I have. What can you tell me about it?" Rowan asked.

"I know they're active, that they meet regularly. Look, I'll be honest with you, Rowan. I don't want it known to anyone that I've been speaking about Hollow Kin with you," Margaret said, looking concerned.

"Absolutely not. You have my word."

"Thank you. Hollow Kin believe in the God, Veritas. Veritas is everything to them and they do everything in their power to protect her and her island."

"Would they kill for this Veritas?"

"Yes, I believe they would. For some people, it's easier to deny their existence but they all know how much control Hollow Kin have on the island. If they found out I was talking to you – they would come after me . . . You don't know what you're dealing with. They're evil."

"You've probably heard that Martin's body was found with three symbols. I think they belong to Hollow Kin. If

I brought pictures of them for you to see, would you recognise them?"

Margaret Warren nodded. "I would."

"How can you be so sure?"

"Because I used to be a member. I left Hollow Kin years ago."

"I'm surprised you were allowed to."

"It was under extremely strict conditions. Which I will not discuss with you, Detective Inspector."

Rowan raised his hand. "It's fine. I won't ask you to," he said, not wanting to push Margaret too far. He could see how tense she'd become, how uncomfortable she was.

"You must have known about Hollow Kin growing up, Rowan. What do you think?" Margaret said, her tone calming.

"When I lived here as a kid, growing up, I heard things. But I wasn't interested. Since moving away from the island years back, I've forgotten all about it."

"Did you ever see Hollow Kin for yourself?"

Rowan shook his head. He didn't want to tell Margaret that as a teenager, he saw lots of strange and weird and wonderful things. An intense relationship with drugs influenced that. Instead, he said: "Who's involved with Hollow Kin around here?"

Margaret shook her head. "I won't say, Rowan. It would put me in danger. No one can know I've been speaking to you."

"You'll be fully protected. You have my word."

She shook her head again. "Why don't you ask Sergeant Jennings? Rowan, I won't say any more. Sergeant Jennings knows."

Tim Thorn

"You go home for the day, Little Liam," Tim said. It was ten forty-five in the morning. They'd just had their fingerprints taken – a formality, as Sergeant Jennings had said. Little Liam seemed very nervous, so Tim decided that he'd be better if he had some time off. As for himself, he felt pretty good. He had no previous so his prints wouldn't be on record, and coming into the station voluntarily should keep DI Black off his back for a while.

Just as he was about to follow Little Liam down Quayside Lane, Tim heard Sergeant Jennings' voice. "Tim," he said. "A word, please."

Rather than go back in the station, Jennings walked over to Tim and motioned for them to walk. They headed towards Tide Fall Beach.

"Anything to report?" Tim asked quietly.

"Nothing to you, Tim."

"Steady, Frank. Remember what we've got on you. You'll do what I say unless you want Rowan Black to find out about your colourful past." Tim paused, turning to smile at Mrs. Benn and her corgi, Dennis. He took the opportunity to mention the progress he was making on her table. Once she was out of earshot, he said: "And how is your daughter these days? Well, I trust?"

"You know very well how she is. You're not going to blackmail me. I did what I had to. It wasn't right but it was essential. Tim, she was being abused. You bloody well know this," Jennings said through gritted teeth.

"Calm down. The last thing you need is someone talking to DI Black, saying it looked like we were arguing. Wouldn't look good now, would it?"

"You've got nothing on me, Tim. I've settled my debt to you – a thousand times over."

"The thing about your debt to me and Hollow Kin, is that you'll never be able to repay it. I'm afraid that's the deal you signed up for when you wanted me to plant those drugs."

Sergeant Jennings said nothing.

"My point's made . . . Now, what's the focus of DI Black's investigation?"

"Did you murder Martin Howler?" Jennings asked as they turned onto the seafront. They walked along the promenade; despite the tension between them, they looked like two old friends catching up on a sunny spring morning.

"I'm not obliged to give you that information. But it's sufficient to say, we – Hollow Kin – have everything in hand."

"You know who did it?"

Tim stopped and placed his hand heavily on Jennings' shoulder – shattering their old-friends-catching-up illusion. "You need to figure out whether or not you want to press me on this. Keep asking, and I'll see your career and reputation are fucking ruined. You want to end up in jail? No. I thought not."

"Promise me you'll leave my daughter out of this."

"You'll do as I ask?"

"I did it for my daughter. And I'd do it again to save her. You wouldn't know what it is to love someone that much. You're a fucker, you are."

"Again, you'll do as I ask?" Tim asked.

"Yes," Sergeant Jennings said – his voice, a whisper.

"Now, tell me everything. Where's DI Black going with his investigation? Who does he suspect? Any leads?"

"He wants to know how you hurt your hand."

"I told him already. You tell him I hurt it Tuesday. That's all he needs to know!"

Rowan Black

"That's *The Mark of Veritas, The Binding of the Kin*, and *The Tongue of Silence*," Margaret had said when Rowan went back to see her with the photos of the symbols found on Martin's body and in his home.

"What do they mean? Why these ones? What makes them significant?"

"*The Mark of Veritas* represents the truths that lie within, and the balance between life and death. It's a mark of judgement. When it's found on the body, it means someone or something has been judged, unveiled, or sacrificed in the name of truth."

"Meaning Martin has been judged – or sacrificed?" Rowan asked.

Margaret nodded slowly. "*The Binding of the Kin* represents entanglement. The unbreakable bond between Hollow Kin and Wraith's Hollow. It can be worn as a punishment or to signify inclusion. The individual is bound either as a follower or as an enemy."

"And the last one?"

"*The Tongue of Silence*, well you can probably guess where this is going. It represents the sealing of deep truth, of Hollow Kin. And the silencing of dissenters."

"How does that relate to Martin, do you think?"

Margaret looked at him. "They wanted to make it obvious: he's been silenced."

After their conversation, Rowan didn't want to go straight back to the station.

He had to get some air.

The cult was obviously active on the island and, it would appear, had an active part in Martin's murder. Occupying his mind further was Margaret's insistence that he spoke to Jennings about Hollow Kin.

Rowan walked through the town centre. He was like a pendulum, swinging between happy reflections of his time growing up on the streets he was now walking and feeling anger towards Sergeant Jennings. Clearly, if what Margaret had said was true, Jennings hadn't been honest. He had deliberately misled Rowan – lied to him – about Hollow Kin. There must be a reason, but he couldn't yet figure it out.

The question at the forefront of his mind as he headed

towards the seafront was whether he should challenge Jennings or play it cool for the time being, at least until he understood the reason for Jennings' behaviour.

DI Black crossed the road and stepped onto the promenade. To his left, in the distance, heading north, and not far from the lighthouse, were Jennings and Tim walking along. He stood for a moment observing them, noticing Tim placing his hand on Jennings' shoulder. Despite the distance, it was clearly an uncomfortable moment between them. Tim looked as though he wanted to bury Jennings in the ground. It wasn't long until they were walking again, heading away from Rowan.

Making a mental note about the exchange he witnessed, Rowan went to Diane's Coffee Pot. He needed a coffee.

Also approaching the door to Diane's was Little Liam. He and Rowan had an awkward exchange at the door – each of them insisting the other go first, but neither of them moving.

"Little Liam, we haven't had the pleasure of meeting properly yet," Rowan said and smiled. "Rowan Black," he said extending his hand. Little Liam took it with a firm grip. "Please, after you."

"Thank you, sir," Little Liam said.

"Rowan's fine." They entered Diane's and joined a small queue. "My treat," Rowan said. "Choose whatever you want. The cakes look good."

"Thank you," Little Liam said, leaning into the counter to get a closer look at the cakes and pastries.

"Better choose soon. We're next."

"I'll have a piece of millionaire shortbread and a hot chocolate if that's okay?"

"Of course, take a seat and I'll bring it over."

Bringing their drinks and food to the table, Rowan sat opposite Little Liam, noticing that his cheeks had reddened.

"Tuck in," Rowan said. Little Liam took a huge bite of his shortbread and was then self-consciously rubbing the crumbs from his lips. "Looks good." Rowan took a sip of coffee. "I bet it tastes better."

"Awesome," Little Liam said.

"Wait until you're my age – you'll only have to look at that kind of thing to gain weight!"

"I've a fast metabolism, apparently."

"Didn't we all. Anyway, how'd it go at the station this morning? You had your fingerprints taken, didn't you?"

"Mm-hmm. It was fine. Glad it's over. I were worried about it but didn't need to be. Made me think of those CSI programs . . . You lived on Wraith's Hollow, didn't you? So they tell me."

Rowan wondered who they were but figured it could have been anyone on the island. Everyone was into everyone else's business.

"That's correct, I did."

"Why'd you leave? I don't think I'd ever leave here," Little Liam said between mouthfuls.

"I just had ambitions beyond what the island could give me, you know?"

"I think I get it."

"The island offers lots of things the mainland doesn't, don't get me wrong. You can live a great life here–"

"Unless you're Martin Howler," Little Liam said, flushing redder.

"This is true. I guess, well, you're training to be a cabinetmaker, aren't you? That's good. You've enough people on this island to keep you in business for the rest of your life – assuming you want your own business. There's nothing wrong in that."

"Mum and Dad think it's good."

"Absolutely, and you'll be good, no doubt. I imagine Tim's good to you."

"He's the best there is. I love working for him."

"He's a good man," Rowan said. "Are you making your own furniture yet?"

"Not yet. I can sand, varnish and wax and help cut bits and use the lathe a bit. I'm good with tools. Still got lots to learn. I'm handy though."

"I bet Tim relies on you more than you can imagine. Especially now that he's hurt his hand."

"I know. I've done loads. I think his hand's getting better though."

"You've got to be careful working with lathes and hammers. Nasty injuries. When did you notice he hurt his hand?" DI Black asked, sipping some coffee.

Little Liam had the last bite of his biscuit and looked out of the window as though he'd find the answer to Rowan's question there.

"Umm. Yesterday . . . Yeah, pretty certain it was yesterday."

"What makes you so certain?" Rowan asked having remembered that Tim said he'd hurt it on the Tuesday.

"Because yesterday we got a delivery of cherry wood in the morning, and I helped carry it in as Tim couldn't because of his hand. It was fine Wednesday."

"Cherry wood. Sounds expensive."

Little Liam's eyes lit up. "It's going to be a table for Mrs. Benn. Don't know if you know her. Nice lady. I'm going to work so hard on it. It's going to be lush. Cabriole legs. Polished finish."

"It sounds amazing."

"It gets me fired up thinking about it. She's paying a lot for it, but it will last her for years and years."

"I might have to get you to make me one – or something similar. I could do with a nice coffee table."

"Yeah!" Little Liam said swigging down his hot chocolate. "That would be awesome. We'd need to chat to Tim about it but, well, you could be my first proper customer."

"I'll absolutely be that. Whenever you think you're up to it – when you've learned everything you need to, to make a cherry wood coffee table, you let me know . . . I just want to draw your attention back to Tim's hand. Did he not hurt it at work then?"

Little Liam shook his head. "Nope. Came in like it on Thursday. Certain of that."

"So, we think he did it Wednesday evening then? If his hand was fine Wednesday day, and he didn't hurt it Thursday – it has to be Wednesday evening."

Little Liam shrugged his shoulders. "I guess."

"Did he say how he hurt it? Did you ask?"

"I took the piss out of him for it. He was useless. Looked nasty. But I don't think, or I don't remember asking him how he did it."

"I don't suppose he enjoyed you taking the micky," Rowan said.

"Nah, Tim's fun. But he does get angry sometimes. Especially if he can't get something right."

"You ever seen him get angry?"

"A few times. Scary. He gets in a right mood if he gets something wrong."

"What was he like the last time you saw him in a mood?"

Little Liam looked out of the window. Then: "Well, it wasn't a work thing – like something he was trying to fix or make. But he got angry at Martin last Saturday."

"What happened?"

"They were arguing in the workshop. I was supposed to be going for a walk with my hot chocolate – I bought one, Martin sent me here to get him a coffee. I went outside but came back in. I was going to get my jumper. It was sunny but not very warm. They didn't see me, I don't think . . . It was something to do with Martin wanting the bookcase finished and delivered on Saturday and Tim saying he didn't wanna work over. I remember Martin said something like if Tim wanted paying then he'd get the job done."

"Anything else happen?" DI Black asked, jotting some notes in his book.

"Yeah. Tim told Martin not to threaten him – but I don't know what he meant by that. Something about Tim seeing something at Martin's house. Don't know what. Then Martin just squared up to him."

"To be clear, Liam. Martin squared up to Tim – not the other way round?"

"No. Definitely, Martin squared up to Tim."

"Thank you. What happened then?"

"Martin said he could fuck Tim up in a second."

"Did you believe him? Was he being serious, do you think?"

"He was. Well serious. Tim picked up a hammer. Martin told him to put it down. I mean, if Tim hit him with that, he would've killed him there and then."

"He would've done," Rowan said. "What happened next?"

"I think, yeah, before Martin grabbed Tim's throat – they said something about brain implants, or chips, or whatever you call them. I don't really know, to be honest. I think that was it."

"Brain implants? What do you think they meant by that?" DI Rowan Black asked, aware of how surreal it sounded.

Little Liam shrugged. "No idea."

"You're sure that's what you heard? Exactly sure? Who said it?"

"Yeah, I reckon so. Tim said about the implant thing. I know what I heard. But after Martin grabbed Tim's throat – Tim threw him off. Tim's strong."

"I'm sure he is. And how did the situation resolve itself? End, I mean."

"Martin left pretty much after that."

"And how did Tim seem after?" Rowan asked.

"He was furious. He went to his office – you know the office in the workshop? – and slammed the door. I reckon he didn't know I were there at all."

"Thank you, Liam. You've been a great help."

"Tim's not in trouble, is he? Because of the hammer?"

Rowan shook his head. "No. You've done the right thing in telling me. Off the record, what did you think of Martin Howler?"

"I didn't like him. Didn't know him, but I know people round here didn't have time for him. And he'd walk in and out of Tim's workshop like he owned the place. Talked down to me loads."

"Sounds like you didn't think much of him."

"Not really, I fucking hated him."

*

Rowan Black spotted Nathan Waters from a good distance before Nathan seemed to notice him, despite the fact that he was standing at the door to Nathan's lighthouse.

"Saw you coming," Rowan said.

"Umm, hi," Nathan said. "Sorry, I didn't recognise you. Well, I did, but not from back there. I'm in my own world most of the time. Especially near the sea. Nature happy me."

"Yes, how can you not be when you've got a view like that coming home? The sea's beautiful today." Rowan extended his hand.

Nathan gripped it, weakly. "And the beach. I love it all year," Nathan said, releasing his grip and wiping his hand briefly on his jeans before putting it in his pocket.

"Does it ever look bleak?" Rowan said, motioning to the beach and the sea.

Nathan was quiet for a moment. Rowan noted how absorbed and internalised Nathan had become. It was as if DI Rowan Black wasn't there at all. He was about to prompt Nathan when he suddenly said: "Yes. I find it can be quite bleak at times."

"Owing to?"

Snapping out of it, Nathan said: "Nothing really. Just gets me sometimes . . . I'm afraid I'm really busy–"

"Yes!" Rowan interrupted. "I do remember you. I said to Sophie, when I spoke to her yesterday, that I couldn't place you. But I can! You're younger than me but I remember you a bit growing up here. Didn't you used to bring your Dalmatian to the beach? You must've been about, I don't know, ten – I was in my twenties by then."

"I did. Denny. I loved him . . . I'm really sorry. I've got lots to do."

"Must've been all those seaside walks with Denny."

"What was?" Nathan asked, looking confused.

"That got you into nature. I'm told you're the man for all things nature around here."

"I'm a marine biologist." Rowan detected pride in Nathan's voice.

"For the layman like me, what's a marine biologist? I'm not even sure I know what it means. That alone tells me you're far cleverer than I am!"

"Not at all. I study marine ecosystems – organisms that live in coastal and underwater environments. It basically means being out all day, wading through water, getting bitten by bugs, and overanalysing every minute detail."

"Sounds a bit like my job – change the water for shit, and the bitten for getting hit. Keep the over analysis part . . . You could be a detective, Nathan, and you don't even know it. Look, ten minutes of your time, and I'll be out of your hair."

"I am really busy – but I could do with a break. Come up."

Rowan followed Nathan Waters up the spiral staircase of the lighthouse and into the living room. It was untidy and it smelt musty, stale. A window needed opening.

"Here, let me get this," Nathan said, pulling clothing and a wooden box off the sofa. "Please, take a seat. Sorry about the mess. I wasn't expecting anyone, and I've been a bit lost in my work."

"No problems, Nathan. I'm just the same. Stuff everywhere when I'm on a case – especially a murder enquiry. All I can think of is catching the person responsible – I get a bit obsessed." Rowan observed Nathan. Nathan's eyes didn't meet his, not once. "What's your latest work obsession, then?"

Nathan grabbed a sterile jar from the table by the tall window. It was sat near a broken model lighthouse.

"You've no doubt seen this around the island?" He handed Rowan the jar.

"Yes, it's everywhere!" Rowan said, holding the jar up to inspect it. "It's bizarre."

"It's aggressive."

"Where did you get this sample from?"

"Off the rocks, near Tide Fall Beach. Under the scope it's fascinating."

"Really. It's pretty fascinating now. Coloured like a rainbow. Iridescent – you call it that, don't you?"

Nathan nodded. "Iridescent, indeed."

"Looks like something out of a sci-fi film!"

"It could be. This is strange enough. I've never seen a species invade and take over so quickly before."

"Strange how?" Rowan asked.

"Well, I haven't fully sequenced it yet, so I don't completely understand it, but what's unusual is how aggressive it is. The spore output is raging – reproducing at an abnormal rate. Nothing like I've ever seen in a marine fungus."

"Okay, but what does that mean to people on the island?"

"That it's both special and potentially dangerous."

"Dangerous – you mean dangerous to Wraith's Hollow's ecosystem?" Rowan Black asked.

"Most definitely!"

"Would you say it's dangerous to humans?"

Nathan paused and then took the jar from Rowan, moving slowly as though he was carrying the only available sample. "Umm. Not sure yet. I need more time to understand it."

"Well, I'll take your advice on the best course of action. We don't want animals or people ingesting this. We don't want a return to the sixties," Rowan said, laughing.

"Yes, people getting high on Wraith's Hollow!" Nathan said, though his tone didn't match the joke he was telling.

"Is this, if it was ingested, one of those psychedelic type drugs?"

"Potentially. I can't say for certain. If ingested in the right concentration, it could disrupt normal neurological function. But the compound would have to be properly extracted and isolated."

"That's way over my head, Nathan."

"Ah that kind of thing just takes patience. It's not too hard," then: "Drink, DI Black?"

"I've not long since had a coffee. Maybe just a glass of water. Thank you."

Whilst Nathan went to the kitchen, Rowan looked around. The place was a mess – student accommodation came to mind. The sun streaming through the window not only lit the iridescent fungus in the jar on the table, but it also revealed dust and dirty fibres on the faded cream carpet.

"Here you go," Nathan said, handing Rowan the glass.

As surreptitiously as possible, Rowan checked the rim for cleanliness. He then took a sip, having decided it was okay.

"How well did you know Martin?" he asked as Nathan angled a chair to face him. Sitting down with his glass of water, Nathan leaned on the table, his elbow almost touching the top half of the broken lighthouse. The sunlight illuminated one side of his face.

"I guess I didn't know him."

"It's funny – most people, if not all, have implied the opposite. Everyone seems to know everyone round here – whether they want to or not. The hazard of living on a small island, I guess."

"Yes. I suppose that's true. You'd know. You used to live here," Nathan said.

"I did. Sorry, just to be sure. Are you now saying you did know him, or at least only in the way that other people have claimed – due to the island thing?" Rowan said, notebook ready.

"Umm. I'm, yes. I knew him a bit, but I didn't *know* him."

"Yes, it's an important distinction . . . Do we ever really know anyone? Anyway, did your paths cross much?"

Nathan shook his head. "Not a great deal." He sipped some water and looked at the fungus in the jar.

"I still can't get over how alien it looks," Rowan said. Then: "Did you get on at all? When you met?"

"Not really."

"In what way?"

"I thought he was reckless. That he didn't care about Wraith's Hollow – about our landscape or our shores."

"Why reckless?" DI Black asked.

"Reckless in expanding his empire. He'd have built everywhere if it wasn't for me. People never stood up to him apart from me," Nathan said. Rowan saw tiny particles of spit coming from Nathan's mouth as he spoke, firing into the sunlight between them.

"Did you ever argue?"

"Sometimes . . . but not for ages. Can't remember the last time."

"What about?" Rowan asked.

"Like I say, he treated everyone and Wraith's Hollow appallingly. We argued about his building plans and anything else he was doing to rape our land."

"Did you ever physically argue or just verbally?"

Nathan looked at his arms briefly and then said: "Look at me. Martin would've killed me in a fight. I'm not stupid. I don't get into battles I can't win."

"You'd be surprised – it doesn't take much force to injure or even kill a person. Especially when they don't expect it."

"I'm not the fighting type."

"It's not always the *type* who get into fights . . . You mentioned that you're pretty much the only one who stood up to him. In what way did you stand up to him?"

"I was vocal about what he was doing to our land. I held meetings. Got petitions organised."

"Did you argue over these petitions? Must've annoyed Martin," DI Black said.

"Yes. He hated me because I wouldn't just let him do what he wanted. I gave him my best shot. And those idiots at the Island Trust. They rolled over whenever Martin told them to."

"You said that you haven't argued in a while – you can't remember when the last time was. I take it the latest petition was unusual in that it didn't cause you two to disagree – or did Martin not know about it?"

"You've seen it then?"

"Actually, no. I've spoken to Margaret Warren this morning and she mentioned your petition incidentally. We were chatting about lots of things."

"Oh," Nathan said, sipped some water and then folded his arms. "I don't know if he saw it, but he certainly knew about it. I wanted to stop him building more flats on his most recent site until I've fully understood this fungus. I said to him on the phone, we don't know how destructive, no, invasive, it could be."

"Were you in the habit of phoning?"

"Not really. Only when it was essential."

"When did this essential call take place?"

Nathan looked thoughtful. "Last Saturday morning. Can't remember the time. It was early. I wanted to catch him before he left for work."

"Were you in the habit of knowing his comings and goings?"

"I know how it looks–"

"How what looks?" Rowan interrupted.

"That I had a rough idea of his routine. But it wasn't for any reason other than my desire to speak to him on the phone when I could. It was trial and error. I've learned that if I caught him early, my call would have the maximum impact on him . . . I don't suppose in reality that it made any difference."

"Did you quarrel on the phone last Saturday?"

"Yes and no. I was mad at him, but I didn't let on that I was."

"Do you think he knew you were?" DI Black asked.

"Possibly."

"How so?"

"Tone of voice – I was short with him. But it wasn't a full-blown clash."

Rowan scribbled in his notebook and then said: "Just so I'm clear. You've fallen out in the past over land developments – your point of view is to protect the land whereas Martin's was to build as much as possible? You've challenged him on every idea he's had–"

"No, not on everything."

"Oh, okay. I've been informed that you've spoken out against everything Martin's tried to do."

"Be careful who you listen to," Nathan said.

"You were apparently vocal about Martin at your nature meetings – so I'm told."

"I won't lie to you, yes. I've spoken openly about what I think of him."

"Thank you, Nathan. Just one more question."

"Of course," Nathan said and sipped some water.

"Where were you Wednesday night, into the early hours of Thursday morning?"

"I was here. In bed."

"Can anyone confirm this?"

"I live alone. So, no."

DI Black stood up. "Thank you for your time, Nathan. I'll be in touch if I have any more questions." As Rowan was leaving, he looked at Nathan's jacket hanging over the back of the sofa. "Nice," he said.

"Yes. I've got another around somewhere. Keeps me warm when I'm out and about gathering samples – studying."

"I bet it does. That reminds me, you've got a lab on the island, haven't you?"

Nathan nodded. "A field station – not far from here. Ten-minute walk."

"Perhaps you could take me there one day soon. This fungus is fascinating."

"Welcome to my world," Nathan said, his face softening. Their conversation had caused Nathan to become tense. DI Black didn't yet know the reason.

Jasper Flint

Jax had spent the early part of the morning catching pollock off the coast for Moira and her fishmongers, aptly named Moira's Catch. He had been selling to her ever since he'd started fishing Wraith's Hollow's shores. She'd done right by him over the years.

"You okay, my love?" she asked as he placed the second crate of pollock on top of the first. They were in the back of the shop, where the smell of lemon and vinegar cut through the salt and fish in the air. Jax went to the back door and lit a cigarette.

"Absolutely living the dream, Moira. Nothing wrong with me."

"That's good. You just seem a bit . . ." Moira said, making a start on gutting the fish. "Reg popped in earlier, before ferrying back to the mainland – said the sea was choppy, he did."

"It was a bit strange – can't put my finger on it, but it didn't feel settled, you know?"

"The sea is beautifully strange at times," Moira said without looking up.

"Uncanny," Jax muttered, drawing a long pull from his cigarette.

"What about this Martin business, then? Terrible."

"That it is, Moira. Who'd have thought it? Murder on Wraith's Hollow?"

"Bloody awful. Never would've believed it could happen here. Still. The world's shifting and sliding all over the place. Who knows what's coming next. Who do you reckon did it?" Moira inspected a fish. "You bled these good."

"Thank you, I do try. As for Martin, I don't know. He wasn't liked."

"I liked him – sort of. He was arrogant, but never rude to me. He was one of my best customers. Liked his fish, he did."

"Don't we all," Jax said, finishing his cig, stamping it out on the stone.

"You seem, I don't know, not quite your usual, happy self."

"I'm fine, ta. Busy morning, that's all."

"You know where I am, if you need anything."

"I do," Jax said, already halfway out the door.

Jax cruised along the coast road in his van, heading to Silver Cove Marina. Don Henley's *The Boys of Summer* was playing. He turned it up and drummed his fingers. The toolbox in the back of the van slid a little as he went round a corner – he didn't think he was driving fast enough for it to do that, but he slowed down anyway.

Nathan's lighthouse was in his mirror.

Soon enough he was driving through the iron gates of the marina. There were cars everywhere – none that he recognised. Police cars as well.

Jax parked in the corner and, leaving his toolbox in the van, made his way to the reception, observing his reflection in the glass door as he approached. He couldn't see what it was Moira had spotted, but he arranged himself accordingly.

Roger Stone opened the door for him. "Jax, I'm so sorry. I forgot you were coming to do my boat."

"What's going on, Roger?" They went inside, walked over to the windows on the other side of the room and looked down at the marina.

"They've been here a while now," Roger said. "Some kind of underwater team, unit thing. See there, they've cordoned off the dock."

"I do. Did they say what they were doing?"

"Looking for evidence. They're looking under where Martin's boat was moored."

"Yes, I see that. What evidence?"

Roger shrugged his shoulders. "No clue. Just PC Everett, that other detective, him there . . . Yes, that's the one. What was his name? DS Hooking, no that's not it. Hocking. DS Hocking. Big bugger. And Sandra Mead. She's a no-nonsense type; I can tell you."

"What does she do?" Jax asked.

"Some kind of forensics. She did say but, I think it was investigator. Although to look at them now, you'd think DS Hocking's the one in charge down there. Watching like a hawk."

Jax agreed. Then: "I count two divers," Jax said. "Any more?"

"Don't think so."

"What's on that," Jax said, pointing to a foldable table covered with gear.

"Other than that plastic tub, no idea. Evidence bags?"

"Could be. Have they pulled anything up?" Jax asked.

"Not to my knowledge but I haven't been watching them all the time. Danny came in earlier – flashed his warrant and took the laptop."

Jax turned to face Roger. "I wonder why that was. Don't suppose he said?"

"I spoke about this with Danny yesterday. It's likely whoever shut the CCTV and alarm system down on the night they damaged Martin's boat, came back and did the exact same thing on the night Martin was murdered."

"Really?"

"Yes, sir. It's speculative. But seems sound to me, Jax."

"But why would they come back on the night he was murdered?" Jax said, returning his gaze outside. One of the divers surfacing caught his eye. It looked like they were holding something they'd found on the seabed.

"Young Danny reckons that the murderer must've known Martin was going out on his boat and that someone else was with him. You see otherwise, they wouldn't've needed to disarm the CCTV and alarm. Nothing suspicious about Martin getting his boat alone. But if he was taking someone out on the water with him who didn't want to be recorded – well, hence the need to shut down the system."

"They think there was more than one person involved?" Jax asked.

Roger shrugged. "Who knows. Like everything, us normal folk are the last to know . . . I don't know what they'll find on that laptop."

"All sorts, Roger. When you think you've deleted stuff, you really haven't. It all depends on who's doing the searching."

"Oh, yes. I forgot you're a bit of a computer whizz."

"Not really. I dabble. Technology's moving on too fast for me to keep up."

"You know a lot more than I do. That laptop of ours has been showing messages about system failures and whatnot for a while now. I think I told you before, didn't I? Should've got you to look at it. I didn't understand it. I mean, I know what these things mean, but how they relate to what's on the computer, who knows. I told Martin about it, but he didn't care."

"That was Martin for you, Roger. Thought himself invincible. He didn't give a damn about anyone. Look how he ended up," Jax said.

Roger didn't seem to hear.

"They'll find out what it all means, I'm sure," Roger said. "The police will have the right people examine it, no doubt."

"They will. What do you think it was that that diver grabbed from under the water?"

"Not sure. Couldn't tell from here – looked like a tool of sorts."

"Yeah, maybe something like that."

"I couldn't tell. Sun's shining right in my eyes," Roger said and chuckled a little. "They bagged it pretty quickly whatever it was."

"They did. Must've been important," Jax said.

Nathan Waters

Nathan Waters knocked Ellie Crick's door on Old Beacon Way. It took forever for her to open it.

"Nathan," she said. "What're you doing here? This isn't a good time."

"Have you been crying?"

"It's nothing, really. Can you come back some other time?"

"I need to talk. I can't think of anyone else. I need someone I can trust."

Ellie sighed. "Ten minutes."

Nathan followed her into the living room. "Why're you limping?"

"It's nothing. Make a drink if you like," she said, flopping on the sofa. She winced as she moved her leg.

"Do you want something? Tea? What's up with your leg?" Nathan asked.

"Please. Tea first. Then we'll talk," she said softly.

"Right."

Nathan made the drinks and sat next to Ellie on the slate-grey leather sofa. "I've fucked up, Ellie. I'm fucked," he said not looking at her but at the black and white photograph hanging on the wall. It was the photo he'd taken for her of his own lighthouse.

"What do you mean?"

"I don't know what to do. I can't tell you everything . . . but Martin. Martin's–"

"Nathan, are you involved?" Ellie said, sitting up on the sofa.

Nathan nodded. "Promise me you won't say anything to anyone? Not to Rowan, not to the police."

"I promise."

His impulse to tell her overrode his concerns about what she might do or what she might say. "I'm, I can't tell you all of it, but I'm involved, partly responsible for Martin's death."

"How!? Why?"

"I hated him. Hated him for what he did to you. Hated him for just walking around here for years getting away with raping you . . . I'll never forget the day you told me. I wished I'd killed him then."

"Nathan you idiot. I need to know everything," Ellie said.

Nathan stood up. "No! No!" He glanced at the open laptop on the small table by the window. Had he been able to concentrate properly, he would have seen on the screen: Crick Eco Trust – Portfolio Forecast.

"Why not?" Ellie asked.

"Because he said he'd kill you. If I go to the police or involve you in any way, then he'll kill you. I'm not risking telling you anything. I did this for you."

"Did what? Kill Martin?"

"Yes!" Nathan said, sitting back down and gripping her hand. "I love you. I've never said it before. But I've been wanting to tell you for years."

"You love me?"

"Yes."

Ellie was silent for a while. "I don't know where to go with that, Nathan. What am I supposed to do with that?"

"I don't know. But I needed you to know in case I'm arrested and sent to prison."

"Let me help you. What *have* you done? Don't tell me who else is involved. Just exactly what you've done."

"I helped poison him."

"This is crazy! What are you talking about?"

"The fungus. I used it to poison him – get him high. Then the other two did the rest."

"Rest, as in kill him?"

"Yes."

"So, you didn't actually kill him on the beach?" Ellie asked.

"I didn't touch him – physically. Didn't see him on the night. But I'll be sent down for murder – conspiracy to commit or whatever. I'm an accessory."

Ellie stood limping a little, went to the kitchen and brought back two glasses of wine. "Here, drink this."

Nathan downed it. "I'm fucked."

Ellie nodded slowly and downed her drink. "Get the bottle of wine. It's in the kitchen. I need to think."

Nathan went to the kitchen, wiping his eyes, brought the bottle back and filled their glasses.

"Shit," he said, collapsing on the sofa.

Ellie was silent.

"What about you. Why were you upset?" Nathan asked, wanting to escape the thought of prison.

Ellie pulled up her dressing gown, showed Nathan *The Mark of Veritas* on her leg and explained everything that had happened in the crypt the previous night. Nathan knew about Hollow Kin from his conversations with Ellie in the past. He had, at one point, wanted to be involved with them; but now he was relieved they rejected him.

"Fuck," was all he said, reaching for more wine.

Ellie Crick

If Ellie was being honest, the wine had totally gone to her head. Kissing Nathan felt good, despite everything they'd discussed and everything that she'd experienced recently. It was a moment without a single thought getting in the way. His facial hair tickled and his tongue against hers was arousing. She hadn't had sex for what seemed like an eternity.

Suddenly, someone knocked the front door. She ignored it at first but, whoever it was, tried again – louder than before.

"Fuck! Let me get rid of them," Ellie said, standing.

"Sure. I'll pour more wine."

Ellie opened the door, the handle springing back loudly as she let it go. "Yes," she said.

"Ellie Crick?"

"Yes," she said, sharply.

"DC Mike Mann. Nice to meet you. I wondered if I could take a few minutes of your time?"

"Why! I've already spoken to Sergeant Jennings, PC Everett, and DI Black. I haven't got anything left to say."

"I appreciate that, Ellie. I do. I just wanted to follow up on a few things regarding your business relationship with Martin Howler – Beech Heights, was it?"

"It was. But, again, I've nothing left to tell you about Beech Heights."

"Perhaps I could come in . . . Oh, am I interrupting?" DC Mann asked as Nathan came to Ellie's side.

"You are," Ellie said. "You–"

"It's fine, Ellie. Speak to him. I'll call back later," Nathan said.

"You don't have to go anywhere," Ellie said.

"It's no problem. I'm best out the way. I've got a few things to take care of anyway. DC Mann, nice to meet you. Nathan Waters."

"Hi, Nathan. I'm sorry. I don't want to intrude."

"Well, perhaps this should be the last time you do," Nathan said. "As Ellie's mentioned. She's spoken to the police already."

"I won't take much time."

Nathan kissed Ellie on the cheek, she recoiled – only minutely, but it was enough to be obvious to DC Mann; Ellie knew that.

"Come in," she said, walking back to the living room. "Excuse the mess."

"I see you've opened a bottle already." DC Mann pointed to the bottle of wine and glasses.

"Like I said. You *are* interrupting."

"May I?" DC Mann asked and then sat down on the sofa.

Ellie sat on the sofa, too. "What do you want?"

"Beech Heights – what was your plan?"

Ellie described the original idea behind her housing project.

"They sound like a great idea. It's all about the environment these days, isn't it?"

"It is kind of important."

"Yes, I take your point. We don't often think properly, do we? We're not often aware of our surroundings," DC Mann said.

Ellie didn't know what DC Mann was getting at. There seemed to be something in his tone – was he prodding her? But, then again, did she think that because she was irritated?

"Why did the development end up as luxury housing?"

"Martin Howler. He had other ideas."

"And what were they?"

"He basically didn't like the fact that eco-housing wouldn't turn over as much profit. Luxury attracts wealthy people. Martin wanted wealthy people on the island. Cut me out of the deal. Cost me a small fortune – I could've earned loads out of that."

"That must've been hard to take. How did you manage that at the time? Six years ago, that's right, isn't it?"

"Yes. And it was horrible. I won't lie, I hated him then and I hate him now – even though he's dead."

"You're not sorry he was murdered?" DC Mann asked.

"I know how it looks. I know how it sounds, but no. I'm not sorry. He treated me terribly. In my eyes, he got what he deserved." Ellie finished her glass of wine.

"Pain is worth letting go of, Ellie, if you can . . . Can you walk me through how he cut you out of the deal? How did he do it?"

Ellie was quiet for a moment. "I did the groundwork. He let me do all that. Pitched the concept, drew in the green investors, got the planning through . . . But the land was never registered to our joint venture. Bastard bought it through a shell company – I didn't even know it was him. By the time I realised, it was his. So, when the time came to build, he changed the specs, said the eco-focus wouldn't sell. Beech Heights suddenly became everything he wanted. Go up there yourself and see what he did . . . Anyway, it's all in the past."

"Pardon me for saying, but it doesn't sound like it's in the past, Ellie."

"It still hurts. Bastard offered me hush money – didn't take it. I wouldn't."

"Must've been a very stressful time. What was your relationship like after?"

"Told you. I hated him – he knew it. But he didn't care."

Ellie reached for the bottle of wine, glanced at DC Mann and withdrew her hand; but then reached for it again. There wasn't much left, but she wanted it.

"Anything else?" she asked.

"Was that the end of your professional relationship with Martin?" DC Mann asked.

"Yes. Professional or otherwise."

"Was there more to your relationship – other than professional, I mean?"

Ellie, because the wine had both loosened her tongue and boosted her confidence, said with ease: "Yes, but that's nothing to do with you."

DC Mann raised his hand – reassuring her. "Did you feel you could trust Martin, after what happened?"

"What do you think?"

"Fair point. Did you ever challenge him over what had happened between you?"

"Martin is . . . was very powerful. Who could I have gone to? My word against his. No. He was a real fucker. He had me, and he knew it."

"And Martin was–"

"Look! I haven't got anything else to say. Can we please stop talking about Martin Howler!" Ellie exhaled forcefully.

"Of course."

Ellie looked into DC Mann's eyes. "Martin Howler was a fucker and a rapist." Standing up, she went into the kitchen, leaving those words behind her. Ellie opened another bottle of wine and swigged it straight away. She returned to the sofa.

DC Mann said: "Ellie. I know this is unpleasant, but I need to confirm. Did Martin Howler rape you?"

"Yes, he did. But what the hell does it matter? It was years ago."

"Did you report it?"

"You're really not getting this, Detective. You don't go against someone like Martin. Never. No . . . Justice was served without the police. He deserved everything he got. Rapist fucker."

"Ellie, can you confirm where you were on the night Martin was murdered?"

"In bed. Alone."

Rowan Black

It was coming up for one-thirty. Rowan hadn't had lunch yet – but, then again, he wasn't hungry for anything. A sandwich, fish and chips, a piece of fruit . . . nothing was exciting him.

He was on his way to Havenmoore Port – Jax was on

his mind. He was hoping to find him there, figuring that Jax was a fisherman, the port was probably the best place to find him. Approaching, the sea air was strong, but it was as welcome as it was refreshing. The sign that once read *Havenmoore Port* was weathered. The flaking white paint now read *Have oor Po*. Probably fall down in the next storm, Rowan thought. The port itself was small, but it was just as much of a working port today as it had been when Rowan used to live on the island.

DI Black paused – watching Reg's boat slip towards the mainland – tuning into the sounds the port had generated for decades. Engines rumbling softly, seagulls calling overhead, the sea lapping at timber, and the occasional soft clang of a loose ring or drifting chain, held and carried on the wind. There was something peaceful in the air, something Rowan, breathing deeply, took just a second longer to enjoy. The peace only slightly sullied by the scent of diesel and fish.

Jax was stepping onto his fishing boat, carrying some kind of box and hadn't yet noticed him. As Rowan approached, he saw the boat was called *Hollow Rose*. He searched his memory for why Jax might have chosen that name and found nothing.

The stone quay was slippery underfoot – the tide having crept up earlier that day. The *Hollow Rose* rocked gently in place and Rowan was practically climbing aboard before Jax registered him.

"Rowan!" Jax said, putting the box down. "Sorry, didn't see you."

"You're obviously busy at work."

"Just cleaning out these – went fishing this morning. They needed another rinsing. What's up? I won't shake your hand – I'm all fishy."

Rowan Black raised his hand and grimaced. "Thank you for sparing me that fate, Jax. Can I step aboard?"

"Of course. Watch your step."

Rowan saw the boat was tied to both mooring points – the rope relaxed, but there wasn't much excess.

"Can't even offer you a drink," Jax said.

"No problems, I'm all good. How long you had the boat now? She looks in good nick."

"Take a seat," Jax said, watching Rowan sit on the wooden seat at the back.

"Thank you, this is pleasant." Rowan raised an arm, resting it on the gunwale. "I could get used to this!"

"You could, ay? What about when it's pissing it down and the wind's knocking you sideways?"

"Well, when you paint a colourful picture like that! Maybe I'll just settle for this now, in the sun."

Jax turned a green cool box upside down and sat on it.

"So, you had the boat long?" Rowan asked.

"A good few years now. She's steady. Good motor. Strong. She's in good nick, as you say, but don't look too closely. There's plenty of scuffs and scrapes."

"You must be good at covering them up."

"I'm handy, I guess. You work with boats long enough."

"I've always been jealous," Rowan began, stretching one leg out, relaxing into the seat.

"What of?" Jax asked, stretching one leg also.

"People like you – good with your hands. Able to build, fix things. I'm useless at that."

"I bet you don't really get the time, though."

"Yeah, but that's no excuse. I should've learned something skilful."

"Being a detective has its skills. Not everyone can do that – but everyone could be a boat mechanic or a carpenter."

"I disagree, Jax. Not everyone could be a carpenter. Or a boat mechanic. Or a cabinetmaker. It takes real skill, patience. You need a certain mind for it. Be good with spaces – having a vision."

"You need to have a certain mind for police work. Catching criminals all day . . . now that takes patience and skill. No way I could do that. Wouldn't want to," Jax said.

"I think you'd be surprised at what you could do, Jax – put your mind to it and all that . . . Look, I wanted to thank you for not bringing up Sophie last time we spoke."

"Don't mention it, Rowan."

"No, honestly. It was good of you. A lot of water's travelled under the bridge since then with Sophie and Cynthia . . . but being back here, it feels like yesterday," Rowan said.

"It was a difficult time for us all."

"It was," Rowan said and faced the midday sun with closed eyes.

"Don't want to be rude, Rowan, but I've got a few things on today. If you wanted to catch up, we could one evening."

"Right," he said, opening his eyes, slightly dazed from the light. "No, I won't keep you long. Straight to business." Rowan smiled and looked in his notebook for a moment. "I just want to remember what you said, yes . . . When we last spoke about Martin, you characterised your relationship as, well, why don't you remind me."

Jax pulled his leg back into the side of the box. "We spoke about how him having loads of cash changed him. Made him an arsehole. I remember saying that to you."

Rowan checked. "You did . . . Go on."

"There isn't much left to say, Rowan. We drifted apart. I fixed his boat when he needed it doing. That's it."

"Did he like fishing?"

Jax shrugged. "I guess. We went out on the water years ago. Had some nice times out at sea. Some good laughs – but that were years back. We hadn't done anything like that for ages."

"Do you miss him at all?"

Jax pulled out a pack of cigarettes from his pocket and lit one up, leaving the packet on the deck. "Haven't thought about it, really."

"He obviously had his own boat – he must've liked going out on the water."

"Martin Howler liked showing off. He didn't like the sea, didn't respect her. He couldn't give a damn about her."

"It was a money thing then?"

Jax nodded and hummed lightly through his cigarette as he pulled on it.

Rowan left them in silence for a moment. He looked over Jax's shoulder into the cabin: a large, white wheel, worn shiny in places; a rusted throttle lever; a thick, waterproof jacket hanging by the door; and a few coils of rope gently swaying from their hooks.

"You're right. Money changes people."

"It does. Turns them into arseholes. Look, Rowan, I'm not sure what you're asking me. Why you're here."

"What did Martin think of your profession – fisherman."

"And boat mechanic," Jax said, sitting upright.

"Sorry, yes. Did he value your services?"

"Not really. Can't says we spoke about it."

"Never spoke about the fact that you're just a fisherman and he's, sorry was, a multimillionaire businessman?"

"I don't get your point here, Rowan."

"You said his money made him ten times worse. Must've been difficult to navigate. Him being rich and you just a fisherman."

"It was. It really pissed me off. But not for the reasons you're thinking–"

"I'm not thinking anything, Jax. Just looking for clarity."

"Whatever. It did annoy me, but I weren't jealous. It was because it changed him. He didn't care about people!"

"Did this, let's say, economic difference between you cause you to argue?"

Jax was silent. Rowan observed him shifting in his seat a little before looking over Rowan's shoulder back at Wraith's Hollow.

Rowan copied, making a quick glance. "Beautiful. Even Havenmoore Port has its own kind of beauty."

"It does," Jax said and remained silent – silently looking back at Rowan.

DI Black waited. The silence escalated between them, until a seagull flying overhead squawked.

"No. I wouldn't let it get to me – not in front of him."

"Was there ever a time when you weren't able to hide your frustration around him?"

Jax shook his head.

Rowan flicked through his notebook, then: "I want to call your attention to a week ago, last Friday in the pub."

"I already told you what happened in the pub."

"Remind me." Rowan closed his notebook and placed it on his lap.

"That I told him about his boat – how someone might've damaged it on purpose. Nothing more to say."

"How did he respond to what you told him?"

"I've told you already," Jax exhaled. He finished his cigarette and lit another. "Told me just to fix his boat – didn't believe that someone would've wanted to damage it on purpose."

"And then nothing happened – you went your separate ways, so to speak. You didn't argue?"

"Nope – wouldn't waste my breath on him."

"I'm conflicted here, Jax. You see, I've received information that you *did* in fact argue with Martin in the pub on Friday and–"

"Who the fuck said that!" Jax stood, and then immediately sat down again.

Rowan waited for Jax to visibly calm down. "Please, confirm whether or not you and Martin argued."

"We did *not*."

"I wonder why my source believed you did?"

"Couldn't tell you, Rowan. Maybe you should be questioning them – not me."

DI Black ignored Jax's last words. "I'm led to believe that things looked heated between you, that you looked angry after your exchange. My source heard Martin calling you 'just a fucking fisherman' – saying that you needed to keep to your station."

"Did they *hear* anything else?"

"Not exactly. They saw Martin lean in and say something that only you could hear. What was that?"

Jax shrugged his shoulders. "Beats me. I don't remember any of this. It's my word against theirs."

"I'm not accusing you, Jax. But I do have a problem with not being able to verify what happened between you. I'd appreciate it if you confirmed one way or the other: did you or did you not have some kind of confrontation with Martin Howler last Friday in the pub?"

"Absolutely not."

"Great. Thank you. That was all . . . No, wait. Sorry. One more thing – for now. You remember you told me that Sophie and Martin argued about something? You said that you couldn't even tell Martin on the phone in the morning about his boat because he was furious from having rowed with Sophie."

"Yes. What about it?"

"When I asked Sophie about it, she denied having quarrelled with Martin. What made you think they did?"

"I told you, Rowan. Martin said he'd been rowing with that bitch Sophie. His words, not mine."

"Well, it doesn't seem like you could've interpreted the situation differently from that description . . . You're sure that's what he said?"

"Definitely. Sophie isn't a bitch – that pissed me off at the time, he shouldn't be calling her that."

"Why didn't you tell me this – what he said – before when we spoke?"

"Must've slipped my mind. I didn't *not* tell you on purpose if that's what you're thinking."

Rowan raised a hand and half smiled: "Not making any assumptions here, Jax . . . So, to be clear, you didn't remember to tell me something that Martin said that clearly makes you angry because it slipped your mind?"

Jax nodded.

"Okay. I want to confirm all this with you, Jax. You state that Martin told you he and Sophie had been arguing last Friday morning, but Sophie says she definitely wasn't. It's been reported to me that you and Martin argued in the pub Friday evening, but you state that you definitely didn't either."

"Quite the quandary," Jax said quietly.

"It is, Jax, you see. Someone is lying about what happened with Martin. I just need to figure out who."

"Not me. Besides, Martin told me he had an argument with her, maybe he was just saying that."

"But for what purpose?" Rowan Black asked.

Jax shrugged.

"Nothing comes to my mind either."

"What does it matter, anyway, if she argued with him? Doesn't mean she's the one who murdered him."

"No. You're right about that. And the same goes for you. If you rowed with him in the pub, it doesn't mean you murdered him."

"You're definitely right about that, Rowan. I didn't murder him. I'm not that stupid."

"It would seem that it's your word against Sophie's as to what the truth is around her argument with Martin. But what about you? I wonder if there was anyone else in the pub that evening who could verify my witness's account."

"I don't know. But I'm telling you we didn't fall out. And I didn't murder him."

DI Black stood up; the boat rocked. "Perhaps we'd better leave that beer for now, Jax. I'll be in touch if I need you." Rowan stepped onto the damp stone quay. Turning towards the boat he said: "Jax. Can you tell me where you were in the early hours of Thursday morning?"

"Of course. In bed."

"Can anyone confirm this?"

"No such luck, Rowan. I live alone. Haven't got time for relationships."

"Thank you. I'll be in touch, Jax," he said and walked away, gripping his notebook.

*

Three-thirty. Rowan was back at the police station drinking a much-desired coffee. This investigation was one of the most challenging he'd faced. It seemed to be sprawling in all kinds of directions. He'd updated his team about the conversations he'd had with Margaret, Little Liam, Nathan, and Jax. The cult was very much alive and kicking, Margaret had identified the three symbols; Little Liam reported seeing Martin grab Tim's throat over something to do with brain implants; Nathan's behaviour was peculiar, he was clearly stressed, and had ongoing conflicts with Martin – he was also studying the mysterious fungus that had possible psychedelic qualities; and Jax or Sophie or both of them were lying about the arguments they'd had with Martin in the last week before he was killed.

Sergeant Jennings filled DI Black in on his brief meeting with Tim when he'd come to the station to give his fingerprints. "Said he hurt his hand Tuesday – despite what Little Liam claims," Jennings said.

"Did you get the feeling he was telling the truth?"

"Too hard to be sure – but possibly."

"How did he seem? Was he certain about it, unsure, evasive – did he leave the station quickly, normally, anything that piqued your interest?"

"When I finished his prints and talking to him, he just left. Didn't seem anything other than normal. Plain old Tim Thorn."

"You didn't see him after he left the station?" Rowan asked.

"No, sir."

Rowan was quiet for a minute, watching Jennings. Then: "Who do we believe, Frank? Little Liam claims Tim came into work with his hand injured Thursday morning. They had a delivery of a type of wood which Little Liam was excited to use. It would be odd that he got this wrong, wouldn't you agree?"

"I'm not sure, Rowan. I'm more inclined to believe a proper adult."

"Isn't Little Liam trustworthy?"

"I didn't say that. You know what kids are like. None of them have their heads screwed on right these days."

Rowan thought about how best to respond. "I think you're right. I'll leave it for now – we may need to come back to it. Okay, if we believe Tim's story about when he injured his hand, he didn't do it trashing Martin's house. We need to wait for more evidence."

Sergeant Frank Jennings unfolded his arms. He let them relax by his side. "I agree, sir. Smart move. I'll do some more work on the cult – perhaps catch up with Margaret, see if an old face gets her chatting."

"Actually, leave Margaret for now – but carry on digging for me," Rowan said, remembering that Margaret told him he should ask Jennings about Hollow Kin. He knew he needed to tackle Jennings about this but now wasn't the right time.

"Really? Why's that?"

"Just leave her for now. I will speak to her again if necessary."

"Fair enough, sir. Just thought a familiar face etc."

"That's fine. I didn't mean to snap."

Sergeant Jennings placed a friendly hand on Rowan's shoulder and headed out of the incident room. Rowan placed his finger and thumb on the bridge of his nose and pinched it tightly for a moment.

"Sir," DS Hocking began. "Sandra Mead sent the pliers they found at Silver Cove Marina straight to the lab. Fast-tracked."

"Thank you. Anything on the pliers? Do we know if they're a specific type?"

"They're stainless steel, red rubber handles – good for grip in wet conditions – the cutting edge had the marks of frequent use," DS Hocking said.

"The kind a fisherman or marine biologist would use?"

"Reckon so, sir. Maybe even a cabinetmaker."

"Good work . . . Can you review the statements taken so far – including the door-to-door enquiries. Cast a fresh eye over them. Prioritise timeline gaps, inconsistencies, anything that hints at Hollow Kin's involvement."

"Sir."

Rowan finished his coffee, noticing DC Mann approach him quietly.

"Sir, may I have a word in your office?"

"Of course. Come through." They sat down at Rowan's desk. "Everything okay?" Rowan asked.

DC Mann told Rowan what he'd learned about Ellie and Martin's housing project, the way in which Martin screwed her over, and about how freely she claimed to hate him.

"Was there anything else?"

"Yes. She told me Martin raped her six years ago."

Rowan looked surprised. "She didn't tell me that when I spoke to her."

"To be fair, sir. I'm surprised she told me. But she'd been drinking. She wasn't alone when I got there."

"Who was she with?"

"Nathan Waters."

"Really. He must've gone there soon after I spoke to him. Interesting."

"There's something else. She told me she didn't report what Martin did to her."

"Did she say why?"

"Ellie said that she couldn't – basically implied it was useless to go against someone like Martin Howler. All his money and power. She was afraid that nothing would happen to him."

"Must've been difficult to swallow seeing him walking around knowing what he did to her."

"Definitely, sir. She looked angry. Whenever I mentioned his name, she looked at me with fire in her eyes. She said an odd thing at the end of our interview. She said: 'Justice was served without the police. He deserved everything he got. Rapist fucker'."

"Does she have an alibi?"

"Said she was in bed, alone."

"I'm hearing that a lot. Let's bear it in mind. She has a motive – revenge. But the timing is odd. Why wait six years?" Rowan was thoughtful for a moment. "Anything on the restaurant front?"

"Yes. The Ram's Head confirmed Martin ate there Wednesday night – table booked for seven. John Michaels, the owner, said Martin had his usual table, in the corner of the restaurant."

"Was he alone?"

DC Mann nodded. "He was."

"Did John say how Martin was? Did he seem unusual, preoccupied?" Rowan asked. The letter Martin sent him was in his mind. He still didn't have the reason Martin sent it – who spooked him? Threatened him?

"John said he was just the same as normal. Funnily enough, he said he didn't mind Martin. Didn't really have a bad word to say against him."

"Puts him in a minority round here. So, ate alone, finishes around eight, eight-thirty. Then the trail goes cold. We've got no account of his movements post meal."

"Someone somewhere knows something," DC Mann said.

"Yes . . . I want you to focus on this brain implant line of enquiry. I don't know what the hell it's about. We've got nothing to go on yet. Maybe when DCI Hargrave comes back with Martin's bank records, it'll shed some light. But until then, do what you can."

"Sir," DC Mann said and then turned to leave Rowan's office but paused at the sound of his name.

Rowan said: "Send PC Everett in, will you."

"Sir."

Rowan Black stood and went to the window. He spent a minute looking at the harbour – then the ocean.

"Sir?" PC Everett said at the door.

"Ah, Danny. Come in. Take a seat, would you?"

"Thank you, sir. Everything okay?"

"Yes," DI Black said, sitting opposite.

"God, you had me worried for a minute!"

"It's probably nothing, Danny. But can you refresh my memory as to what Ellie told you about her and Martin's relationship?"

"What do you mean, sir?"

"Just what she said. About Beech Heights etc. I'm just mulling it over – I need refreshing, so to speak."

"Sure, sir. She didn't *really* tell me that much – probably as there's nothing to say. I know they had that Beech Heights project – like I told you – but Ellie didn't say much else. Told me it went sour. That was it."

"Are you sure, Danny? It's important we get this straight now."

Danny looked down. Then nodding: "Yes, that's it."

Rowan was quiet. About ten seconds went by. Danny held his stare for half of it, then smiled nervously and looked away. Rowan wasn't trying to intimidate him – that wasn't his style. He waited for Danny to speak.

"I'm sorry, sir. I've fucked up."

"Go on."

"I told you she didn't say much. I was protecting her – she asked me not to say anything. I don't know why I listened."

Rowan knew exactly why but didn't interrupt.

"Ellie didn't want me to say anything, but Martin screwed her out of the deal. She lost loads."

"Why didn't she want you to say anything?"

"Because it makes her look guilty – like she wanted revenge or something," Danny said.

"What do you think? Is she guilty of murdering Martin?"

Danny Everett shook his head quickly. "No way, sir. I know Ellie – she isn't up to anything like that. She's too nice for one thing."

"Was there anything else you need to tell me?"

Danny sank into his chair. "Martin raped her, sir."

"DC Mann's just told me. What I would like to know is why you chose to keep this from me, Danny. What were you thinking?"

"I'm sorry, sir. Ellie asked me to. I know it was stupid . . . I'm sorry. I was just trying to protect her."

"Danny! This is a murder investigation. You've deliberately withheld information." Rowan exhaled. "It's misconduct."

"Misconduct?"

"Of course! Misconduct. To be clear, she asked you not to say anything?"

Danny nodded.

"Jesus Christ, Danny. You understood what was being asked of you?"

"She said it would make her look guilty – like she was the one who killed him."

"And what if she did?" Rowan smacked his palm off the table and then stood. He went back to the window. The scenery held no answers.

"Sir, I really don't–"

"Enough!" DI Black said. "This looks bad, Danny. You've neglected your duty."

"I'm sorry, sir. I didn't know what to do. I think I love her. I thought I was doing the right thing."

"How could you have possibly believed that!?" Rowan said, turning to face him.

Danny shrugged his shoulders.

"Not good enough, Danny. I should report you for this."

"I understand if you do, sir. I fucked up. Made a mistake."

"Take the rest of the day. See me in the morning. I need to decide what to do with you."

"Sir," Danny Everett stood up, turning to leave.

"Danny," Rowan called after him. "Please tell me you sent the laptop from Silver Cove off to forensics."

"I did, sir. Yes, I did."

*

Rowan had just stood up from his desk intending to head out of the station at five, when his phone rang – DCI Hargrave. Martin Howler's bank records had come in. He pulled up the latest flagged entries, logged by the MIR on the mainland. Analysts had highlighted payments received from different companies, ranging from tens-of-thousands to millions of pounds. *NVB Capital Partners, Shoreline Biotech LTD, Wraith BioTechnologies LTD* – all linked to someone named Naomi Bennett. The last payment of sixty-five thousand landed four days before Martin was murdered.

Rowan called DC Mann and said: "Get what you can on Naomi Bennett. Companies, investments, bankruptcies. Run her through Companies House, Land Registry. PNC as well. See if there's a link to that brain implant project."

"Yes, sir. If there's something there, I'll find it."

Sergeant Frank Jennings

The Ram's Head was not as busy as it normally was at eight o'clock in the evening on a Friday – which was odd, Jennings thought as he carried two pints of Guinness towards his table, given the current situation at Wraith's Hollow. He thought everyone would be in there gossiping about Martin. When Rowan said about going for a pint, Jennings had had his reservations – thought everyone would be trying to probe them for information. But, so far so good.

He placed Rowan's pint before him, having scanned the room for Tim Thorn. Jennings sat down with a sense of relief having been unable to spot him. He'd keep an eye on the door. The last thing he needed was Tim thinking he was clever by joining them, leaning on him, applying pressure – especially when he wouldn't have been able to do anything about it, not in front of Rowan.

"Cheers, mate. I needed this," Rowan said, drinking down three big glugs. "What a couple of days."

"Yes. I'll be glad to go to bed tonight that's for sure."

"As much as I hate to agree with you – an age thing, I guess – I'll look forward to flopping into bed, too."

Both sat in silence drinking for a few minutes.

Frank Jennings was hesitant, but he went for it and committed himself to broaching the topic of Sophie Marlow.

"Yes," Rowan responded. "I can't believe that Sophie's the way she is with me after all these years."

"Why would she still be upset with you? What've you done?" Jennings asked.

Rowan sighed. "She obviously still believes I was responsible for Cynthia's death, Frank. Even though I wasn't even there when it happened."

"I remember it. We concluded she was alone – why she *was* alone at that time of night, I don't know. But she was high on drugs and fell off Ghost Cliff Point. What the hell've you got to do with that?"

"I was seeing her, wasn't I. Sophie hated it for some reason. Never found out why. She didn't like me at all. But I was on the wrong path back then. Maybe Sophie saw that in me. Thought I was wrong for Cynthia . . . I loved her you know."

"I know you did. I remember you telling me. You've forgotten our chats in the past?"

"Of course not. Probably what helped me get back on track."

"It could've gone either way with you, Rowan. Drugs have a way of screwing people up pretty badly. You're one of the lucky ones. You got away," Jennings said, lifting his pint.

"Sophie believes I got Cynthia into drugs."

"Did you?"

"I don't know, Frank. Maybe, maybe not. We were kids back then. All of us were on something: Jax, Martin, Sophie, Cynthia. We used to meet up – there wasn't anything else to do."

"Other than get high, you mean?"

"Pretty much. We weren't doing anything that other generations haven't. Nothing unique about smoking spliffs and doing coke."

"No, I suppose not. I've never done it. My Penny got caught up in it until we got her straight."

"Shit, sorry, Frank. How is your daughter?"

"Fine, thank you . . . Did you tell Sophie you weren't there, the night Cynthia died?"

"Of course. But I couldn't prove it, could I? You even asked me where I was more than once . . . I know now you were just doing your job. Sorry if I gave you a hard time."

"You were just doing your job – angry young man," Jennings smiled.

"It was just a horrible accident. One that I can't help feeling guilty about – if I was there, she wouldn't have fallen. I'd have protected her." Rowan paused. "It's funny, I always thought we'd get married. But life has a way of shitting on your best laid plans."

"Do you think Sophie will ever forgive you?"

"No. She's the main reason I couldn't, wouldn't, come back to Wraith's Hollow, Frank. Couldn't imagine seeing her every day. I think she'd kill me."

"I know I just said we concluded that Cynthia was alone that night, but I've often wondered if she was, Rowan. I've got no evidence to prove otherwise. I've just always felt that someone round here knows something about Cynthia's death. You know when your gut tells you something?"

"I do. I've wondered the same thing, Frank. Never been able to prove it . . . I remember Jax never had an alibi for that night."

"Do you think he was there?" Jennings responded.

"I knew they were having an affair behind my back. Jax and me argued, had a fight – all that stupid stuff – after she died. I was convinced he was there. Can't prove it."

"You think he had something to do with it – you mean she didn't fall?"

"No nothing like that. If anything, they were both off their faces, too close to the cliff edge – it was a disaster waiting to happen. No, if he was there, he was guilty of not looking out for her – like I said, if I was there, she wouldn't have fallen."

Sergeant Jennings had some of his pint and took a quick glance around – still no sign of Tim.

"You okay?" Rowan asked.

"Oh yes, absolutely."

"Good. Look, Frank, can I speak to you about something?"

Jennings' heart sank. A sick feeling washed over him. Did Rowan know something about him and Tim – the cult?

"I had a thing earlier with Danny," Rowan said. "It came to light that he lied about a conversation he had with Ellie."

"What about?" Jennings said.

"He covered for her. She didn't want him to tell me – one, how Martin really screwed her out of the Beech Heights deal, and two, that Martin raped her."

"Shit . . . Because it makes her look suspicious?"

Rowan nodded. "I'm angry with him."

"Can I help?"

"I've only just found this out, so I'm not going to do anything with it yet."

"No, good decision," Jennings said. "Best to think it through. Do you want me to have a word with him?"

"No. It needs to come from me. He knows he screwed up."

"But why cover for Ellie?" Jennings asked.

"Bit naïve there, Frank. He thinks he's in love with her."

"I see."

"Exactly. Wasn't thinking with his head was he."

"No. So how're you going to handle this?"

"Like I said: he knows he's done wrong," Rowan said.

"I don't think he'd have been covering something up about Martin's case. That would be different."

"Frank," DI Black began. "He might've only covered for Ellie because he loves her; but he could have inadvertently helped her get away with it – if she's guilty."

"Did you ask Danny if he thinks she's guilty?"

"I did. He believes she isn't."

"And what do you think about Ellie?"

Rowan was thoughtful. "My gut says not. But she has a motive: revenge. He raped her financially and physically. I've known people who've killed for less."

"That's true. But is she capable of it? I don't believe she is."

"I've met many people who you'd think weren't capable of committing serious crimes, Frank. This job's taught me to never underestimate anyone."

Sergeant Jennings nodded. "We know Danny did what he thought was right – I think he just got it wrong."

"Alright then, if it was down to you, what's your call?"

"There's no need to take it higher. Keep it between ourselves. Give him a slap on the wrist – a stern talking to . . . Danny's not a bad lad, Rowan. We've all made mistakes. He's young, bit foolish. And he's in love."

"A fool in love," Rowan said and drank the rest of his pint. "I'll take it on board, Frank. Keep this between us . . . Listen, there's something else I want to talk to you about."

"Go on. Actually, hold that thought. I'll get us another in."

Rowan checked his watch. "You know what. Don't worry, I'll catch up with you another time. I need an early night," Rowan said, standing. He placed a hand on Jennings' shoulder: "We'll catch up soon."

Before Jennings had a chance to say any more, Rowan left the pub. Jennings finished his pint and went to the bar for another one. Rowan knows something. He bloody knows something!

Rowan Black

The door of the Ram's Head closed with a creak. Rowan stood outside and breathed in the sea air. He decided to go back in the pub. He met Jennings at the bar.

"Make it two pints, Frank," he said, retrieving his bank card from his wallet. "I'll get these."

"Sir, I thought you wanted an early night."

"Everything okay, Frank, you look, I don't know, a bit stressed?"

"No, I'm all good. Just waiting for John here to organise our drinks."

Something about him, not sure. "Take a seat, Frank. I'll bring them over."

Rowan eyed Jennings carefully from the bar. He looked a million miles away.

"Cheers," Frank said, taking a big swig. "So, to what do I owe the pleasure – thought bed was calling you?"

"It still is," Rowan said, taking a more measured drink of Guinness. "That thing I wanted to talk to you about before I left."

"I'm all ears."

"Something's bothering me. It's about Hollow Kin."

"I told you I'm on it."

"And that's what I expect of you – seeing as I asked you to do that. But there's something else. Why would Margaret Warren tell me to ask you about Hollow Kin?" Rowan waited but Jennings said nothing, he just rubbed his lips with his fingers and then folded his arms. "You see, I'm starting to think two things here: one, you know more about this cult than you're letting on – meaning you are compromising yourself to the point of royally fucking up. And two, you've actually been honest with me about what you know – meaning you've had your head in the sand for decades where the cult is concerned. You see what I'm getting at, Frank?"

Frank Jennings was silent.

"It's one of those options, Frank – which is it?"

"You're looking for something that isn't there, Rowan. I've already told you that I've heard people talking about a cult for years and years; but it's a load of rubbish to me," Jennings waved a hand. "If there is one, I'm not involved. As for Margaret – I've no clue why she'd say that. Not a clue."

"It's an odd thing for her to say," Rowan said. "Maybe she got her wires crossed."

"That's it right there."

"She told me she was in Hollow Kin years back – but she left."

"Did she now. Do you believe her?"

"I've no reason not to. Besides, she was able to identify the three symbols."

"Could come in handy," Jennings said, drinking his pint. He took his time, eyeing Rowan out of the corner of his eye.

Rowan maintained eye contact. He knew Jennings was lying – that was perfectly obvious. He was trying to decide how to play this out.

"Why could it come in handy, Frank?"

"I was just meaning if they link back to someone–"

"From the cult?"

"From Hollow Kin – yes. Doesn't mean it will, and it doesn't mean I believe in them."

"No, fair enough." Rowan Black stood slowly from the table. "If you're lying to me, Frank, I'll see to it that you're ruined."

And then he left – his pint half drunk.

Ellie Crick

It was just past ten p.m. when Ellie struggled drunkenly to draw her curtains. She was successful on the second attempt. She thought about opening the last bottle of wine but decided against it – her head was swimming.

She sat on the sofa and turned the TV on. It was all rubbish. She was halfway through a ten-part crime series, but there was no way she was going to be able to concentrate on that. Knowing that Nathan was involved in Martin's murder was at the forefront of her mind. Nathan!

Her phone sounded – incoming text from Danny. He'd messaged earlier seeing if he could come over, but Ellie had rejected him. She'd messaged back saying she'd see him tomorrow. Whatever he needed to talk to her about was not important right now. Danny could wait.

Mrs. Appleby, I didn't kill him . . . If I can somehow prove it to you that it was someone else . . .

Her words to Mrs. Appleby swam through her mind. She could now prove that she didn't have anything to do with Martin's murder. But Nathan had confided in her. Was her friendship with him worth more than her ties to Hollow Kin?

Nathan told her he loved her. That was worth something. Maybe she loved him too? They could leave Wraith's Hollow, find somewhere a million miles away from this madness.

What the hell was Nathan thinking?

What the hell was she thinking telling DC Mann that Martin raped her? Rowan bloody Black would want her back at the station, spilling her sullied, regretful past to him. She wasn't going to dig all that up again. No fucking way. She didn't have to, and she wouldn't – it was none of his fucking business.

But should she tell Mrs. Appleby about Nathan? Was there a way to tell her and not screw Nathan over? God her head hurt – closing her eyes made it ten times worse. She couldn't think straight having drunk her own bodyweight in wine. It was a good job Danny didn't come over – she'd probably just vomit on him.

Hell, why'd she drink so much?

And then, whilst deliberating whether to tell Mrs. Appleby about Nathan, therefore getting herself back in with Hollow Kin, she passed out.

Sergeant Jennings

Sergeant Frank Jennings knocked DI Black's door on Quayside Lane. The number *12* was bathed in silvery moonlight, and the frosted glass reflected the moon behind him.

It was coming up for midnight. Jennings wasn't sure if this was a good idea. But everything was becoming too much – he didn't know what else to do. He'd been living a lie for too many years. And it wasn't as if he was just lying to other people: he'd been lying to himself. The worst kind. Convincing himself that it was all fine and justified.

Penny. She was the one it was all for. He loved his daughter so much.

An interior light went on, puncturing the darkness around him, glowing against his face, providing him with his last chance to bailout.

Jennings stayed.

"Frank," Rowan said, opening the door.

"Sir, I'm sorry it's late. I didn't know what else to do. Can I come in?"

"Sure." Rowan stepped aside and motioned for Jennings to come in. "Can I get you a drink? I haven't been shopping, yet; so, I've only got what Margaret gives to her guests."

"No, thanks. I'm fine. One too many pints as it is."

"Go through, the living room's in there."

Jennings went to the sofa – Rowan sat in the chair in the corner.

"Wood-burner's a beauty," Jennings said. He sat back against the sofa but changed his mind and moved towards the edge of the seat. "I bet that warms the place in winter."

"Frank," Rowan said. "You haven't come here at midnight to talk to me about Margaret's wood-burner – lovely, though it is."

"No, true. That's true. I don't know how to begin . . . that's a first for me. Never been shy with words."

"Start with the truth, Frank. You look like you're up to your neck in something."

Frank Jennings was quiet for a moment, then: "My daughter, Penny. She was in a lot of trouble – about fifteen years ago, around the time you left, I guess. You remember Freddy? Her boyfriend at the time?"

"I do. Went down for possession of heroin, didn't he? Intent to supply."

"He did. Got seven years."

"Big stash, wasn't it?"

"It was . . . Penny was up to her neck in it with him. He was abusing her, Rowan. Real bad. Sometimes physical but mostly psychological. Really nasty – fucking with her head. I couldn't convince her to come to the station to report him."

"She never did?"

Jennings shook his head. "She was terrified of him. I don't know what it was with him. Knew him as a kid. He was always quiet. Never thought he'd turn out to be the monster he did."

"I never knew."

"You wouldn't, Rowan. Bastards like that are clever. Scheming. Manipulative. He convinced everyone he was a saint and that *she* was the problem. I had people coming up to me at the time asking whether they could help her in any way – or if I needed support in *order* to help her. It was madness . . . He told her she was worthless to the point where she believed him."

"Must've been awful, Frank."

"It was. She called me once, at night – God, I thought she was going to kill herself – she sounded empty. Truly, dead and empty. My beautiful girl's life just totally worthless . . . That was an awful time. Never had stress like it. I was desperate. I wasn't thinking straight." Jennings stood up and paced a couple of steps before sitting down again. "I tried threatening him – leaning on him, told him I'd destroy him if he carried on. But he didn't care. He knew I couldn't – man of the law."

"I feel like you're coming onto something, Frank."

"Rowan, I framed him. Stitched him up. Screwed him over. And you know what, I'm glad, too. I'd do it all over again if I had to."

"What're you talking about?"

"Planted the drugs in his shithole flat. Dirty bastard, he was."

"Fuck, Frank."

"I know, I *know!*"

"Shit. To be clear: *you* planted the drugs?"

Frank Jennings breathed deeply. "Not me. I got help."

"Who from?"

"Hollow Kin," Jennings said.

Now Rowan stood up. "Hollow Kin! The cult you've claimed doesn't exist. Frank, you've been bullshitting me!"

"I'm sorry. I didn't know what to do!"

"Why'd you do it?" Rowan asked.

"I was desperate, on my knees, no one to turn to . . . How far would you go to save someone you love?"

"Don't give me that crap!"

"No. It's important. Now you know how far I'd go."

"Yes, I do – to jail." Rowan sat down. "Was it Tim who helped?"

Jennings nodded.

"I saw you both earlier, at the seafront, talking. Something wasn't right – it looked uncomfortable. Now I know why. What involvement did he have?"

"I got the drugs and Freddy's keys – Tim did the rest. All I had to do was arrest Freddy . . . Tim's trying to blackmail me. Wants to know about the case, what you're up to. If I don't tell him, he says he'll tell you about the deal."

"Well, you've told me now – that's stripped him of his power." Rowan was silent. Jennings could barely look at him. "We need to play this cool. Our priority is finding

Martin's killer. That's what we're here to do. For now, I need you on the case. That makes me complicit, I know that, but I'll worry about that later. You don't breathe a word of this to anyone. Do you understand me? And definitely don't let on to Tim that I know. I can't see how yet, but we might be able to get some leverage out of this. As for you, I think you know you need to face the music on this once it's over, Frank."

"I do," Jennings said, sombrely. Then offered: "I reckon Tim knows who's responsible for Martin's murder."

"Did he give you a name?" Rowan asked.

"No. Just said Hollow Kin have everything in hand."

"Right. Lean on him – but don't make him suspect anything. Do you believe Little Liam about his hand now?"

"I feel terrible about this, sir, because I've lied to you. Look, I don't know what to think. Maybe Little Liam is right. Tim came in Thursday with his injured hand. But Tim didn't tell me anything about it. Just wanted me to reaffirm that he hurt it on Tuesday. I'll press him on it, sir. You have my word."

"Tell me, Frank. With what you know about Tim Thorn, is he capable of murdering Martin?"

"Yes," Jennings said without hesitation.

"Right, we better get a drink of something. You need to tell me everything you know about Hollow Kin."

Chapter Eight

Interviews

Rowan Black

Saturday.

Along with reviewing the statements, Rowan called DS Hocking and asked him to trace Martin's movements after he left the Ram's Head, leading up to his death.

"We've still got six hours unaccounted for," he said. "Speak to forensics, see if they've pulled his phone's location data. Might give us a trail."

That morning, he was up early despite being up late last night with Jennings – who had left at two in the morning. Rowan had two cups of coffee – his first, watching the sun rising over Wraith's Hollow – before he left for Mrs. Appleby's at eight-thirty a.m. Taking a slow walk, he let Jennings' words about Hollow Kin flow through his mind. If what he said was true, then they might be responsible for Martin's murder. Tim Thorn, nasty, violent, entered his thoughts. It wasn't hard to imagine him beating Martin to death on the beach to protect Wraith's Hollow. But what were Hollow Kin protecting? Sooner or later, the world would eat into all that Wraith's Hollow was – and its old ways would die.

Would Veritas die too? He wasn't so sure. But he was certain the members of Hollow Kin would do their best to ensure she didn't.

Wraithmoore Lane was a long, steady climb, and Rowan took it at an easy pace. He opened Mrs. Appleby's gate, glancing at the sign: Hollow Crest. She really needed a new one.

He didn't need to knock the door. "Rowan Black. How are you?" Mrs. Appleby said. "I saw you coming up the path there."

"Mrs. Appleby. Lovely to see you. I'm very well – under the circumstances."

"Yes. It's an awful time for Wraith's Hollow. Probably the lowest point in our long and colourful history."

"Have you got five minutes for an old friend?" Rowan asked at the doorstep. "I couldn't help noticing, but your sign on the gate there needs replacing."

"Everyone says that to me at the moment – Tim was here recently, he said the same thing," Mrs. Appleby smiled.

Rowan made a mental note. "Do you see Tim much?"

"Come in, come in," she said. "I do. Tim's a lovely, warm-hearted man. The kind that Wraith's Hollow needs." Mrs. Appleby led the way through to the kitchen and asked Rowan to sit at the table whilst she made some coffee.

"Thank you," Rowan said as he took the cup from her. "God, this place hasn't changed much, Mrs. Appleby, since I was here as a kid."

"You're telling me!" She smiled and sat opposite him. "The garden hasn't changed either."

Rowan smiled back. "I used to like coming here – helping. Hard work, mind, going up and down that bloody hill."

"Rowan, please, if you don't mind, refrain from cursing in my house."

"Oh, of course. I'm sorry. Force of habit."

He looked at Mrs. Appleby. Her blue eyes were quite mesmerising – he felt on the back foot. He needed to find a subject for them to come together on.

"I liked my gardening and chats with your George. He was a lovely man. In fact, when I think back to my time here before I left, George is often the first thing I think of."

"That's nice, Rowan . . . George really was the nicest man I could have ever wished for. We had a good life together. A perfect life. I miss him every day."

"I expect you do. I remember he loved space. I always remember talking to him about the magnificence of space – as he put it."

"Is that what you used to talk about? I used to wonder what on earth you could've been talking about. Whenever I looked out the window, you two would be chatting away . . . He never told me, you know. What you spoke about."

"Did he not?"

Mrs. Appleby shook her head, slowly. "I didn't know he liked space so much. I mean, I suppose I did. But he never spoke to me about it."

"Strange. He knew lots about space, the stars, constellations. All that sort of thing."

"I thought I knew him inside out," Mrs. Appleby said.

Rowan took a sip of coffee. "I guess we all have our secrets, Mrs. Appleby." He eyed her for a moment.

"Not us. We weren't supposed to – not one." Rowan watched her knuckles whiten and her thin, aged skin tighten as she gripped her cup. Her tone deepened. "Why're you here, Rowan?"

"I felt guilty. I didn't get the chance to pop round the last couple of days."

"Aren't you busy trying to catch whoever killed poor Martin?"

"I am. But I still wanted to pop in and see you . . . I noticed you said poor Martin. What was your relationship like with him?"

"All of a sudden I feel very much under suspicion, DI Black."

"Of course not, Mrs. Appleby. I've asked the same of everyone. It's very helpful to have people's opinions. They help build a picture of him."

"You knew him. You should have a picture, as you put it, of him already." She stiffened in her seat.

"Not really. The Martin I knew years ago was not the same man who was killed the early hours of Thursday morning."

Mrs. Appleby sipped her coffee, eyeing Rowan between sips, then: "Does a leopard ever change its spots?"

"Sometimes," Rowan said.

"Well, as you're asking. I didn't mind him at all."

"Really – even though he killed George, accidentally, with his car?"

"Oh, you'd be right if you'd said that in the days after George's death I hated Martin. That much was true. But, Rowan, you see, when you get to my age, you learn to let go of the things that embitter you. Do you know what I mean? It doesn't do you any good – in here," Mrs. Appleby said, placing her palm on her heart.

"If only we were all as wise as you. The world would be a better place, that's for sure," Rowan smiled. "There was no ill feeling between you?"

"Not at all. I didn't mind his ways."

"You're in a minority, Mrs. Appleby. Most people I've asked have told me how they hated him – for one reason or another."

"Looks like you've got your work cut out, Detective. Multiple suspects," Mrs. Appleby said, sipping her drink. "Good coffee."

Rowan Black agreed. "But I'm narrowing the circle of suspects."

"Oh really?"

"Certainly."

"Are you good at your job, Detective?" Mrs. Appleby asked.

"I like to think so."

"Tell me, how do you usually catch a killer?"

Rowan considered before he answered. "A combination of instinct and science – forensic science. But the best tool I have is communication – conversation. You see," DI Black edged forward in his seat, closing the space between them, until his chest brushed the edge of the kitchen table, "I find, the guilty reveal themselves through the words they use."

"How interesting. The eyes reveal all, too, don't you think?" Mrs. Appleby said.

Rowan regarded her blue eyes: she was looking at him, but he knew she was elsewhere in that moment. He thought about what Tim said to Jennings about Hollow Kin having everything in hand. The trouble Rowan faced was that he had no evidence. He could go in guns blazing and question Mrs. Appleby about it, but she could easily deny it and he wouldn't be able to prove a damn thing.

"Are you a traditionalist, Mrs. Appleby?"

"That depends on what you mean by traditionalist?"

"Someone who has an affection for the old ways – doesn't like, or resists, change."

"Then yes, by that definition, I am. I wouldn't be without Wraith's Hollow's traditions from the Christmas fairs to the summer celebrations. I love our land, our ways, our ideals, our morals. We are very different from the mainland, Rowan – though I guess you worked that out long ago. What we have here is a community where people truly love their neighbour."

"Unless that neighbour happens to be Martin Howler."

"Like I said: I didn't mind him."

"What about that house of his up the way – Nexus House? Doesn't fit in with the Wraith's Hollow aesthetic, so to speak."

"He was ambitious with that one, to say the least."

"What do you mean, Mrs. Appleby?"

"I think you know what I mean," she said, staring at him.

"Clarify for me."

"Nexus House doesn't fit in with our aesthetic, to use your words. It's a monstrosity of a place. We are tradition – as you quite rightly observed. We are wholesome, and good. It's in our bones and our buildings. But Martin's home, well, that wasn't a home – not a Wraith's Hollow home."

"Did you ever go to his house?"

"Absolutely not. Not even when I was invited. I had no interest – told him as much."

"Do you think that offended him at all, your frankness?"

Mrs. Appleby shook her head. "Not really, it brought us closer together in some ways. You see, he admired the fact that I don't beat about the bush, Detective."

"What about the development, Beech Heights? I've been informed that it had a bumpy start."

"If you're referring to Ellie Crick – I don't know anything about it. And as to the development that now exists, it's appalling."

"Must've been difficult to swallow, that lot going up."

"Rowan, dear, I know what you're up to. I wasn't born yesterday."

DI Black raised a palm. "I'm not up to anything, Mrs. Appleby. Like I said, I'm trying to build a picture of Martin and how he fitted in around here . . . Look, I'm the same as the people I've spoken to. Nexus House, Beech

Heights, Silver Cove Marina – all luxury and antithetical to the island. I'm not happy about them, and I haven't lived here for years. Wraith's Hollow cannot be at peace once more unless every resident is doing their bit for their fellow neighbour. Martin Howler wasn't concerned about his neighbour, was he?"

"Said like a true islander, Rowan Black . . . You're right: Martin had no neighbour in mind. Let me tell you something that may help you. Going back to Beech Heights. I know this much. Martin elbowed Ellie Crick out of the deal – I suppose that's what you get for associating with someone like *him*. But anyway, I know she was angry at the time, I remember people telling me. Imagine how you'd feel losing out on a small fortune to the man you had to see day in day out, year in year out. For years, seeing him floating around, knowing that he was bathing in the money that could've, should've, been yours." Mrs. Appleby paused. "I don't think I could handle that, could you?"

"Are you implying that Ellie Crick had something to do with Martin's death?" Rowan said, knowing exactly what she was doing.

"Oh no, dear. I don't want her to get into trouble. She's a sweetheart, really. I just wanted to do my bit and pass on my thoughts to the police. We need the truth to come out, don't we?"

"Thank you – I'll bear it in mind. Tell me, what did you mean when you said that's what you get for associating with someone like Martin? I thought you got on reasonably well – or at the very least, didn't mind him."

Mrs. Appleby wasn't phased – her answer came quickly. "I suppose I was looking at the situation from Ellie's point of view."

"I'm sorry to press you on this, but it didn't sound like that to me."

"Well, dear, as my answer is insufficient, tell me, how did it sound to you?"

"Like you have some resentment towards Martin – despite saying to me just now that you didn't mind him."

"I didn't mind him socially – but I was referring to him in a professional capacity. I would never associate with someone like him in business."

"Why would that be?"

"Well, it may surprise you, Rowan, but I have no interest in making money. I'm too old. I have everything I need. The mistake Ellie made – one I wouldn't have – was choosing Martin as a business partner. He'd sell his only child if it meant more money. That kind of desire poisons the soul."

"And once a soul becomes poisoned?"

"Judgement must follow. Punishment is given. Loyalty must be demonstrated. A sacrifice must be made."

Rowan thought he detected a faint smile on her lips.

"Mrs. Appleby, what can you tell me about Hollow Kin?"

"We protect Wraith's Hollow. We serve Veritas."

"You're not denying the cult's existence?"

"Hollow Kin's not a cult, Rowan. We are loyal servers of Veritas, and we ensure Wraith's Hollow is guided in the right direction."

"And what happens when Wraith's Hollow is off course?"

"Veritas reveals herself."

"How does she do that?"

"In many ways. Most recently, she's sent a sign to the island – that we're in need of repair. You've seen the fungus growing?"

"I have."

"That's Veritas. But not everyone hears her. I'm the only one who can truly listen. We ensure her desires are fulfilled."

"Would her desires ever involve murder?"

Mrs. Appleby was silent for a moment. "At times, balance must be restored . . . Why don't you ask me outright, Detective."

Rowan leaned back in his seat, rested his arms on the rests, and linked his fingers. "Mrs. Appleby, is anyone from Hollow Kin, that you know of, responsible for the murder of Martin Howler?"

"And how have you come to that conclusion? The symbols, I expect."

Rowan nodded. "Three symbols on his body and three at his home. What can you tell me about *The Mark of Veritas, The Binding of the Kin*, and *The Tongue of Silence*."

"They mark judgement, they bind with punishment, and they seal what must not be spoken. They are tools of balance, Detective."

"Tools of justice?"

"Perhaps, yes."

"And who judges?"

"Veritas," Mrs. Appleby said with a smile. "Veritas is the ultimate judge – she judges, even you, Detective."

"Veritas decides when murder is necessary to restore the balance?"

"Veritas shows us how to be at peace once more."

"You haven't answered my question, Mrs. Appleby. Do you know if anyone from Hollow Kin is responsible for the murder of Martin Howler?"

"All I know," Mrs. Appleby placed her hand on her heart, "is that balance has been restored. That's all Veritas requires of us. Do I know if anyone from Hollow Kin is responsible? I'm afraid Veritas hasn't revealed that to me."

"Someone placed those symbols on him!" Rowan raised his voice, his words bouncing off the kitchen walls.

"I'm afraid, Detective, I don't tolerate anyone shouting at me – especially in my *own* home. I, respectfully, would like you to leave."

Rowan drank the last of his coffee. "That *is* good coffee, Mrs. Appleby. Well, you've given me food for thought. I'll need you to come down to the station – just for a formal interview. You're not under arrest–"

"I know I'm not."

"Like I said. You're not under arrest; but given your knowledge of Hollow Kin, the symbols, and the connection these have with Martin's death, I believe you could provide crucial insights." Rowan Black stood and checked his watch – more for show than anything else. "Let's say tomorrow at ten. I'll send a car for you."

"I'll make my own way there," she said, cuttingly. "I'll be there. Even if the day is one intended for rest and peace."

"Thank you. I'll see myself out."

Sergeant Jennings

When Jennings woke at seven, he was surprised he'd managed to sleep at all. He'd left Rowan's far too late, but having discussed his past with him, Jennings had felt relieved – even good.

He briefly reflected on the direction his police career was taking. But the important part was that the truth had come out (if only to Rowan) – and the burden of his past with Hollow Kin had been lifted.

Jennings got himself together quickly and was heading for Tim's workshop by eight forty-five. He knew Tim would be there working. There was plenty Jennings could say about Tim – none of it particularly wholesome – but he couldn't fault the man's work ethic.

"Frank," Tim said as opened the door. "I'm not usually open at this time to customers, but for you, I'll make an exception."

"I thought you'd stopped smoking," Jennings said, not by way of a pleasantry, just to twist the knife a little. He stepped inside.

"Whether I smoke or not has sod all to do with you. Why're you here?" Tim shut the door, leaving the closed sign on display.

"Little Liam around yet?"

"No. He'll be here shortly. We have time – I presume you're giving me an update?" Tim said. He eased his backside onto the workshop bench and took a deep pull on his cigarette.

"I see you're enjoying that." Jennings wanted to slap the smile off Tim's face.

"I am," he said, blowing smoke in Jennings' face. "Well, come on then. What's the latest?"

Jennings said: "I need clarity on when you hurt your hand."

Tim shook his head. "I don't think so."

"Look, if I know, I can cover for you better."

"Why're you being supportive all of a sudden? It's not like you." Tim took another deep breath, full of smoke, into his lungs.

"We've found a discrepancy. It's been reported that you hurt your hand later than when you said."

Tim scowled. "Who said?"

"Who is irrelevant. The fact is, it's come up, and we need to deal with it. We, as in you and me."

"I told you already. I did it Tuesday. End of."

"I can't help you if you don't let me, Tim . . . It looks bad. We've got an account of you having hurt your hand after Martin's house was trashed – after he was killed."

"Doesn't mean anything. Who is this fucking person you're listening to?"

"I can't tell you, Tim. I'm risking everything by talking to you now. If Rowan figured out that you knew this information, he'd take two seconds flat to link it back to me."

"Well, you just make sure he believes I hurt this," he raised his right hand, "Tuesday. Right. What else you got for me?"

"I need to understand what you meant when you said Hollow Kin have everything in hand?"

"What do you think it means?"

"That you know who killed Martin Howler."

Tim eyed Jennings, suspiciously. "You're up to something, Frank. I can see it. It's in your eyes."

"Tim, I'm trying to help you and help Hollow Kin."

"Bullshit."

"You think I've told Rowan about what *we* did? That I've screwed myself so the truth could come out?"

"It would be bloody stupid – but then again, Frank, it's you we're talking about."

"Don't be so fucking stupid."

"I'm not telling you who's responsible for killing Martin. Hollow Kin protect their own."

"But it was someone from Hollow Kin?"

"Let's just say Veritas revealed who's responsible."

Jennings was thoughtful for a moment. He watched Tim stub out his cigarette and go to the kettle. Tim made one drink.

"Tim," Jennings began. "This is a matter for the police. If you know who's killed Martin, you need to come forward – someone does. What do you mean Veritas has revealed the killer to you?"

"You of all people, Frank, should know that Veritas is everything to Hollow Kin and Wraith's Hollow."

"Yes, but she's not exactly a reliable, credible source of informa–"

Jennings couldn't finish his sentence – Tim had him by the throat and was squeezing.

"Think very carefully before you say another word, *Frank*."

Jennings struggled for air. He tried to break free of Tim's grip – but it was too much. Jennings dropped to the ground as Tim released him.

"Don't speak like that about Veritas," Tim said, watching Frank Jennings on all fours, sucking in air.

"Bastard!" he said once he was able to. "You're a fucking lunatic." He stood to meet Tim's eyes. "Don't touch me again, Tim. It'll be the last fucking thing you do."

"Oh really," Tim folded his arms and relaxed back against the workbench. "I don't think so."

"I know you did it, Tim. You trashed Martin's place and killed him on the beach," Jennings said, realising he wasn't exactly playing it cool like he and Rowan agreed. It took everything he had not to kill Tim right then and there. Never had he allowed anyone to hurt him before – Tim wouldn't do it again.

"Be careful before you go accusing me again. If you do, I'll go to Rowan. Tell him everything."

Jennings ignored this. "You know, we found fingerprints at Martin's – in the bathroom. What's the odds they'll be yours?" Jennings headed for the door, opened it, and turned back to face Tim. He said: "Fuck you, Tim.

It's over for you. You're finished."

Mrs. Benn and Dennis the Corgi

Mrs. Benn had always thought going through the kissing gate at the edge of Wraith Forest was a quaint and fun way to enter. There was something distinctly old-fashioned, something so Wraith's Hollow about it. She loved it. Dennis led the way, his tail wagging.

"Dennis, my goodness. We're nearly there! Slow down, silly thing," Mrs. Benn said. Dennis barked by way of reply, perhaps, Mrs. Benn thought, agreeing with her. It was a lovely morning – the spring sun had blessed the island during its rise, and Mrs. Benn felt its glorious warmth on her back right until she entered the forest. But she'd come prepared. Being a lifelong Wraith's Hollow inhabitant had meant that she, and her many dogs over the decades, had visited Wraith Forest hundreds, if not thousands, of times. Her favourite coat and chiffon scarf were all that she needed. Besides, she knew the sun would reach the path eventually – warming the compacted soil and occasional gravel spots. The path really needed some work, perhaps she would mention it during the next council meeting.

No doubt Tim Thorn would rather keep it natural. He would say as much at the meeting, claiming that it's been there for generations, that it's earth, it's alive, it's part of what makes Wraith's Hollow special. But, Mrs. Benn would counter, I just want it maintained so I don't fall over!

Dennis sat and waited, he was such a good boy, for Mrs. Benn to unclip his lead. They began their lovely stroll. She placed her hands in her pockets, the lead wrapped gently around her knuckles, whilst she played out the 'path' conversation between her and Tim. Despite Tim's stubbornness, she really was fond of him – had been for years. He's a lovely man, if a little hard. And clever! She had no doubts that the cherry wood table he was making for her would be stunning.

She called Dennis back a few times – he was, for some reason this morning, getting a little further ahead than normal. Excited! That's it, she thought. She had just started along one of the paths that would lead them between the beautiful oak trees when she realised Dennis had disappeared.

She could no longer see his white-tipped, sandy tail!

"Dennis!" Mrs. Benn shouted. "Dennis! Oh, my goodness, where are you?" Panic pulsed through her.

A moment later, Mrs. Benn breathed a deep sigh of relief. "There you are," she said, stepping into the undergrowth, away from the main path. Dennis barked. "What have you found?"

Mrs. Benn clipped Dennis' lead back on and gently moved him to one side. "Some kind of jacket, Dennis? Someone's going to be disappointed, having lost . . ." her voice trailed off into the forest – both she and Dennis remained in silence as they realised the jacket was covered in blood.

Mrs. Appleby

Nine-thirty. She'd tried phoning Tim a number of times since that serpent DI Black had left. It was infuriating that he didn't pick up.

What could he possibly be doing?

"Mrs. Appleby," Tim said. "I see you've called–"

"I've been trying to reach you. Where the hell have you been, Tim Thorn? I've had Rowan Black sniffing round here like some filthy dog."

"I'm sorry, Mrs. Appleby. But I've had my own dealings with Frank Jennings this morning."

"What did *he* want?"

"I'll tell you in a minute. What did Black want?" Tim asked.

"He asked me if I know whether someone from Hollow Kin is responsible for murdering Martin."

"What did you say?"

"I told him Veritas hasn't revealed that to me."

Tim paused on the end of the line. "I told Jennings Veritas has revealed the murderer to us."

"Why would you do that? Careless!"

"I didn't say who. I know how to play Jennings, don't worry. What else did Black want?"

"To know about Hollow Kin. I told him the fundamentals but nothing incriminating. He asked about the three symbols and what they meant."

"You reckon he's getting closer?" Tim asked.

"You should be the one to tell me that. Has Jennings given you an update?"

"I'm afraid not. Only about a time discrepancy about my hand – as in when I hurt it. Someone's been talking, telling Rowan I hurt it later than Tuesday."

"Who's been talking?" Mrs. Appleby's tone dropping.

"I don't know, Mrs. Appleby. I want to, so I can pay them a visit."

"No, you don't. Not now. Stick to your guns. You told him Tuesday so stick to it. It's your word against whoever else's. Why the sigh, Tim?"

"I grabbed Jennings."

"You idiot! Badly?"

"No, just by the throat – put him in his place."

"And what if he takes that to DI Black?"

"He won't. I know Frank."

"Damn it, Tim. Anything else happen that I should be aware of?"

"Frank accused me of trashing Martin's place and of murdering him."

"What did you say to that?"

"That's not all, Mrs. Appleby. He told me they found prints at Martin's. Frank's betting they're mine."

"You've been to his house. It's highly likely your prints are there."

"Yes, but the prints were found in the bathroom. I told Rowan I didn't go anywhere in his house other than up the stairs with the bookcase . . . But it's fine. I'll claim that I forgot. It doesn't prove anything anyway. Frank's trying to scare me – empty threats."

"I don't like where that's going, Tim. Have you, or have you not, got Frank under control?"

"Of course."

"Let's hope so. Because if you haven't . . ." Mrs. Appleby let the threat hang. Then: "DI Black wants me at the station tomorrow for a formal interview."

"You're not under arrest."

"Yes, I think I'm aware of that."

"What was his reason?"

"Because of my knowledge of Hollow Kin, the symbols and their relationship to the case. It might be because I threw Ellie under the bus a bit too."

"Why? We said we'd handle it. Hollow Kin and Veritas will handle Ellie."

"Modify your tone, Tim. Remember who you're talking to. Besides. I didn't give him anything really. Just that Ellie might have cause for revenge against Martin because of what he did to her."

"I hope you're right and that it doesn't come back to bite us on the arse."

"Anyway, the *reason* for my calling is to get your thoughts about how to play this interview at the station."

"Then listen carefully. This is how to play it."

Rowan Black

Nine-thirty. Rowan Black was on his way back to the station. He'd called in to Diane's for a coffee after his conversation with Mrs. Appleby. Veritas, the symbols, and

Hollow Kin, were circling in his mind. His thoughts were interrupted by his phone ringing.

"Sir," DS Hocking said. "Got some info back from forensics. They pulled the location data from Martin's phone. He left the Ram's Head at twenty past eight. GPS tracked him home – connected to his Wi-Fi at eight-forty."

"No detours?"

"None, sir. But here's the thing: call log shows Sophie Marlow phoned him at nine twenty-three. Conversation lasted just over five minutes."

"Sophie?" Rowan repeated. "What's she playing at? She kept that quiet . . . What else?"

"No more activity. Phone stayed put until SOCO bagged it Thursday. Forensics are running it through GrayKey to extract messages and emails etc, but we're going to have to wait for that."

"Thank you. Clearly, Martin *did* leave his house that night – he ended up dead on the beach. Did Sophie arrange to meet him? And why not take his phone?"

"Want me to pull Sophie in, sir?"

"Yes. I'm heading in now. Bring her in. I want you with me on this one."

*

On entering the station, Rowan nearly bumped into PC Everett. He was waiting for Rowan, looking anxious.

"Sir, you wanted to see me this morning," he said, keeping his voice low to prevent Gerald, the part-time desk clerk – who'd been called in beyond his regular hours to assist with the murder enquiry – from hearing.

"I did. Follow me." Rowan walked through reception, heading to his office with Danny behind him.

"Oh yes, sir, we've had a call this morning from Mrs. Benn."

"Right," Rowan said over his shoulder.

"Yes, she, she's found a jacket in Wraith Forest with blood all over it."

Rowan stopped in the incident room and pulled out his phone to call Sandra Mead. "Where's Mrs. Benn now?" he asked Danny. Danny said she was waiting at the entrance to Wraith Forest. "Sandra," Rowan spoke into the phone, "a jacket's been found with blood on it at Wraith Forest. I need you to go and collect it, make a sweep of the area. I'll send PC Everett to meet you. Call me as soon as it's bagged. Thank you."

DI Rowan Black led Danny into his office. "Let's make this quick as you've got work to do. Take a seat," Rowan said, taking his.

"Sir, I want to apologise for what I did. I'm sorry. I've thought about it and–"

Rowan put his hand up to stop Danny's pleading. "Danny, if I believed you acted purposefully to steer the outcome of this investigation, you'd be facing suspension and a misconduct charge. But I don't believe that. I believe you acted stupidly, but not with malice. Above all else, you know you made a mistake. Although you should've known better. Ellie is a potential suspect. You thought you were protecting someone you care about."

Rowan let his words hang in the air. "You're lucky I still think you're a decent copper. Don't make me regret that, Danny."

"Sir, I promise I won't. What can I do? I want to help." Danny sat taller in his seat.

"Go and meet Mrs. Benn at Wraith Forest. Support Sandra when she arrives. Then, once you're done, find out if anyone else, other than Margaret Warren, witnessed Jax arguing with Martin that Friday evening in the pub. Jax told me they didn't – let's see if we can catch him off guard."

"Yes, sir," PC Everett said, springing to his feet. Rowan allowed himself a knowing smile as Danny turned and left.

DS Carl Hocking

Interview Room One was small – especially so, now that DI Black, DS Hocking, and Sophie Marlow were sat around the table. The room still held its characteristic cottage charms, but the formality of a recorded interview taking place dominated the atmosphere.

With the presence of DI Black and DS Hocking established for the record, Sophie confirmed her full name and date of birth. DS Hocking then reminded her she was being interviewed under caution and explained her rights.

"You are entitled to legal representation–"

Sophie stiffened in her seat. "Don't need any. I haven't done anything wrong."

"Are you sure you don't want a solicitor present?" DI Black said. "Miss Marlow, this is serious."

"I've already said I don't. Play the recording back and you'll hear what I said."

"Right," DS Hocking said – remembering DI Black wanted him to take the lead. "We've reviewed Martin Howler's call log from his phone. A call was made at nine twenty-three p.m. from your number the night he was killed. It lasted around five minutes."

Sophie was silent.

DS Hocking watched DI Black flick through his notebook.

"Miss Marlow?" Hocking prompted. "You need–"

DI Black cut in. "When I spoke to you two days ago on Thursday, Sophie, you stated that the last time you saw and spoke to Martin was on the Friday of the week before. To remind you, you said that you didn't argue because you were tired – do you remember?"

Sophie just nodded.

"Miss Marlow nods," DS Hocking said for the benefit of the recording. "Why did you fail to mention that you phoned Martin on the night he died?" DS Hocking asked.

"I guess I forgot. It was only a quick call."

"What was it about?" Hocking asked.

"Can't remember."

"It would save us a lot of time and trouble, Miss Marlow, if you could answer the questions to the best of your ability." Hocking glanced at Black.

"I'm trying to remember. Look, it was a quick call. About the studio, I think. The one he wanted to build. I just phoned to tell him to forget the idea." Sophie looked at Black. "Rowan, you know me. I'm being honest, here."

"Miss Marlow, I'm here in a professional capacity. Please don't imply that there's more to our relationship than there is. For the record: I did know you because I grew up on Wraith's Hollow, but I stopped knowing you when I left the island fifteen years ago." DI Black paused. "I remain professional and impartial."

"Whatever," Sophie said.

"Bringing your attention back to the phone call," DS Hocking said. "Had you not told Martin before that you didn't want a studio built? Was there a need to say it again?"

"I obviously felt there was."

"What else did you talk about on the phone? You've got about another three minutes to fill," DI Black said.

"The weather, the spring sun – it's been lovely, you know."

"Did you arrange to meet Martin Howler after your call took place?"

Sophie looked away.

"Did you meet Martin Howler?"

"No, I did not meet him. I didn't arrange to either. Do you really think I'd be that stupid to phone him hours before I was going to kill him?"

"Believe me, criminals aren't immune to stupidity – especially in the heat of it," DI Black said.

"I'm not a criminal, Rowan."

"I never claimed you were. But you're yet to tell us what else you spoke about."

Sophie exhaled sharply. "I didn't arrange to meet him, I don't know what else to say."

"Try telling the truth!" DI Black raised his voice.

"After you spoke about the studio," DS Hocking said, his tone light, "what did you speak about next? It was only two days ago – try to remember."

Sophie said nothing for a short while. DS Hocking noted that she was looking everywhere except at DI Black. "I told him I didn't want to see him again – that he's not welcome at my home. I wanted to cut ties with him."

"Pretty hard to do on an island as small as this one," DI Black said, folding his arms.

"Yes, you're right. But that's what I told him."

"Was there any reason for this? Did something happen between you leading up to the time of his murder that prompted your call?" DS Hocking interlinked his fingers, resting his hands on the table.

Sophie shook her head. "Just didn't want him in my life anymore. That's all there is to it. He tried to convince me otherwise, but I was adamant about my desire not to see him again."

"Not to see him as in never?"

"Absolutely not. I had nothing to do with his murder."

"Okay," DI Black said. "I want to remind you, Sophie, that this is your chance to tell us everything you know. If it comes to light later that you've been lying, protecting someone else, you could be arrested and charged with perverting the course of justice."

"It's very serious," DS Hocking added. "You understand, Miss Marlow? You could end up in prison."

"I do. What I've told you is accurate. I'm not a liar. I didn't kill Martin Howler."

"Fine. I am requesting a DNA swab and prints from you–"

"But why, Rowan?" Sophie cut in.

"It's standard procedure," DS Hocking said. "It will help with our enquiries."

"And what if I refuse?"

"It won't look good for you," DI Black said, leaning forwards, looking into her eyes. "It never looks good when someone doesn't willingly support us."

"Is that a threat?"

"No. Just letting you know how things work."

Sophie Marlow

It didn't take long for her prints and DNA to be taken, and it took even less time for Sophie to leave the station. She hated that swab thing in her mouth – it made her feel sick! And she hated Rowan Black even more for putting her through it.

Approaching the end of Quayside Lane, the following thought formed slowly at first then whirled with the speed of a tornado in her mind: my blood was on the boat!

Shit!

Why did she let them take her fucking DNA? She was done for. Shit.

But.

But wait. Nathan said he cleaned it. Didn't he? He did! Did he get it all off? Jesus Christ, she hoped he got it all off. It was nauseating knowing her potential freedom hung on how well Nathan cleaned that damn boat.

She looked at the sea – felt nothing.

Her fingers trembled as she got her phone out of her bag. She dialled the number – the only number she knew off by heart. Please pick up.

"Thank God," she said at the sound of the familiar voice. "I'm in trouble. Real trouble."

"Slow down. What's happened?"

"He said he cleaned the boat. Did he clean it? Did he clean it enough?" she said quickly. "Was there a lot? Did he get it all, would he–"

"Just stop! Breathe. Breathe!" After a pause: "Now, slowly, tell me what the fuck you're on about."

"Don't swear at me! This is you! This is your fault. I did this for you."

"How's this helping? Calm down so I can help you."

"Isn't it bloody obvious? I'm talking about the blood on the boat. My blood!" Sophie walked quickly along the seafront in the direction of her home. She caught her breath suddenly, having nearly stepped into the path of child peddling like mad on a tricycle. Their parent said something as Sophie went by, but she didn't pay attention. She was too focused on Nathan's lighthouse up ahead – fuck, her life was in his hands.

"Did you hear me? Did you hear what I said? The blood that Nathan said he cleaned?"

"Yes, the fucking blood Nathan said he'd cleaned," Sophie replied.

"Sophie. Important part: he said he cleaned it. He *cleaned* it."

"But what if he missed a bit? Shit."

"Why this now? Why're you panicking?"

"I've just been interviewed by Rowan Black. He took my prints and DNA."

"Shit."

"Don't do that. Don't you dare do that to me."

"Okay, okay, okay. Why did he interview you?"

Sophie quickly summarised the conversation about the phone call and the reason she gave for phoning Martin.

"Perverting the course of justice? That's not the half of it . . . Right. Let me think. Give me a minute." The brief pause took forever! "Right. You've done nothing wrong. They can't prove anything about the phone call. It's no more than a coincidence. I know we said about a burner phone, but I still think Martin wouldn't've answered. They could've traced that back to you anyway. Then you'd be trying to explain why you didn't use your phone to call him . . . We did okay there. I promise. And you're right: refusing to give your DNA at this stage just makes you look guilty. You did the right thing, okay?"

Sophie nodded. "Okay."

"Now, about the boat. Suppose Nathan missed a bit – he didn't, I know that for certain – but suppose he did:

if they match it with the sample you've just given, again, it doesn't prove anything. It just means that at some point, you were on his boat, and you cut your leg."

"But what about the evidence I've given? I didn't say anything to Rowan about being on his boat."

"I don't know yet, let's cross that bridge when–"

"Oh yeah, cross that bridge means when I'm in custody. You can't exactly swing by and help me out then. No. This needs sorting now. Help me!"

Rowan Black

"Sir, update from forensics. No match yet from the blood sample Sandra's team recovered inside Martin's boat. Forensics say it'll need manual comparison," DC Mann said, appearing in the doorway to Rowan's office. "Marine report's in as well. Essentially, Jax was right: multiple holes below the waterline, deliberately hit, patched up by him. The prop shaft was out of alignment, just like he described."

Rowan nodded. "He said a damaged shaft could've played havoc with the steering and propulsion . . . Jax reckoned it could've been the reason Martin's boat ended up on the rocks. That checks out. We need digital to get back to us. See if there's any salvageable CCTV, anything on the laptop from the marina. Who shut the alarm system down? Once we know that we start getting somewhere," Rowan said, then, thinking out loud: "So, Martin takes the boat for a spin at night. Why? Someone to impress? They ended up smashing into the rocks, dragging themselves to the shore." He paused, resting his chin on his palm for a moment, then with eyes back on DC Mann he said: "Sophie? Was Sophie out with him, the one he was trying to impress?"

"Too early to say, sir," Mann replied. "No evidence to suggest that."

"True. How're you getting on with Naomi Bennett?"

"Still working through. But I've linked her to a couple of bio-tech firms – one's registered offshore, and another looks like a shell. She's got a background in genetics; has a PhD in Biomedical Engineering. I'll keep digging," DC Mann said with a nod before returning to his laptop.

Midday approached fast. Rowan needed to stand up, move his body, get some fresh air into his lungs – and, most importantly, get away from his computer. A headache was approaching but, he figured, a short walk along the seafront would sort that out.

Jennings had briefed him earlier on his meeting with Tim at his workshop. Jennings really didn't play it cool, but at least he'd got it out of Tim that Veritas had revealed to him who the murderer was.

Rowan crossed the road and stepped onto the promenade, giving two seagulls – flapping and shouting in dispute – a wide berth. He had to be careful with this Veritas business. It would never hold up in court and, therefore, should be treated as nonsense. Divine revelations weren't evidence: they couldn't be traced, tested, or cross-examined. But if members of Hollow Kin were willing to kill for their beliefs, then he needed to tread carefully. What did he believe? Saying he didn't know felt like a cop-out – but it was, at least, the truth.

A few minutes walking along the pathway and a few more standing on the beach, looking out at the sea, served him well. He breathed deeply a number of times, allowing some half-baked thoughts about what the ramifications were if Sophie was somehow involved, but, but . . . he didn't know her anymore. The Sophie he knew was from a long time ago, and even then, that was only because she was Cynthia's sister.

He missed Cynthia. Out at sea, he spotted a lonely bird flying into the distance, toward the horizon. It slipped out of sight as quickly as a single folding wave.

Walking back into the station, feeling somewhat refreshed, Rowan stood by DS Hocking's side at the whiteboard in the main office. His eyes scanned the recent additions: a photo of the bloodstained jacket found in Wraith Forest; a note beside Sophie's name: 21:23 call – five minutes; and a fresh line added underneath Tim's notes, stating: match confirmed – Tim Thorn.

Hocking turned and said, "Prints from Martin's bathroom just came back. They're a match for Tim Thorn, sir."

Tim Thorn

Tim Thorn's Saturday had already – frustratingly – been interrupted by Sergeant bloody Jennings, and now that DI Black had called him in for an interview, Tim was even more pissed off. He was sitting opposite Black and DS Hocking – loathing both in equal measure.

When Rowan had read him his rights and told him the interview was being recorded, Tim felt certain that Rowan was enjoying it. Tim snapped back and told them he didn't need anyone representing him. He represented his own interests, and he'd done absolutely nothing wrong.

"Please," DI Black started. "Remind me of where you went inside Martin's home the day you and Little Liam delivered his bookcase. What day was that firstly?"

"Last Saturday, one week ago."

"Thank you," DS Hocking said. "About eight in the evening?"

Tim agreed the time with a nod as short as his verbal reply. He then looked at Rowan's notebook. "You can remind yourself of what I said. Presumably it says it in your little book?"

"It does. But I need you to confirm."

"I said something like–"

"No," Rowan interrupted. "Where you went in the house, not merely recalling where you *said* you went."

"Fine." Tim folded his arms. "We carried it through the front door, struggled through the living room with it to the stairs and up to the second floor. We then went straight to the office."

"And where did you go once you'd installed it?" Rowan asked.

"The same route but in reverse . . . This all seems ridiculous. Why're you asking me this?"

"Did you go anywhere else in Martin's house, Mr. Thorn?" DS Hocking asked.

Tim shook his head. "Like I said before. Our mission was to get in and out."

"So," DS Hocking shifted in his chair. "You didn't use the bathroom for anything?"

"Not at all. Look, Rowan, you asked me this before. I'm *not* a liar."

"Well," DI Black moved forwards in his seat, leaning his forearms on the table. "How would you explain the fact that your prints were found in the first-floor bathroom near the tap?"

Tim was silent. He'd known this was coming – Jennings had, even if unintentionally, given him the heads up. He shrugged his shoulders, saying: "Looks like I forgot. Sorry."

"You just stated that you didn't use the bathroom. Now you're saying you must've forgotten that you used it. Please clarify whether you did or not," DS Hocking said.

"Must've done."

"What for?"

"A piss."

"Little Liam was present–"

"Not in the toilet, he wasn't."

DS Hocking ignored Tim's interruption. "Could he verify that you used the bathroom?"

"You'll have to ask him."

"We will," Rowan said. "Don't you worry about that . . . I think I need to remind you, regardless of what else you've done, lying to a police officer during an investigation is a serious offence."

"Isn't lying to one any time serious?" Tim smiled, he was getting to DI Black.

DS Hocking said: "DI Black's right. From here on in, honesty's your best course of action."

"I'm an honest, God-fearing individual."

"The trouble I'm having, Tim," Rowan said. "Is that you look like you're lying, that you know full well where you went when you delivered the bookcase; I think you're confusing this occasion with another visit."

"And when would that be? I'm all ears."

"When Martin's house was wrecked, trashed by you on the night of his murder."

"Nothing to do with me. Why would I know anything about that?"

Don't raise your hand at me, Tim thought, as Rowan began to speak again:

"You told me previously you knew the code to get in Martin's – which you needed when you delivered the bookcase."

"I did. He said he'd change it afterwards. I don't know if he did or not."

"The time between you delivering the bookcase and when he was murdered was relatively short. You were in his house Saturday, a few days before he was killed. We believe the break-in happened sometime Wednesday night or in the early hours of Thursday morning. If you still knew the code, you could've gone in there easy enough, smashed the place up . . . Sound about right?"

Tim chuckled. "You're clutching at straws, Inspector, really. You've got nothing on me."

DS Hocking said: "We've got forensic evidence placing you at the scene and we're waiting on further evidence."

"So?" Tim said.

"So," Rowan started but left it hanging.

"You didn't like Martin, did you?" Hocking asked.

"No. He was an arsehole. Not going to pretend otherwise. Doesn't mean I trashed his house or killed him. Most of the island have motive for killing him."

"It's been reported that you had an argument with Martin on that Saturday morning," Rowan said.

"Might've. Wasn't an argument, not really," Tim replied.

"Martin grabbing your throat wasn't the result of you disagreeing?"

"I know what you're doing, Rowan. I know what it looks like. But I come from a generation that's rough and ready, you know what I mean? So what, he grabbed me. I chucked him off just as quick. I'm not going to make a song and dance about it."

"Would you like to tell us why he assaulted you?" DS Hocking said.

"Assault," Tim scoffed. "I can't remember."

"You're having issues with your memory, aren't you, Mr. Thorn? But you are of that generation. Perhaps you should see a doctor," Rowan said. "Let me try and jog your memory: it was something to do with you seeing something you shouldn't have at Martin's. Martin got the hump about it, threatened you."

"You're barking up the wrong tree, Rowan." Tim eyed him.

"Allow me to jog that forgetful memory of yours again. The reason why you argued in your workshop is because you saw paperwork pertaining to brain implants. And as soon as Martin left that morning, you went into your office furious and concocted your plan to trash his house." Rowan paused for a moment, then: "Tim Thorn, did you murder Martin Howler?"

"Absolutely not! That's the truth!"

"Okay. Let's just calm things down a bit," DS Hocking said. "Tim, what can you tell me about Hollow Kin and the three symbols?" Hocking named them, and continued: "They were found at both Martin's house and on his body?"

"Nothing. I mean, I've got no idea why Hollow Kin symbols were at his house or on him."

"What do you know about them?"

"In general?" Tim clarified.

"Yes," Rowan replied before Hocking got the chance.

"Not much. As I said to Rowan before. The cult is a load of rubbish. If there's one, I've got nothing to do with it."

"You wouldn't know why *The Mark of Veritas* was spray painted onto the bathroom mirror and *The Binding of the Kin* and *The Tongue of Silence* were also found at the property? One being found in the secret compartment of the bookcase you made."

Tim shrugged.

"For the benefit of the recording, please confirm yes or no," Hocking said.

"No idea."

Rowan Black leant back in his chair. "We're interviewing Mrs. Appleby tomorrow, Mr. Thorn. I wonder if she'll be able to shed any light on this."

Tim paused – he knew what Rowan was trying. He played it cool. "You'll have to ask her, Rowan. Nothing to do with me."

"You're not connected to her and Hollow Kin in any way?" Rowan prodded.

"Not at all. But I'm a decent neighbour, so to speak. I visit an old, frail woman to see if she needs help with anything – quite frankly, Rowan, I think it's appalling you're dragging her in to interview her. Ridiculous."

"And why would that be? Does her age make her exempt from questioning?"

"No, but it at the very least commands some respect."

Rowan's eyes narrowed. "I'll drag anyone in here and interview them if I feel it necessary. I see you've spoken about it with her already – fast work."

"She rang me in a terribly upset state. Like I said, I'm a good neighbour."

"Right. I want to bring your attention back to something that didn't sit right with me. Something you said when we talked before. I asked you whether you saw at Martin's house when you visited – to measure up for or to deliver the bookcase – a Celt-like symbol with intricate patterns. Maybe somewhere lying around. Do you remember that?"

"Yes."

"Good. Your reply to my question, which I have in my notes here, was 'No, no. I'd remember them. I like that sort of thing'," Rowan paused.

"And?" Tim prompted.

"Well, I only mentioned *one* symbol, did you see *a* Celt-like symbol. You replied as though I asked you about multiple symbols, i.e. more than one, say . . . three."

Tim was silent.

"Why did you respond as though DI Black asked you about seeing more than one symbol? Like you knew there was more than one at Martin's house," DS Hocking said.

Tim was quick to respond. "Must've heard you wrong. Hearing's a little off sometimes."

"Would your GP confirm that?" Rowan asked.

"Haven't had it looked at proper, I'm afraid. Sign my age's catching up with me. People tend to ignore those things."

"You're claiming that your response was due to you mishearing DI Black and not because you actually knew how many there were . . . because you put them there?"

"Of course I didn't put them there. It's nothing to do with me."

"Just for the record, Mr. Thorn. Where were you the night Martin was murdered?" DI Black asked.

"Like I told you before: in bed."

"Can anyone confirm this?" DS Hocking asked.

"Afraid not. I live alone, sleep alone."

"Mr. Thorn, what about the brain implants – the topic of your argument with Martin?" Hocking said.

Tim was thoughtful. "That part is true. I caught a wink of something to do with a project about brain implants." He wanted to give them something – even if only to validate his testimony so far. "But what it was about, I've no idea."

"Where and how did you see this?" Rowan asked.

"It was on the mahogany table next to his sofa."

"Just left out on the side?" DS Hocking asked.

"Apparently so. I glanced at it, that's all."

"If we found this document, your prints wouldn't be all over it?" Rowan asked.

"Nope," Tim said, knowing they wouldn't find it because it was located at Mrs. Appleby's house. "And I can't tell you any more about it. Look, are we done here?"

DI Black shook his head. "One more question – concerning Hollow Kin–"

"Rowan! I've said all that I've got to on that subject."

"Won't take you a second then . . . What did you mean when you said to Jennings that Hollow Kin have everything in hand? That Veritas has revealed the murderer to you?"

Tim stared at Rowan. You little prick.

"Mr. Thorn, answer the question," DS Hocking said.

"No comment."

"Again," Rowan said, "What did you mean when you said that Hollow Kin have everything in hand? That Veritas has revealed the killer?"

You bastard. "*Again*, no comment."

"You're choosing not to answer. That will be noted."

Tim was silent.

"We have your fingerprints; we also need a DNA swab from you before you leave," Rowan said.

"What for?"

"To eliminate you from our enquiries. If you've done nothing wrong – you have nothing to worry about," DS Hocking said, reassuringly.

"I *haven't* done anything wrong."

"Prove it and cooperate with us. We would appreciate it," Rowan said.

Tim bubbled inside: he wanted to kill Rowan Black there and then.

Mrs. Appleby

Sunday morning. Nine forty-five.

Having spoken to Tim yesterday morning, she'd felt better about everything; but having spoken to him last night – about his interview with Rowan – she was now feeling on edge.

Breathe, this is all part of Veritas' plan. No one, not even Rowan Black, could stop Veritas. And just like that, her faith placed entirely in Veritas, Mrs. Appleby stepped outside her front door and approached Tim, who was waiting to take her to the station.

"Dusted this off," she said, closing the car door and tucking her walking stick by her side. "Haven't used this since my last hip operation."

"It's a good idea to bring it. Remember what we said?"

"Of course."

*

"Oh, thank you, Tim," Mrs. Appleby said, stepping timidly over the station threshold. PC Everett greeted her. "I see he's got you working on this day of rest, Danny?" She held her free arm up for Danny to take.

"I'm happy for the overtime, Mrs. Appleby. Are you okay today? You seem a bit wobbly on your feet."

"I'll be okay, thank you. Sweet of you to ask. No DI Black this morning?"

"Not this morning. You've got DS Hocking and DC Mann speaking to you," he said.

"Oh, you are a good, boy, Danny."

As they walked through the station, Mrs. Appleby spoke lightly but enthusiastically to everyone she possibly could. She behaved as though everyone was there working on her behalf.

She tapped her walking stick on the ground harder than necessary, the sound echoing through the interview room as she entered.

"Mrs. Appleby, I'm–"

"Now, dear, hang on a minute. I can't hear you. Wait a minute. Just give me a minute to settle down." Her back was stooped and her steps painfully small. "Now, just let me sit in this seat . . . Owww!"

"Are you okay?" PC Everett asked.

"It's my back, young Danny. Been playing me up this morning."

"What's best, Mrs. Appleby? Standing or sitting? I won't let you go, don't worry."

"I don't want to make a fuss. Just help me into this seat. I'll be alright once I catch my breath." She looked at the detectives opposite. "I'm not as young as I used to be – believe it or not."

"Mrs. Appleby, I'm DS Hocking and this is DC Mann."

"Pleasure to meet you DS Hogarth and PC Manley." She extended her hand weakly.

"No, Mrs. Appleby, that's DS *Hocking* and *DC Mann* – Hocking and Mann," Danny Everett said.

"Oh, how silly I feel. Sorry boys. I'm such a silly old woman."

"It's fine, really," DS Hocking said.

She watched DS Hocking closely but made a show of looking around the room as he told her she was under caution, that she didn't have to say anything, and she could have legal representation if she wanted. "We will also be recording the interview. Do you understand?"

"Oh, why yes, dear. I might be old, but I'm not stupid. I don't need a lawyer, thank you," she said, smiling sweetly. "Boys, will this take long? I've got my lunch to prepare – I'm not as fast as I once was."

"No, no. Won't take long. Why don't we start with you telling us about Hollow Kin."

"But I don't know what to say. What is it you want to know? I really don't think I'll be much help."

"It's okay," DC Mann said. "Are you a member of Hollow Kin, Mrs. Appleby?"

"I wouldn't say a member. I know of them, but I don't like interfering in other people's business."

DS Hocking sighed just loud enough for Mrs. Appleby to hear. "What do you know about Veritas."

"Sorry, dear, could you repeat the question?"

DS Hocking obliged using a louder voice.

"Violet? Who is Violet?" she said, leaning in and putting her hand to her ear.

"No. Veritas. Hollow Kin's God. When you spoke to DI Black you said Veritas reveals herself – she is the ultimate judge," Hocking said.

"Did I? When was this? Did I speak to Rowan Black?"

DC Mann took his turn. "Yes, Mrs. Appleby. Yesterday morning. DI Black spoke to you at home."

"At home? My home?"

"Yes. Do you remember?"

"Yes. I remember he comes to do the gardening for me – he helps my George out. They spend ages talking to each other." Mrs. Appleby purposefully struggled opening her bag. She eventually picked out a small, oval-framed photograph. "This is my George."

"Mrs. Appleby," Danny began, nervously. "DI Black came to your house yesterday, but he wasn't doing the garden with George. He interviewed you."

"He wasn't out in the garden?" she said.

"No. Neither was George. Mrs. Appleby – you remember George has died?"

Without a second's pause, she said: "Of course I know George's dead. Martin Howler's responsible for that."

"Sorry," DC Mann said. "I think PC Everett took it that you were a bit confused about why DI Black was at your home."

"Me? I'm not confused, dear. I've got all my marbles. But I am starting to have bad days . . . What did DI Black talk to me about?"

"About Hollow Kin . . . Let's start slowly," DS Hocking said, calmly. "What did you mean when you said, 'Veritas reveals herself'?"

"I don't recall saying that at all, my dear."

"Mrs. Appleby, for the benefit of the recording, you are now stating that you do not recall a conversation about Hollow Kin or Veritas with Detective Inspector Rowan Black yesterday morning. Is that correct?"

"That's right, dear. But if that's what he said we spoke about – then I guess we did."

"What do you recall about your conversation?" Hocking asked.

"I think we spoke about George. How Martin Howler was involved in the accident. But that's all in the past. I forgave Martin for what he did."

"What do *The Mark of Veritas, The Binding of the Kin*, and *The Tongue of Silence* mean to you?" DC Mann asked.

Mrs. Appleby repeated the names twice, slowly. "I think. Something to do with Hollow Kin, but I can't be sure . . . I really think I'm being such a silly old woman."

"Mrs. Appleby, you're doing fine," PC Everett said.

"When did DI Black used to come and do the gardening for you?"

"Oh, that was years ago – when my George was alive. Did I show you?" she paused, looking at the picture on the table. "I didn't realise I showed you George's photo already. Wasn't he charming?"

"Yes, thank you for showing us. It's a very special picture. A tragic loss for you – what happened with Martin. You say you forgave him?" DS Hocking asked.

"Oh, yes, dear. I'm not one to hold a grudge. I couldn't. It doesn't do you any good."

"Was it easy forgiving the man who, accidentally, hit George with his car?" DC Mann asked.

"True forgiveness is far from easy, but I was able to put it all behind me. I wasn't angry with Martin Howler, and he didn't deserve to die."

"Wraith's Hollow is such a pretty town," DC Mann said. "It would be a shame if it lost its olde-worlde charm. What about these newer developments around the place – linked to Martin, I believe."

"It doesn't bother me in the slightest. You get to my age, dear, and things don't bother you liked they used to. Age has to have some benefits – I'll take wisdom any day of the week."

"I guess Hollow Kin has plenty of olde-worlde charm?" Mann asked.

"I wouldn't know. It doesn't really concern me."

"Which part of Hollow Kin is it that doesn't concern you?" Hocking asked.

"All of it. Me and George would never have anything to do with whatever it is."

"So, it is something. You're aware of it."

"Oh, yes. But it's none of my business – like I said to you earlier. You see, I'm not a mad old woman."

DS Hocking stood from his chair. "It's evident there're some discrepancies between what you said to DI Black yesterday and what you've said today. We'll conclude the interview for now, but we may be in touch again."

"Oh, of course, dear. I will always assist the police. You boys do such a good job protecting people like me." Mrs. Appleby began to stand, shakily, relying on PC Everett's arm for leverage. "Between us, I think people forget who needs protecting in a place like this – Wraith's Hollow has its own ways."

Rowan Black

It was late Sunday evening when Rowan decided to call it a day. He'd manned the phones and sent everyone else home for a rest ready to start again Monday morning. His interview with Mrs. Appleby and her subsequent one with DS Hocking and DC Mann was circling in his mind. They'd said Mrs. Appleby had played the sweet-old-woman card, but he wasn't having any of it.

"Put a pin in it for now," he had said. "We don't have anything, but she'll slip up."

Rowan turned off the light in his office and walked through the incident room, making a single, half-hearted scan of the whiteboard. He paused for a second as he eyed the photograph of the dark green jacket that had been found by Mrs. Benn and her corgi and was currently being processed by forensics.

Of course.

It seemed so obvious now – the recognition rang loudly in his mind in the otherwise perfect silence of the station.

Of course!

Chapter Nine

Evidence

Rowan Black

Monday.

Eight-thirty. Briefing. Rowan had just asked DC Mann for updates on Naomi Bennett.

"Sir, I've confirmed her financial links to *NVB Capital Partners, Shoreline Biotech,* and *Wraith BioTechnologies LTD* – the ones flagged by the analysts. *Wraith Bio's* registered address is a shuttered office in Bath. *Shoreline's* listed director is a non-starter. Might be a nominee – typical shell structure."

"What about *NVB*?" DI Black asked.

"That's linked directly to her – she's a founding partner. NVB's account made multiple transfers into Martin's personal account. That's where the sixty-five grand came from."

"Where's she based?" DS Hocking asked.

"She's not local," DC Mann said, flicking through some notes. "Based in Oxfordshire. No obvious ties to Wraith's Hollow – except Martin Howler, of course. Nothing on PNC. No charges. No cautions – not even a speeding ticket. But when I did some background digging, I found she's not that clean. A research scandal in the US in 2020: unethical methods, testing on animals, controversial methods on humans. The information I got showed she relocated to the UK shortly after that."

"Proving herself to be a worthy partner of Martin's," Sergeant Jennings said.

"Here's where it gets really interesting. She's listed as a research consultant on several questionable, ethically speaking, biotech – rather neurotech – studies: brain enhancements, neural integration, some flagged by the Health Research Authority."

"I want her spoken to," Rowan Black said, looking at DC Mann. "Contact Thames Valley. Send them everything we've got: financials, genetic enhancement information, the lot. Get the interview recorded, too. I want to see her." He paused and then said to the team: "She has to be linked to Martin's brain implant project."

"Yes, sir," DC Mann said.

DS Hocking rubbed his chin, frowning: "It's bugging me that SOCO didn't find any sort of document relating to this project at Martin's place – not even the one Tim said he saw. Where is it now?"

"You mean did someone take it?" Sergeant Jennings asked.

"It's possible," Rowan said. "But why? Other than to keep the whole thing a secret. But if Martin left it lying around, as Tim claimed, *he* wasn't that bothered about it being seen. Therefore, it wasn't Martin who moved it – or took it. Okay, bear it in mind everyone. Someone around Wraith's Hollow knows where it is." Rowan scanned the whiteboard as he asked DS Hocking, "Anything from the statement review?"

"Afraid not, sir," Hocking said, looking disappointed. "Nothing jumps out so far. Hollow Kin's been mentioned a number of times but there's no link, they–"

Rowan interrupted: "Let me guess: no one's naming anyone or giving us anything?" he asked. Now that Jennings had told him everything he knew about Hollow Kin, Rowan felt the need to move Hocking onto something more productive. "Chase up forensics – see if they've got anything on the symbols. On his body or the ones found at his house."

"Sir," DS Hocking said.

"Danny, any witnesses to the argument Jax had with Martin on that Friday?"

"Yes, sir. I've taken statements from a couple of people, but the landlord, John, said he saw it. He was serving someone at the time, and he couldn't be sure what they spoke about, but said it looked heated. He said the same as Margaret: Martin squared up to Jax."

"Good work, Danny. Jax is lying. He swears blind he didn't argue with him – we need to find out why. Danny, keep working on it – you've made a good start." Rowan offered PC Everett a small smile.

"Sir," Sergeant Jennings said.

Rowan nodded at Jennings. "One second, Frank. Everyone, we're expecting updates from forensics to start filtering in. The boat, the body, the house – so pay attention. If anything stands out, bring it to me immediately."

"Sir?" Jennings prompted.

"Frank, you're coming with me. We need to speak to Nathan Waters."

Nathan Waters

Nathan was gathering some bits together – petri dishes, sealed glass jars of spores, a portable centrifuge, and a well-used notebook – ready to take them to the field station, when a knock sounded at the door.

He descended the spiral stairs and opened the door. "Rowan. Frank. What're you doing here?" He fought hard to sound surprised rather than nervous.

"If everyone knew we were coming, Nathan, we wouldn't catch any bugger now, would we?" Jennings said.

"No, no, I guess not. But I'm not, I can reassure you, someone who needs catching."

"It's fine, Nathan. Frank's feeling frivolous this morning. We just wanted to have a brief catch-up."

"I'm just off to the lab – my field station. You remember the one I told you about, Rowan. You said you might want to come and visit. Not now I'm afraid, I've got so much on – perhaps we can schedule another time though?"

"For the visit, yes. For our chat now – no."

"We need to come in," Jennings said. "Put a brew on, Nathan."

Nathan led them upstairs – God he wished he'd tidied. It looked a sodding mess. Then showing them to the sofa, a horrible thought pulsed violently through his mind: had Ellie told them? Did she tell the police what he told her? That he created the poison that sent Martin firmly on his way to being killed.

Shit. Oh God. He must come clean. He must tell them everythi–

"Everything okay, Nathan," Jennings asked. "You look a little lost. We only want a brew. Think you can get that organised?"

"Ummm. Of course." He left the living room to go to the kitchen but came back in suddenly. "So sorry about the mess. I'm snowed under at work. This fungus on the island. A number of projects on the go." He headed back to the kitchen.

"You need to learn to juggle," Sergeant Jennings called after him.

"You *are* in a frivolous mood," Rowan spoke quietly but Nathan could just about hear.

"I feel great, sir. After what we spoke about. A weight's been lifted. The noose around my neck, loosened."

"Yes, but you know where your career's heading, Frank."

"Of course, I know exactly what's in store for me. But, for now, I'm going to enjoy this little bit of freedom."

Nathan had no idea what they were talking about. Coming back with their tea he asked: "How can I help you?"

"How're you getting on with researching this fungus? Any updates we need to be aware of?"

"I mentioned before about the incredible reproduction rate – it's spreading wildly. I've seen it practically everywhere. The compound isn't exactly benign."

"Oh, really?" Sergeant Jennings asked. Nathan could tell he didn't have a clue – which was good.

"There are signs of psychoactive metabolites."

"Meaning," Jennings said, rolling his hand to encourage Nathan to explain.

"Let's just say, don't go picking any for your dinner."

"Right. We need to get a health warning out, Frank. Can't have people ingesting this – if they haven't already."

"It would make them very ill if they did. But surely people wouldn't be stupid enough?" Nathan said.

Frank Jennings laughed. "Of course they are!" he said to Nathan, then to Rowan: "Leave it with me, sir. I'll sort it."

"What kind of things are you doing with this fungus? I mean, how exactly are you studying it?" Rowan Black asked.

Nathan eyed Rowan for a second. He couldn't decide if his question had an investigative undercurrent or if he was genuinely interested.

"I'm analysing its neuroactive compounds. They're a match for serotonergic psychedelics. I'm running toxicity tests too. All boring stuff, really."

Rowan sipped some tea. "Not at all. It's fascinating. Could you write something for us to put out to the locals about the dangers of ingesting this stuff? I think if it comes from you, people might actually listen."

"Of course. Is that what you wanted to see me about?"

"No. But, on this fungus, please keep us updated with information – especially the effects it could have on people."

"I will, of course."

"The reason we're here is because I wanted to know if you found your jacket yet?"

What was Rowan Black on about? "Sorry, I'm not sure what you mean."

"Do you remember, last time I was here, I said you had a nice jacket? It was folded over the back of the sofa. And you said you had another one just like it somewhere."

"Yes, I do now you've mentioned it . . . But I can't figure out why you've mentioned it."

"Is the other one still lost?" Jennings asked.

Nathan nodded. "I'd lose my head if it wasn't screwed on at the moment."

"Oh, really?" Rowan sipped some more tea. "What makes you say that?"

"It's nothing, really."

Nathan watched as Rowan put his cup down on the faded cream carpet, right next to the brown, watery stain shaped like an apple. It was obvious Rowan saw it because his eyes scanned the rest of the carpet before meeting Nathan's. "No. It is. I'm interested in why, at this current time, you'd lose your head if it wasn't screwed on."

Nathan swallowed. "Figure of speech, Rowan."

DI Black was silent – Nathan really wanted him to say something, anything, to fill the ghastly silence.

"I suppose I'm just a bit shattered. Burning the candle at both ends and not sleeping in between."

Rowan stayed silent, Jennings too. Nathan's gaze flicked between them and the floor.

"I don't know why I'm not sleeping well," Nathan said, his heart pumping faster. He attempted a smile. "Trouble is, I'm getting to bed later, needing to get up earlier, and drinking more caffeine in the day to compensate for the tiredness, which interrupts my sleep."

Continued silence.

Sergeant Jennings looked at DI Black. DI Black looked at Nathan. Sergeant Jennings looked back at Nathan.

"Well, if there's nothing more to say, I'll–"

"Has something happened, Nathan?" Rowan asked.

Nathan replied quickly. "Not at all. Nothing. Why'd you ask?"

"The symptoms you describe only usually occur because either you're chronically overworked, and have been for months, if not years; or because something chaotic, something dramatic has crashed into your life . . . Now, I may be wrong, but I don't suspect it's the first option because you're a man who loves his work – it's your passion. It probably doesn't even feel like work does it when you're out and about sampling this leaf, observing that flower?"

"It can be quite hectic, but I get your point."

"The former being out of the question, would you like to tell us what's interrupted your life's balance so much it's playing havoc with your sleep?"

Nathan looked at the model lighthouse, crossed his legs, folded his arms. "Really, there's nothing to say. I'm just going through something personal. Relationship issues. Draining me a bit."

"Who's the lucky lady, or man?" Jennings asked.

"She," Nathan asserted, "is someone on the island but my business is my business."

"Fine. No problem." Rowan smiled warmly and stood; Jennings followed suit.

Nathan was taken aback. "Oh, yes. Sure. I'll see you out."

"Thank you, Nathan," Rowan said at the door. "Let me know if you find your jacket. Dark green, isn't it? The kind that's perfect for those colder mornings when you're out and about."

"Yes. It is dark green. You haven't got it have you?" Nathan laughed, nervously. "Honestly, I don't know where I've left the bloody thing. I can't even find my best pliers. See what I mean when I say I'd lose my head if it wasn't screwed on?"

"What sort of pliers?" Jennings asked.

"Stainless steel kind, red handles – I use them for everything. I'll find them sooner or later."

Rowan looked him in the eyes – DI Black could see into his soul. "Look after yourself, Nathan. Remember, keep us posted about the fungus and write a piece we can publish round the island. We don't want hysteria – so something euphemistic."

"Of course, DI Black, Rowan."

"Oh, just one more thing. Do you ever dive – when getting samples?"

"I have. But I hate it. Qualified a while ago. I haven't been diving for ages. It's cold and oddly claustrophobic. There's plenty for me above the surface!"

"But you could, if you had to?"

"Of course. But I don't usually do the diving."

"Why's that?"

"I told you; I have a problem with it. Anyway, if it comes up, which isn't often, Jax does the diving – he's better than me."

Rowan Black

The lighthouse door closed – loudly. DI Black and Sergeant Jennings turned away and began walking along the promenade, heading towards the station.

"So, the question is, does he really think he's lost his jacket and pliers?"

"I don't know, Frank. What're your instincts telling you?"

"Gut reaction? I think he genuinely has no idea where his pliers and jacket are. And I think it's safe to assume they're what forensics are analysing for us right now."

"I agree. Once the Pier Road footage comes back from digital, we might be able to match the jacket to the one found in Wraith Forest."

"Placing Nathan en route to the crime scene at one thirty-five a.m., wearing his own jacket, where he murdered Martin and then–"

"Dumped it in the forest. I know. It doesn't make sense. Nathan's not stupid. He wouldn't dump it for it to be discovered later," Rowan said.

"No, he'd burn it. Destroy it."

"Something's not right. If it's *his* jacket, someone *else* wore it, wanting us to think Nathan's the killer. And walked past the right CCTV cameras wearing it."

Jennings frowned. "But then how'd his pliers end up at the bottom of the marina? They stole them, too? Planted them when they damaged Martin's boat, just hoping we'd find them?"

"Exactly," Rowan said. "I genuinely believe Nathan thinks he's lost them. He's too scatty. He'll have no idea when they went missing."

"Where does this leave us?"

"We focus on the evidence. We'll wait to hear back from forensics. If they belong to Nathan, his DNA will be all over them."

"And, if we're right about this, whoever stole them, planted them, would be clever enough to wear gloves and protect themselves."

"I agree," Rowan said, slowing his pace and pulling out his phone. "I'll call Hocking to chase up the footage from Pier Road."

*

Entering the station, Rowan and Jennings headed straight into the incident room. DS Hocking approached them and said: "Digital pulled this from the footage." Hocking handed Rowan a still image of the man walking away from the Pier Road camera, captured just before the murder. "Dead ringer for the jacket we found in Wraith Forest. Same hood, structure, length. Look, same reflective strip on the arm – you can just make it out. Colour, dark green, looks about right."

"Good. Whoever this is," Rowan held up the enhanced still – grainy at the edges but sharpened – "most likely murdered Martin. We're waiting for forensics but it's not a massive leap that the blood on the jacket is Martin's, and the synthetic fibre Connie found at the postmortem is also from this jacket." Rowan stuck the image to the whiteboard. "Now, Nathan says he doesn't know where his jacket or pliers are. Me and Frank believe him – for now at least."

"Meaning, someone else took them?" DC Mann asked.

"Yes. It's possible someone's framing Nathan. I don't think he's stupid enough to dump his own jacket without destroying it or leave his tools at the marina. Plus, he says he hates diving."

"Odd thing for a marine biologist – shouldn't he love water?" PC Everett said.

"He should – but he says Jax dives for him. Ask Jax about that, Danny, when you talk to him about his argument with Martin."

"Yes, sir," Danny said, promptly.

DI Black turned to DS Hocking. "Anything on the symbols?"

"Yes. The stone sigil in his mouth was hand-carved from island shale. It had traces of salt and algae, indicating exposure to the air. No trace evidence of blood or fingerprints – but the DNA matches Martin's. Microscopic clay residue was also found – likely from a coastal cave."

"Placed post-mortem. Leading us to think it was Hollow Kin?" Rowan said, thinking out loud. He wasn't waiting for an answer. "What about the one found in the bookcase at Martin's house?"

"Same island shale – but less weathered. Smoother surface, no algae. Trace evidence of wood fibres, no salt, no fingerprints. But it definitely matches the other one."

"Meaning it's been made ready for some kind of ceremony?" DC Mann suggested.

"Could be," Hocking replied. "Now the vine necklaces are made from the same kelp and island flax. Tight weaving on both – suggesting they've been made recently. The one on Martin's body contains his DNA and yellow lichen spores embedded in the fibres. Unfortunately, the necklace in his home contains no DNA but forensics found the same wood fibres that were on the stone sigil. And, get this, microscopic traces of varnish."

"The kind you'd stain wood with if you're a cabinet-maker?" Sergeant Jennings questioned.

DS Hocking nodded. "Toolmark analysis of the stone shows the angle, depth, and scoring patterns are consistent with flat-edged chisels, the kind used in fine woodwork."

"This is starting to stack up against Tim and Hollow Kin. We're still waiting on the blood results from the bathroom. Let's see if it's Martin's or, as I'm starting to suspect, Tim's," DI Black said. "Tim's DNA was taken Saturday. Chase that up: I want it back ASAP. If Tim's is a match, we bring him in."

*

Rowan asked Jennings into his office. "It all points to Hollow Kin being involved. Agree?"

"Agreed. The question is, to what extent."

"Which is hard to figure out when Tim's answering 'no comment' to anything about Veritas or the cult."

"It's my word against his," Frank Jennings said, folding his arms in his seat.

"It is at the moment. Divine revelations wouldn't hold up in court. And besides, I'm not throwing you under the bus, Frank. Your past with Hollow Kin complicates what we need to achieve here. But we'll cross that bridge when we come to it."

"Thank you, Rowan."

"It's fine," Rowan said. He didn't want to think about the ramifications of not reporting Jennings for what he did to save his daughter. But he did save her; Rowan admired him for that. He looked out of the office window at the blue sky before saying: "I've been playing with the idea that whoever trashed Martin's house also killed him. One continuous sequence."

"Me too," Jennings said gently rubbing his chin. "But what if they're not connected? Where does that leave us? We've got Nathan – or someone posing as Nathan –

heading towards the crime scene. But we also have someone else tearing through Martin's house."

"Tim? We've got his fingerprints at the house; he knew the entry code; wood fibres and varnish on the symbols suggest his workshop; tool marks consistent with chisels; he's tied to Hollow Kin; and he knew about the brain implants – which he argued with Martin about."

"And he's probably the only one on Wraith's Hollow who could've scared him."

"He could've been the reason Martin sent me the letter in the first place," Rowan said. "So, Tim trashes Martin's place. Someone else kills him later?"

"Maybe," Jennings said, thoughtfully. "But if Tim planted the symbols at the house, are we still thinking someone from Hollow Kin murdered him? Why else would there be symbols on his dead body?"

Rowan was quiet for a moment. "What if they wanted us to think Hollow Kin are responsible? We can't take Tim's word that he knows the killer – that could lead us up a blind alley. But someone framing Hollow Kin . . ." Rowan let his words hang.

"Possibly. What about the blood on the boat, it wasn't matched, was it?"

Rowan shook his head. "Talking of blood, toxicology results from Martin's blood should be back soon."

"Evidence is coming in, sir."

"It is. We just need to fit it all together. Let's keep a focus on Tim for the house but we need to keep looking for the killer."

*

Rowan knocked Ellie Crick's door on Old Beacon Way and checked his watch: just before midday. He'd decided to call in and speak to her for two reasons: first, he felt a quiet sense of duty after she disclosed to DC Mann that Martin had raped her; and second, he wanted to understand why Mrs. Appleby was keen to implicate Ellie in Martin's death by pushing a narrative of revenge – albeit euphemistically.

"Yes," Ellie said, answering the door.

"Hi, Ellie. I wasn't sure if you'd even be in."

"Well, I am. What do you want?"

"Please, may I come in?"

Ellie stepped aside and extended her arm by way of invitation.

Rowan walked into the living room. The place was a mess. All the signs of someone not coping were present – typified by the empty wine bottle and full ashtray.

"I'll open a window," Ellie said.

"Honestly, I don't mind." But having said that, opening the window was a great idea.

Ellie stepped awkwardly, kicking an empty takeaway container across the carpet. "Shit!"

"Ellie, I'll get the window." Rowan opened the side window, gulping in some fresh air. He went back to the sofa. "Is that a photo of Nathan's lighthouse?" he asked.

It took Ellie a moment to engage. "It is. Yes."

"I think the black and white really shows the solitude of the lighthouse."

"I guess," she said, sitting down at Rowan's side.

"Ellie," he said, shifting on the sofa to put a bit of distance between them. "I wanted to check in on you. It can't have been easy telling DC Mann what happened between you and Martin."

"What, that the fucker raped me?"

"Yes. It must've been difficult for you."

"Getting raped or telling Mann?"

"If there's anything we can do – someone to talk to. It wouldn't be a problem to organise."

"I don't need any help," she said.

Rowan looked around the room but avoided making comment. "How have you been coping would you say?"

"Just fine. It's a bit of a mess now but you know what, I've worked and worked and worked. Worked myself to death. I'm taking it easy. I can live with a bit of mess. I have wine and cigarettes."

"I noticed you were limping – what happened there?"

Ellie looked away, then at the lighthouse, then said: "Muscle strain. I did it on my last run. Don't know how."

"You like to run, don't you. How's that going, considering your current lifestyle of wine and cigarettes?"

"I've packed it in for now. Couldn't think of anything worse than running around this place – this fucking island."

"That's a shame – running's good for you. But a break is equally good . . . Ellie, I wanted to ask, why do you think Mrs. Appleby would–" DI Black paused, noticing a change in Ellie's expression. "Why would Mrs. Appleby suggest you had reason to hurt Martin – she suggested that seeing him day in and day out bathing in money that should've been yours would be impossible for you to handle? She remembers you being angry at the time the deal fell through."

"Would you find it impossible to handle?"

"Knowing that he cut me out of a deal that I was an equal partner in? Yes, I'd struggle. Did you struggle?"

"Of course. But I've been over this with Mann. What're you getting at?"

"What did you mean when you said to DC Mann: 'justice was served without the police. He deserved everything he got. Rapist fucker'."

"My meaning's pretty unambiguous if you ask me."

"Do you believe justice has been served?"

"Yes. By some twist of fate. Yes."

Rowan looked at the lighthouse again. "Are you close with Nathan Waters?"

"Umm . . . I guess, well, yes, I guess we are – why'd you ask?"

"I just remembered that Mann saw Nathan here when he interviewed you."

"I'm allowed visitors. It is *my* home. What's it to you who visits me?"

Rowan noted her reaction. "You're right. It's your place." He paused, hoping the atmosphere would settle. "We know Hollow Kin are involved in Martin's murder in some capacity, Ellie. You previously told me that you didn't recognise the symbols that you saw on Martin's body. Is that still the case?"

Rowan noticed Ellie glance at her leg before saying: "Yes. I didn't recognise them then and I wouldn't recognise them now."

"You have absolutely no knowledge of, or have never seen, anything or anyone from Hollow Kin on Wraith's Hollow?"

"Correct."

"Ellie, why do you keep looking at your leg when I mention Hollow Kin?"

Her eyes narrowed as she looked at him. "I don't."

Realising this line of enquiry wouldn't get him anywhere, Rowan asked: "Have you ever come across the name Naomi Bennett?"

"Not really."

"Not really?"

"No, I meant no. I just said not really because my mind was elsewhere. No, I haven't."

"Are you not going to ask why? Who she is?" Rowan asked.

"No. I don't know her, so I don't care."

Rowan exhaled quietly. "Fair enough. I didn't know if you'd ever come across her in any of your business ventures – I've heard you're quite the entrepreneur."

"It may not look like it now, but I know how to run a business and make money."

"Undoubtedly. If you hear of her, let me know."

Ellie made a short *hmm* sound.

Rowan stood. "To reiterate, if you would like some support, someone to talk to – you don't have to make a formal report – I can put you in contact with someone."

"I'll go see my GP if I feel I need to."

Rowan looked at Ellie's leg – she did too. "Ellie, the option to tell me what really happened to your leg is always open. If there's something you know, someone you're protecting," this last part was a punt in the dark, "please, come and find me."

"I've already told you everything."

"I'll see myself out."

*

Having spoken with Ellie, Rowan decided he wasn't hungry for lunch but that a walk would do him good. Old Beacon Way wasn't far from the seafront, so he headed there, via the town centre. He let his gaze wander, content to follow where it took him, across passing faces and busy shop windows.

There was the question of whether it was Tim's blood in Martin's bathroom; of the potential framing of Nathan – his jacket, his pliers; of the wood fibres and varnish on the symbols; of Ellie's declining mental health, her evasiveness, and connection with Nathan; of Hollow Kin. These thoughts, circling and circling, kept Rowan company on his way back to the station.

One o'clock. As he entered the incident room, Rowan caught the tail end of DC Mann and DS Hocking's conversation about an article on the case in the news. He put his hand up to DS Hocking, indicating he wasn't interested in that right now. He turned to DC Mann.

"Sir," DC Mann stood a little taller and pulled his shoulders back. "Toxicology's back on Martin's blood."

"And," Rowan said.

"They found a psychoactive compound in his system – similar to LSD. Though, not an exact match. Lab thinks it's come from a fungal alkaloid."

"Could be why he crashed his boat – that plus the dodgy prop shaft," DS Hocking said.

"So, he was either on drugs, or he was drugged."

"Yes," DC Mann said. "If someone gave it to him, they probably knew it'd cause hallucinations – confusion. Make him vulnerable. I reckon someone's worked on that fungus here on the island."

Rowan was thoughtful. "Which circles us back to Nathan. He's the only one that we know of with the knowledge to do this. When we hear back from digital about the marina laptop, we might then know who shut the alarm system down before Martin took his boat out – whoever that was, they could've been the one to drug him . . . But I'm struggling to believe Nathan's the mastermind behind this."

"His jacket and pliers have been found," DS Hocking said.

"Only found. Could've been planted."

"I think we're wrong to just assume he's being framed."

Rowan looked at Hocking. "Point noted. For now, we'll keep Nathan on our radar. It's possible someone used his field station, kit, worked on extracting the drug from the fungus without him knowing."

"Possible, but likely?" DS Hocking questioned.

"We know Jax does his diving and, presumably, sampling when he needs to," Jennings said.

"Getting samples is a bit different from extracting hallucinogens from mushrooms."

"Thank you, DS Hocking," DI Black said. He turned to Mann. "Anything else?"

"Yes. The synthetic fibre found on Martin's clothing – it's a match for the type of fabric used in the jacket we found dumped in the forest. Same composition and weave. It's stained with his blood. Forensics are running detailed comparisons. We'll know for sure if it's the same jacket in the next day or so."

Rowan Black nodded. "Good. Between the blood in the bathroom, the blood on the boat, and the blood on the jacket, it's only a matter of time." Rowan nodded to disperse his team. He called PC Everett into his office.

"Sir," Danny Everett said.

"Take a seat, Danny," Rowan said, taking his behind the desk. "Have you spoken to Jax?"

"I have. Couldn't find him at Havenmoore Port so I went to Moira's – you know the fish shop?" Rowan nodded. "I know he sells fish to her. Anyway, she said he was on his way. But before he got there, she started telling me when she spoke to Jax, last Friday, he seemed a bit odd. Not his usual self."

"Change of behaviour coincides with when Martin was murdered. Did she say how?"

Danny shook his head. "I asked but she said he didn't say anything. She just thought he wasn't his usual, happy self."

Rowan noted it in his book. "Could be for a number of reasons. How did he seem to you?"

"Fine – right up until I asked him about his argument with Martin in the pub . . . if looks could kill."

"Go on," Rowan Black said.

"Well, I started asking him about his diving, you know, how often he does it, that sort of thing. He said he loves it; he's got all the gear. He wants to go to the Norwegian Fjords, apparently there's a load of World War Two wrecks there, you can go down and–"

"Focus, Danny, I'm not booking a holiday."

"No, sir, sorry. He's into diving, anyway. I steered him onto whether he dives for Nathan, but he didn't give me much. Just that he's done it in the past. He didn't mention anything about taking samples etc when I asked. He was fine at this point, but the second I mentioned someone else has said they witnessed him arguing with Martin, his eyes, what do you say, burned, not burned, I don't know, but he was angry, and his jaw tightened. He said, 'I've told you already, I *didn't* argue with Martin!'"

"Did you push back?"

"I repeated what I said – but nothing. He just looked at me."

"Right. It doesn't prove anything, but he's continuing to be evasive."

"Do you think he did it?"

"It would be an error on our part to conclude anything right now. He's a person of interest that's for sure. Thank you, Danny. Now look, do me a favour. Keep an eye on Ellie. I spoke to her earlier, she's not coping. I'm not asking you to go round there and start questioning her, I just want you to find a reason to call in. A friendly chat – something like that. This is not about the case: it's about her wellbeing. Come back to me when you've seen her."

Ellie Crick

What it was that compelled Ellie to go and see that bitch Mrs. Appleby, she wasn't sure. It wasn't the salmon and scrambled eggs! Seeing her cottage – Hollow Crest – near the top of Wraithmoore Lane, she wondered if she should just walk straight past. But where would that lead her? Up to Martin's shithole? That could be fun. Go to his house, burn the fucking thing down.

Ellie glanced at the ocean – it was so mysterious. It watched her.

She opened the gate, pushing it back on its hinges, causing the wooden sign to fall to the ground. It landed face up. Ellie stepped on the words 'Hollow Crest' as she headed towards Mrs. Appleby's front door.

The door opened just before she got there. "Well now, dear. Isn't this a lovely surprise? Come in," Mrs. Appleby said, smiling. She looked like the wolf from Little Red Riding Hood. "Go through to the kitchen. Sit down. I'll make us a pot of tea."

"Thank you," Ellie said, angry with herself for saying it.

As the kettle boiled on the side, Ellie watched Mrs. Appleby arranging the cups and yellow teapot. She opened a cupboard. "Biscuit, dear?"

"No, thank you."

Mrs. Appleby, seeming to ignore Ellie's reply, got out a pack of chocolate biscuits, opened them and put some on a plate.

"I know you didn't want any, darling, but I fancied one, and I'm sure, when you saw me eating a biscuit, you'd want one, too. They're positively delicious."

Ellie smiled; she hated her.

The kitchen table being set with tea and biscuits between them, Mrs. Appleby said: "Now, a pleasure that it is, why have you come to see me?"

"I wanted you to–"

"How is your leg, by the way," Mrs. Appleby interrupted.

"Very painful – but healing."

"That will be Veritas," Mrs. Appleby said with a knowing nod.

"Sorry, what will be?"

"Oh, darling. Veritas has taken pity on you. She understands you're repentant, sorrowful. She's guiding you now. Your physical healing is the manifestation, the symbolic representation of Veritas' desire to support you . . . This is good for us all. For Hollow Kin."

"Yes, she's guiding me. She wants me to tell you, you're wrong about me being the killer," Ellie said.

"Come now, dear," Mrs. Appleby replied, pouring tea into their cups. She took her time, looking directly at Ellie. Methodically, slowly, Mrs. Appleby added some milk. "Sugar?"

"Yes. Two, no one, sorry." Ellie had momentarily forgotten how much sugar she normally had. Too much wine, too much stress, too much of knowing how Nathan was involved in Martin's murder had unsettled her. She was adrift.

"Have a sip of tea, and a bickie. Go on."

"No really, I don't want a biscuit," Ellie said, though she did take a sip. It was hot but not burning.

Mrs. Appleby slid the small plate of biscuits towards her. "Have one."

"No."

"Eat one now, darling. Veritas is with us. She's watching you – I can feel her. You see, that's the difference between you and I. I know when she is truly here and when she is *truly* guiding us. This fanciful, whimsical feeling you have about Veritas is wrong. She wouldn't communicate with you – only me."

Ellie took a biscuit. She felt a surge of power. "It's not the difference between you and I; it's actually correct to say between you and me." Correcting Mrs. Appleby was huge. She didn't show it, but her heart was racing. "These biscuits *are* delicious."

"You're a clever girl, aren't you?"

Ellie shrugged. For the first time ever, she had some control. Normally, Mrs. Appleby won. "Veritas came to me, Mrs. Appleby. She came to tell me–"

Although she was arthritic, Mrs. Appleby was able to swipe her hand through the air as quick as someone half her age. The sound of her slapping Ellie's cheek reverberated long after in Ellie's ears and mind.

"Foolish little girl."

Ellie stood and threw her cup of tea at Mrs. Appleby's chest. "You crazy bitch. Hollow Kin's fucked up. None of this is true. I didn't kill Martin."

Mrs. Appleby remained seated, she didn't shout, nor did she react to the hot drink now soaking through to her bare skin. "Ellie, you are a disappointment. Detective Inspector Rowan Black and me have become rather close. Perhaps I'll give him a call, ask him to pop round as I have some news about Martin's killer. Ellie," she said. "Ellie," she said again. "Ellie's your killer. She confessed to me."

"It's Rowan Black and I, you stupid bitch."

Ellie stormed out, slammed the front door, kicked the sign from the path onto the garden. She had feelings for Nathan, but her desire to ruin Mrs. Appleby and Hollow Kin was stronger. If she told the police about Nathan, it would prove that Veritas was bullshit and she'd be free: that would kill Mrs. Appleby from the inside out.

Jasper Flint

Three o'clock. The *Hollow Rose* was bobbing gently on the water. Jax left the cabin, spanner in hand – heading for the damn bolt on the outboard that wouldn't come loose

– causing the boat to rock with each heavy step. He was about to lock the spanner in place when Rowan Black's voice stopped him.

"Need a hand?" Rowan said.

Not from you. Not ever. "No, I'm all good. It's a one-man job."

"Is she alright?"

Jax hated it when people who knew fuck-all about boats or fishing or sailing started calling a boat *she*. They hadn't earned the right. They didn't have a lifetime with the sea behind them.

"Just replacing this sodding bolt – bastard's rusted."

"That'll be the salty air and water." Rowan stepped aboard.

The boat rocked. "And if I don't get this sorted, the engine could rip right off, Rowan, so I'm a tad busy. I need to be out on the water early tomorrow – if I'm not, I don't earn."

"I won't take too much time, Jax."

Jax exhaled. "What is it? I've spoken to Danny this morning already."

"That's exactly why I'm here, Jax." Rowan motioned to the wooden seat. "May I?"

Jax nodded. "I need to crack on here, though."

"By all means. Oh, before I forget, your assessment of the damage to Martin's boat and prop shaft was spot on."

"Like I say, I know my boats." Jax knelt and focused on the rusting, crumbling bolt – showing his back to Rowan.

"You haven't had any more thoughts on who'd want to damage his boat, have you? I'm at a loss on that one, I'm afraid."

"Afraid not. Haven't thought about it, if I'm honest. Anyway, did I not answer Danny's questions to your satisfaction?"

"No, no, it's nothing like that. Just following up. I hear you like diving – Norwegian Fjords, isn't it?"

"It is. Danny told you everything like a good boy, *ayyyy*," Jax said, grinding out the last word as he attempted to free the bolt, shoulders bunching tight. It didn't budge. "Damn it."

"Even if I could help you, I doubt I could get that thing off. I'm best sitting here with the sun and the view!" Rowan said.

He's doing my head in – what the hell does he want?

"How long would you spend out in the Fjords?"

"A week."

"Nice," Rowan said. "World War Two relics in the sea, apparently."

"There is." Jax turned briefly, looking over his shoulder at DI Black. Their eyes didn't meet.

"Fascinating stuff."

"It is."

Rowan crossed his legs and shifted in the seat, facing Jax who continued to work with his back to him.

"It would scare the hell out of me – diving. I think I'd find it cold and claustrophobic. That's something I have in common with Nathan."

Jax's spanner slipped. "Oh yeah?" he said.

"Yeah, it's funny. You'd think a marine biologist would love the water, but he said he hates it. Lucky he's got you to help him out."

"It is." Jax looked at his fractured reflection in the sea.

"Do you need to take any samples for him? I ask because Danny said you didn't tell him much about it."

"Danny wouldn't have remembered what I said, anyway."

"Oh really?"

"Come on, Rowan. You know what he's like. The kid's an idiot. I'm surprised he's allowed in the force."

"I think he's a lot sharper than you give him credit for." Rowan cleared his throat. "So, what about taking samples for Nathan – you any good?"

"I follow Nathan's instructions – doesn't mean I know what I'm doing, and I definitely don't know what to do with it afterwards."

"Have you got him any samples of the fungus?"

Jax swore as the spanner slipped, causing his knuckle to scrape against the bolt. "No, Rowan – fuck that hurt. Look, I've gotta get on here."

"You wouldn't happen to know how to extract a psychoactive compound from that fungus, would you?"

Jax replied: "Odd question. What're you talking about?"

"Drugs. Hallucinogens – you can get them from fungi. I want to know whether you know how to do it."

"Haven't a clue. Why would I?"

"Would Nathan?"

"How would I know?" Jax said, standing, stuffing the spanner into his shorts pocket. He moved round the bench to face Rowan. "What're you getting at?"

"Just consolidating my thoughts."

"No, you think you're onto something. Let me tell you, Rowan, I haven't got a clue why you're asking me these questions. I'm a boat mechanic and fisherman – nothing more to it. I know the sea – not fungus. You want my advice: ask Nathan about it."

"You think Nathan would have the answer?"

"I told you a second ago: I don't bloody know. Jesus Christ."

"Why don't you take a seat, Jax. Plenty of room on this bench," Rowan said.

"No, I'm alright here thanks. Isn't it about time you were leaving?"

"PC Everett also mentioned that you looked pissed off when the topic of you and Martin arguing in the pub came up. Why was that?"

"Because I've told you time and time again: we didn't bloody argue! How many more times? I tell you what, you're one for timewasting – asking me stupid fucking questions when you could be out there finding the killer. Someone somewhere knows something and here you are pissing about with me!" Jax clenched his fist.

Rowan looked Jax up and down. "I see," he said, standing close to Jax – just in his personal space. "Moira, your colleague – for want of a better expression – said you weren't your usual self last Friday. Why was that?"

Jax stepped back an inch. "Not allowed an off day?"

"Of course. I want to know if it was something to do with Martin."

"Like what?"

Rowan looked Jax in the eyes and held his look. Then: "You're probably right, just an off day," he placed his hand on Jax's shoulder. "We all get them."

Jax watched Rowan disembark.

"I'll be in touch – if I need you." DI Black strolled away.

Bastard.

Rowan Black

Rowan was sitting in his office at the back of the police station. It was nearly eight-thirty p.m. He'd been speaking with DCI Hargrave. He wanted to catch her up with the day's events – if for no other reason than to help him consolidate his thoughts.

He rubbed his brow and opened the latest from the MIR: the digital forensic report for Martin Howler's phone. His eyes scanned over the call log information, SMS, WhatsApp, and emails. He then saw an email extract highlighted by the analyst between Martin and E. Hansen:

From: E. Hansen e.hansen@bergenbiomar.no
To: Martin Howler martin.howler@howl-erm.co.uk

Date: 14/2/25
Subject: Shipping Confirmation – *Pseudoteratos Maritima* Cultures

Dear Mr. Howler,

In accordance with your purchase order FE-9147, we have prepared and dispatched the initial batch of *Pseudoteratos Maritima* under controlled temperature logistics. Your shipment includes the following:

- 6 x 500ml liquid culture flasks
- 12 x agar plates (active colonies)
- Storage and propagation protocol documents (in English, PDF attached)

Please ensure these are held at 15–18°C upon receipt. The colonies are active and robust, showing rapid mycelial spread under simulated brackish conditions. As discussed, we disclaim all liability for introduction into non-contained environments. Usage beyond laboratory or designated bio-reactor conditions remains under your exclusive responsibility.

Kindly confirm receipt once cultures arrive.

Best regards,

E. Hansen
Senior Bio-Sales Coordinator
Bergen Biomarine AS
Bergen, Norway

Rowan scanned the email first and then read it a second time. The conclusion was unavoidable: Martin was responsible for the introduction of the notorious fungus now spreading across Wraith's Hollow. This speculation was verified by reading another flagged email – this time between Martin and Naomi Bennett:

From: Martin Howler martin.howler@howlerm.co.uk
To: Naomi Bennett n.bennett@bennettlocke.com
Date: 25/3/25
Subject: Project Genesis + local prep

Naomi,

Updates for you:

1. Fungus deployment: the *Pseudoteratos Maritima* I sourced is spreading like wildfire! It's already gaining momentum inland. Locals are talking about it – calling it strange and mysterious. There's no link

back to me. Its prevalence will render plots commercially unviable for conservation. I have one local up my arse about this, but he won't be a problem.

2. Genesis infrastructure: I've secured preliminary contract bids for Havenmoore Port extension under old maritime exemptions. This will give us discreet cold storage plus plenty of space for your neural assessment suites for phase three. Minimal council interruption so far. I have the Island Trust in my pocket anyway. It will be listed as *Marine Processing and Repair.*

3. Cognitive trials: Your revised microstimulation protocols encourage synaptic clustering around the implant arrays. Good news. The implant coatings are clearly more stable under your latest buffer ratios – the chemical solution must be working beautifully. The project is garnering incredible interest – I'm building a portfolio of high-net-worth candidates. The potential is staggering!

I'll be in touch!

Martin

What followed was Naomi's reply:

Martin,

Good. The fungus is serving its purpose. We are working towards our end goal – I like that. Make sure the Havenmoore build maintains all maritime compliance optics. I've flagged this to Locke's risk counsel. They need a full ingress and egress log up and running – dock manifests, contractor IDs, everything. This protects us down the line.

On the implant front: my team is finalising comparative baselines now. It's useless if neurons just grow extra branches – I need proof of their electrical signalling. It needs to be stronger and better coordinated otherwise it's just pretty tissue with no functional improvement. If these arrays don't show a clear statistical jump in local field coherence, we'll pivot to the secondary overlay.

Interest is irrelevant if the arrays can't deliver.

Naomi.

Rowan shut the laptop and leaned back in his chair. The content was complex – part of him was surprised that Martin knew what the hell it was all about – but from what Rowan could gather, Project Gensis was about implanting chips to force the brain into sprouting more connections, better synchronisation. All of which would equal sharper minds, engineered intelligence. Biohacking's here. Fuck. On Wraith's Hollow – if Martin had his way. The clash between the island's old superstitions and the futuristic world of genetic enhancement was not lost on Rowan. Hollow Kin had a solid motive for ridding the island of Martin Howler.

Martin was building a secret playground for the ultra-rich to upgrade themselves! As Rowan reached for his jacket, a jarring thought halted him: perhaps it wasn't such a bad thing Martin was killed – if this was where he was heading.

Rowan walked out of the station onto Quayside Lane. Naomi Bennett was out of the frame: she absolutely needed Martin alive. Him being dead was no good to her.

*

Rowan Black had got back into the station early Tuesday morning. He'd discussed the contents of the emails between Martin and Naomi with DCI Hargrave, and by the time he'd finished his first coffee, he'd had an Action raised on HOLMES, flagged for Thames Valley's Major Crime Unit. He wanted Naomi Bennett firmly on their radar as he had no doubt that, as Martin was dead, she would find some other rich fool to help her.

He opened the latest HOLMES Action Return and found Thames Valley's submission of Naomi Bennett's interview. It included the DEMS reference. Switching systems, he waited for the secure player to load. Rowan got comfortable in his seat as Naomi's face appeared: long mousey-brown hair curled at the ends; dark, intelligent eyes looked at him as she stared down the camera.

"Ms. Bennett. Thank you for coming in today. You're not under arrest but this interview is under caution. Do you understand?"

"Yes." She nodded, composed.

"I am DI Reynolds and this is DC Stanley."

Naomi introduced her solicitor, Mrs. Redfield, and then waited for DI Reynolds to continue. She looked at her watch.

"We won't keep you long," DI Reynolds said. "We're looking into the death of Martin Howler. How well did you know him?"

There was a moment where Rowan believed a look of surprise manifested in her expression, perhaps indicating that his death was news to her, but it didn't linger. "I knew him. Yes. We had a business relationship."

"Could you explain the many, substantial transfers from entities you control to his accounts?"

Rowan watched as Naomi's solicitor leaned in and whispered something in Naomi's ear.

"Which accounts – you need to be specific please," Naomi said, flicking her eyes at the camera, then at DC

Stanley, and then leaving them fixed on DI Reynolds.

"Of course," DC Stanley said, looking down at his notes. "*NVB Capital Partners, Shoreline Biotech LTD, Wraith BioTechnologies LTD.*"

Naomi folded her arms and looked at DC Stanley as though he wasn't worth her time. "Those are all perfectly standard. *NVB* is my primary investment account. The others are project-specific shells – just safe compartmentalisation for high-risk biotech ventures." Naomi leaned her arms on the table, and arched her back, pulling her shoulders back. "Believe me. I'm very careful about what I do. Everything is documented. If you like, my compliance officer can forward our last three quarterly audits. It might save you a lot of time and resources – I'd rather you used them more effectively."

"Would the recent sum of sixty-five thousand pounds you deposited in Martin's account just four days before his death be included in your audit?"

Naomi's solicitor once again leaned in and whispered to Naomi. "It's fine," she replied. "We have nothing to hide." Naomi turned back to the detectives. "Yes, that deposit will be visible. And I'll even tell you what it was for. It was capital for necessary groundwork, climate-controlled storage, contractor deposits, that sort of thing – but that was Martin's territory. Not mine."

"What was your territory?" DI Reynolds asked. "We know you're working on developing some kind of brain chip – implant. What is that?"

Naomi scoffed at them. "I can see you're way out of your depths on this one, gentlemen. My territory is preclinical research. You obviously know my academic history and PhD interests, so I won't insult you by reciting it. I am developing – with Martin – a neural interface that could improve cognitive performance: faster learning, improved memory, more resilient cognition. It's no different to the kind of research happening at some of the finest universities the UK has to offer. The only distinction is that we're a little bolder." Rowan watched as Naomi put her hand up to DC Stanley – who began questioning what her bolder practices were. "I'll stop you there. Before you try and misconstrue what I've said, I'll make it crystal clear for you. We haven't operated on a single human being. All my research has been confined to the lab. I'll be even clearer here: there's been no breach of UK biomedical law, no regulatory violation. I'm still working on comparative baselines."

"I think we need to cool it a bit here, Ms. Bennett," DI Reynolds said. "We're trying to understand what your relationship with Martin Howler was like – how you knew him etc."

"Well, now you know."

"Yes and no," DC Stanley said. "What we have is a lot of, as far as I'm concerned, rehearsed phrasing and–"

"*My* client has answered every question put to her under caution and has, in fact, provided additional details well beyond what is required at this stage. So, unless you have fresh lines of enquiry directly relevant to Martin Howler's death, we will be concluding this interview," Naomi's solicitor said.

"Ms. Bennett, I appreciate you're busy. How did you feel hearing that Martin, your business partner, has been killed? Do you know of anyone who might have wanted to harm him?" DI Reynolds asked.

Naomi leaned back in her seat and crossed one leg over the other. "To the latter: no. No idea. To the former: I'm sorry for him and for those who knew him, but for me, it's a minor setback that can be easily rectified. You see, gentlemen, my relationship with Martin was purely business. I've made no claims to know him intimately nor, I want to be clear, would I pursue that sort of relationship with him. If I'm perfectly honest, it really makes no difference to my life if he's dead or alive. Any further communication–"

Naomi's solicitor subtly interrupted: "will be directed to me. I'll arrange any subsequent discussions."

Rowan stopped the recording. She was a piece of work; she didn't even ask how he died. But the conversation had verified his initial thinking: for her, Martin alive was far better than Martin dead.

*

It was coming up for nine o'clock and Rowan had just finished morning briefing. He'd updated the team on the emails and Naomi Bennett's interview. His conclusion was clear: their attention needed to move away from her and back to more local matters.

"Danny," he said, once the team had dispersed. "Don't forget to call in and see Ellie – make sure she's okay. Call me if you need anything." Rowan gently touched PC Everett on the shoulder before heading to his office. It wasn't long after he began reviewing the updated witness statements when DS Hocking entered his office.

"Sir, the blood results from Martin's bathroom are back. It's a match for Tim Thorn."

Rowan felt a brief sense of relief that was quickly overtaken by one of urgency. "Bring him in."

Tim Thorn

Being back at the station, so soon after having been interviewed on Saturday really grated on Tim. The interview room felt smaller than last time, as did the table between himself and the detectives. It felt as though both Rowan Black and DS Hocking were breathing down his neck.

"I will state it again," DI Black said. "You are entitled to legal–"

"And I will state again that I don't need a solicitor. I haven't done anything wrong. But this treatment you're subjecting me to is tantamount to harassment!"

"The definition of harassment is very clear, Mr. Thorn. This is a murder enquiry, and we have fresh evidence placing you at Martin Howler's home," Rowan said.

Tim sneered. "We've been over why my fingerprints were found at Martin's for pity's sake."

"Yes. We know. You stated in your last interview that you used the bathroom – which, oddly, you hadn't remembered at first," Rowan said. Tim thought he saw a smug smile register on that bastard's face. "If I remember correctly, you struggled to remember a few things."

"Whatever. Get on with it, if you don't mind."

"The fresh evidence to which I was referring wasn't your fingerprints in the bathroom, it was the blood that we found and matched to your DNA. Now we have your fingerprints and your blood at Martin's house."

Tim was silent. He just looked at Rowan – his right fist clenched over his bouncing leg.

"And do you know what else? Forensics were able to tell me that your blood hadn't been there long. You see, Tim, they look at things like oxidation, dust accumulation, environmental conditions. They can't pin it to the minute, but they can get pretty damn close."

"What's your point?" said Tim.

"My point is that you need to explain why there are traces of your blood at Martin's house deposited around the time of his murder."

"Maybe I cut myself, a finger, and didn't realise – stuff happens, especially delivering heavy objects like that sodding bookcase."

DS Hocking spoke: "We're not talking about when you delivered the bookcase. As DI Black pointed out: your deposits of blood are recent to the murder – if you cut your hand when you delivered the bookcase that would've been too many days ago. The timing doesn't work."

"I don't *know* how my blood got there," Tim said.

The detectives opposite remained silent.

Never had silence been so agonising. Tim was burning to say something to bring the silence to its knees, but nothing would come.

"You look hot," DI Black said. "Glass of water?"

Tim said: "No."

More silence.

"Mr. Thorn, do you know what's being asked of you?" DS Hocking prompted. "You need to explain how your blood ended up in Martin's bathroom."

"I'm not a bloody idiot," Tim replied.

"Answer the damn question then!" Rowan snapped.

"Why don't we come back to that," DS Hocking said. "Give you time to think about it. Now, in your last interview, Saturday, you were certain that Martin assaulting you – grabbing your throat – didn't bother you. Is this still the case?"

"Yes."

"If that were me, I'd have been pissed off," Hocking replied.

"I'm not you – you're you. I know you think I had motive to hurt Martin – but I didn't. Look, he tried intimidating me, I shoved him off, end of story. Why're we going over the same stuff. Over and over."

Rowan Black leant forward: "I find repetition useful for understanding the difference between what people *want* you to know and what they *don't* want you to know. The lies reveal themselves, Mr. Thorn, as bright as day."

"I'm not lying. I didn't touch him."

"Have you got the document relating to Project Genesis?" DS Hocking asked.

"No. Why would I? I told you before. I saw it on the kitchen side. Glanced at it – but that were it."

"You mean the table next to the sofa," Rowan said.

"I'm sorry?"

"You said in our last interview you saw the document on the mahogany table next to the sofa – not the kitchen side. Which one was it?"

"I don't bloody know!" Tim felt his face becoming increasingly hot. His cheeks were burning. "If I said table then I meant table this time. You're just screwing my words up."

Rowan held a palm up. "I'm seeking clarity on what you know and saw. It's important we get these details right because if things change – like where you saw the Project Genesis document – it invalidates everything else you're saying."

"I'm not a bloody liar, Rowan." Tim paused, a devilish thought came, something to steer the power his way. "I remember you when you were a spotty kid. I never liked you even back then. You want to know why I never gave you a job when you left school?"

"Enlighten me."

"Because you were a useless, fuckwit druggie. You had no hope then just like you're a no-hoper now." Tim felt great. "No wonder Cynthia was screwing Jax when she was with you."

Rowan smiled. "You're going to have to do a lot better than that, Tim."

Tim wanted to smash his stupid face – just smash his fist so hard into that smug smile.

"Let's get back to Project Genesis for a minute," DS Hocking said, exhaling.

"What about it?"

"What do you know about it?" DS Hocking asked.

"Nothing. As I said before, I saw it was something to do with brain implants but that's all I know."

DI Black folded his arms. "I'm struggling here, Tim. You see, if I saw something like that at Martin's – or anywhere for that matter – I don't think I'd just give it a cursory glance and move on. Were you not the least bit interested in what the hell it was about?"

Tim folded his arms, too. "I'm afraid I'm a humble cabinetmaker. I know tools. I know wood. I don't know anything about brains and implants or whatever – nor do I want to."

"Don't sell yourself short, Tim. You're not *just* a humble carpenter," Rowan said. "You're a liar, too. It's obvious you sat down and read through that document – only you didn't take it then did you when you went to measure up for the bookcase because Martin would've known you took it. No. You took the document when you trashed the house."

"I wouldn't do such a foolish thing."

"You read all about Project Genesis and–"

"No! I didn't!"

"And it terrified the hell out of you. You told Mrs. Appleby and Hollow Kin, you schemed together and dreamt up your plan to trash his house. Tried to scare him. Because the idea of Wraith's Hollow hosting the world's ultra-wealthy and their biohacking desires terrifies you. I can see it in your face."

"Listen to yourself, Rowan. The only one scheming and dreaming is you with this utter nonsense. You've lost your way."

"How's the hand, by the way?" DI Black asked, his tone shifting to a lighter gear.

"Painful. But not as painful as this conversation. Are we done?"

"Even the timing of your injury fits. Little Liam reckons you came in Thursday morning like it – just hours after Martin was killed. Just after you smashed holes all over his place."

"Little Liam . . . Of course." Tim shook his head in disbelief – at his own stupidity. How could he have forgotten about Little Liam. "What else did he say?"

"You had a delivery of cherry wood Thursday morning, for a table for Mrs. Benn I believe. He had to help carry the wood in because of your hand. He knows it was fine on Wednesday."

"You're believing a kid over me?" Tim snapped back.

"It's just that he was so fired up about helping to make Mrs. Benn's table – I was thinking of putting an order in for one myself – that I believe his account. The point is, you didn't do it on Tuesday like you said."

"It's your prerogative who you believe. I can't change that if you're not going to bloody listen."

Rowan continued: "I didn't tell you before, but it was Little Liam who told me about your argument with

Martin. You say it didn't bother you; Little Liam says that afterwards you stormed into your office, furious. So furious that you didn't even know he was there."

"Like I said. Your prerogative."

DS Hocking jumped in: "From the way I see it, Liam doesn't need to lie to us – has no reason to lie. Why wouldn't we believe what he tells us?"

Tim was silent but shook his head slowly and shrugged.

"For the record, Tim Thorn shook his head and shrugged his shoulders," Hocking said.

"Tim," Rowan began as he pulled two photographs out of a file and slid them across the table. "You stated previously that you knew nothing about these symbols – the ones we found at Martin's house. You had no idea about them. And you said the cult, Hollow Kin, is a load of rubbish. You've nothing to do with any of it. Would you like to change any of these statements, or do they still represent your position?"

Tim looked at *The Binding of the Kin* and *The Tongue of Silence.* Then, looking back at Rowan Black: "I really don't have anything else to say on the matter."

"I'll take it your previous statements still accurately describe your position towards the cult. Can you tell me," Rowan said as he rested his elbows on the arms of the chair and interlocked his fingers, "why forensics were able to find trace evidence of wood fibres and varnish on these symbols?"

Tim swallowed.

"That to me looks as though they came right out of

your workshop. And, like you said, you know wood, you know tools – you're probably one of the few people on this island with the skills to make the symbols. Agree?"

"Whatever."

"They're made of local shale, kelp and flax. Now, tool-mark analysis, Tim, shows that the angle, depth, and scoring patterns on the stone sigil are consistent with the kind of flat-edged chisels you use for woodwork. And on the vine necklace here," Rowan placed a finger on the photograph, "are microscopic traces of varnish – again the kind you'd use when staining wood. Do you stain your furniture?"

There was no point in lying. "Yes."

"Did you make these symbols?" DS Hocking asked.

Tim said nothing.

Rowan leant forwards, lowering his tone. "If you don't start telling the truth, I'll lay every bit of this at Mrs. Appleby's door."

"With what evidence?"

"I'm not obliged to tell you that but, believe me, if it goes that way, she won't spend her last years in peace."

"You wouldn't. Couldn't. Your boss wouldn't let you go after a frail old woman. Bad optics, Rowan."

"You don't think so? They honestly wouldn't give a damn how old she is. If she's guilty of orchestrating the criminal damage to Martin's home and his death, they'll lock her away all the same."

"She didn't do anything!"

"Start telling the truth!"

"Leave her out of this," Tim said. "I'll make you pay if you bring her into this."

"You're not in a position to threaten me," Rowan said. "Tim Thorn, did you kill Martin Howler?!"

"No!"

"Did you break into his home?"

"No!"

"Did you smash up his house?"

"No!"

"Did you plant those symbols so he got the message that Hollow Kin were onto him?!"

"No. Fuck's sake. No!" Tim struggled to control his breathing. He took a few deep breaths – all of which, DI Black and DS Hocking saw.

"Mr. Thorn," DS Hocking began. "We know you hurt your hand damaging Martin's house; we have your DNA and fingerprints there too – your blood places you at the scene close to the time of Martin Howler's death; you knew the door code to get in; you're tied to Hollow Kin; you made the symbols in your workshop; you placed them at Martin's home."

"Look," Rowan cut in. "Tell the truth. I'll see to it your honesty is noted. Tim, I believe you broke into Martin Howler's home with the intention of trashing it and leaving the Hollow Kin symbols as a warning to Martin. That's burglary, even if you didn't steal a thing. You're looking at prison. Not a fine; not a caution. Prison. Two years – could be more, depending on how the judge sees it."

"Custodial sentence without question. I've seen it too many times before," DS Hocking added.

"But start telling the truth, I'll make sure the judge knows you cooperated. They like to hear that sort of thing."

Tim opened his mouth, about to say something. But something held him back.

"The easy way or the hard way," Rowan said. "And just think: who's going to look after Mrs. Appleby when you're inside doing time? She'll get awfully lonely."

Whatever it was that held him back, the thought of Mrs. Appleby, lonely, no one to watch over her and look after her as well as he did, was enough for him. "I did it."

"Did what?"

"I went to his home, wrecked the place."

"What time was this?" DS Hocking asked.

"I don't know – around midnight."

"Was Martin at home?" DS Hocking continued.

"No. Don't know where he was."

"Any signs of him having been there recently before you arrived?"

"Like what?"

"Cup of tea, leftover food, half empty drink, beer, anything?"

"No. Place was practically in darkness – but he'd left a lamp on in the living room."

"Did Mrs. Appleby ask you to do this on behalf of Hollow Kin?"

"Absolutely not. It was my call." Tim's eyes flicked over to Rowan – who was sitting there silently watching him – before settling back on DS Hocking.

"Please clarify why you did what you did. What were your intentions?"

"My intentions were to send him a message that we don't want him or Project Genesis or more luxury fucking houses on Wraith's Hollow. He wouldn't listen to anyone. He was destroying everything we stand for."

"And if he'd happened to have been there when you got there?" Hocking asked.

"Make no mistake, I would've probably killed him. It was a good job he wasn't there."

"I take it no one else was at the property?"

"Like who?" Tim asked.

"Anyone at all."

"No. Just me."

"What time did you leave?"

"I don't know. But it was before one in the morning. Can't be sure."

"Okay. So, you didn't leave his house and then go to the beach with the intention of killing him?"

"No. I went straight home with my fucked hand."

"How did you hurt it?"

"Hitting too many walls – plaster's easy to break but I caught it wrong."

"Did you use any tools?"

"I brought a bag with me. Used my hammer in the end."

"On your way home, did you see anyone else? Martin even – or just someone walking around?"

Tim shook his head. "It was very peaceful. Not another soul."

"Would you've noticed anyone if you were so concerned about your hand?"

"Yes . . . Look, you need to know. I didn't kill him."

"Do you know who did?" DS Hocking asked.

"If I tell you, I want assurances Mrs. Appleby will be sheltered from this. No charges. She's done nothing wrong."

Rowan said: "You have my word. You want Mrs. Appleby safe, give me that name."

Tim was feeling desperate. Did he or did he not trust Rowan? He wasn't sure what to do. Everything was slipping from his grip. "It was Ellie. Ellie Crick."

"Ellie Crick?" DS Hocking double-checked.

"How do you know this?" DI Black asked.

"Veritas revealed it."

"Your God?"

"Yes."

"Is this what you meant when you said Hollow Kin have everything in hand? That Veritas has revealed the murderer to you?" Rowan asked.

"Yes." Tim watched as Rowan shifted in his seat, catching DS Hocking's eye. "It's the truth."

"How did Veritas reveal this truth about Ellie Crick?" Rowan asked.

Tim was quiet for a moment, thinking. Then told them about the night in the crypt but left out Mrs. Appleby's branding ceremony.

"Okay, Tim. Thank you." Rowan's voice was clipped. "You've admitted to breaking into Martin Howler's house and trashing it. That's burglary. But I'll make sure the court knows of your cooperation today."

DS Hocking concluded the interview. Tim slouched in his chair.

"Tim, you'll remain here while we speak to Sergeant Jennings. His role as custody sergeant means he'll decide whether you stay in police custody or are released on bail with conditions."

"Are you sure, Rowan, he's the right man? Are you sure he's as trustworthy as you think?" Tim said.

Rowan shook his head. "Jennings will do it by the book. And I wouldn't keep pushing that line if I were you."

Tim wanted to reply with something smart to let Rowan know that he would continue to push Jennings' corrupt past in his face, but nothing would come. Instead, he watched them both leave the interview room.

Ellie Crick

Ellie was sat with PC Everett at the station waiting for DI Black to be free – comfortably allowing the world to carry on around her. Her stomach rumbled – it wasn't far from lunch, and she hadn't eaten any breakfast. The last few days she hadn't eaten very much, and what she had was total crap. Thinking about it now, this was the first time she'd felt a pang of hunger in what seemed forever.

Maybe the relief of telling Danny everything when he visited her that morning had allowed her body to release enough stress and tension to start the process of rejuvenation.

What pulled Ellie back into the world of the police station was the sight of Tim Thorn. He was walking behind Frank Jennings. She wanted to look away, maybe lean into Danny, strike up a conversation in the hope that she didn't lock eyes with Tim, but she couldn't. Tim's expression of uncertainty mesmerised her. What happened? Why was he here?

"Ellie," Rowan Black said – he seemed to have come from nowhere.

"Hi," she said, focusing on him.

"Sir," PC Everett stood. "I thought it best that Ellie came to you. I want her to tell you what she said to me."

"Of course," Rowan said. "Come through, Ellie. Danny, you as well please."

Ellie followed and was asked to take a seat in the interview room. The weight of what she was about to say pulled her down into the chair.

"Ellie, you're not under caution but I'm going to record the interview."

"That's fine. I, I just want to thank you, Rowan, for sending Danny round. He said you asked him to. That was good of you."

"No problem. Where would you like to begin?" Rowan asked.

Rowan looked relaxed in his seat, Ellie mirrored him. She breathed slowly.

"It's okay, Ellie. DI Black will help," Danny assured her.

Rowan waited.

"I know something about Nathan Waters." She trailed off into silence. She was teetering on the edge of panic.

"Breathe, Ellie," Danny said.

She took a few deep breaths. "I know Nathan's involved with Martin's murder."

"How do you know this?"

"He told me. Told me last Friday. Just before Mann came to see me."

"Okay," Rowan began. "What did he tell you?"

"I know I should've told you sooner. I know that. I didn't know what to do. I–"

"Ellie, the important part is that you're here now. Please, go on."

"Nathan said he fucked up. He was in a right state. He got me to promise I wouldn't tell anyone – not the police, not anyone. I shouldn't be here."

"Yes, you should. You know the truth's important," Rowan said and then waited for Ellie to continue.

"It was to do with that fungus on the island. Nathan said he used it to poison Martin."

"Did he tell you how?"

Ellie shook her head. "No. Just that he used it to get Martin high – then the other two did the rest."

Rowan raised his eyebrows. "Two?"

"Yes. He didn't tell me who."

"Why not? Was he protecting you?"

"Yes. Nathan said one of them threatened him, said if Nathan told anyone or involved the police, he'd kill me."

"You sure Nathan said the one who threatened him was male?"

"Yes."

"Did Nathan tell you why he did what he did, Ellie?" Rowan asked, jotting in his notebook.

"He said he did it for me. That he loves me."

"He did it for love?"

"Yes. And because he knew about Martin raping me. Nathan said he hated Martin for what he did." Ellie looked away. "He wanted to kill Martin when I told him."

"What else did Nathan say?" Rowan asked.

"That he didn't touch Martin, like physically, and he didn't see him on the night. Nathan's terrified about being sent down for murder."

Rowan sighed. "I'm afraid if Nathan's guilty of concocting the drug as part of a plan to murder Martin, he could face life in prison."

"But he didn't touch him!" Ellie said.

Rowan shook his head. "It doesn't matter, Ellie. If he supplied the drug knowing what it was for, i.e. to harm Martin, that's conspiracy to commit or joint enterprise. A minimum of fifteen years. Minimum . . . Nathan's in a lot of trouble. I need you to be really clear with me. Did he say any more to you about the murder or who else was involved?"

"That was it, I promise."

"Ellie, why're you bringing this to me now? If Nathan confided in you – told you he loved you. Why now?"

"I had to."

Rowan eyed her for a moment. "I want to put something to you. Tim Thorn and Hollow Kin believe Veritas revealed you were responsible for Martin Howler's death. Why would they think that?"

"Because they're crackpots," Ellie said, a bit of fire in her voice.

"You stated previously that you knew nothing about the symbols and denied any knowledge of Hollow Kin – is that still the case?"

"No. I lied." The honesty of her words stopped her for a second. It wasn't an unpleasant feeling. "I'm sorry I lied to you. I didn't know what else to do. You can ask me anything about Hollow Kin – I'll tell you the truth."

"Start with telling me why they think you killed Martin."

Ellie took a deep breath and told Rowan about the branding in the crypt.

Although he'd heard it previously, Danny Everett let out: "Jesus," in no more than a whisper.

"Okay. Tim's version of the night in the crypt was different. How can I trust what you're telling me – about Nathan, about Hollow Kin. You've lied to me before."

"Because I don't gain anything from telling you the truth – I only lose. I lose Nathan."

"But you have everything to gain where the cult's concerned."

"Meaning?" Ellie asked.

"By telling me about Nathan, it places you in the clear with Hollow Kin."

"I don't care about Hollow Kin. They can all rot. It proves that Mrs. Appleby is a psycho and Veritas is a joke." Ellie had raised her voice – Danny squeezed her shoulder.

Rowan looked towards Ellie's legs under the table. "Do you feel able to show me the injury? It would help. I can call a female officer if you'd prefer to support you."

"I don't care, Rowan. Danny's here." Ellie stood and rolled down her blue Lycra leggings carefully, exposing her left inner thigh. "Mrs. Appleby did this to me. She prodded that fucking iron thing at me. It's blistered, raw."

"Christ, Ellie, we'll get that checked properly. That's a serious assault. Was Tim Thorn involved?"

"Yes. He held me, cut my robe – others pinned me down."

Rowan looked thoughtful as Ellie pulled her clothing back up.

"Here's what we're going to do. You're going to give me a formal statement, and you're going to make it very clear you want to proceed with charges against Mrs. Appleby, Tim Thorn and anyone else involved from Hollow Kin. I promise you they won't get away with this. Sergeant Jennings will handle it from there."

Rowan Black

Rowan handed Ellie's case over to Jennings and told him they were pressing charges against Tim Thorn and Mrs. Appleby. Then he pulled his team together.

"Tim Thorn's facing two separate charges. One for burglary, the other for his part in the assault of Ellie Crick along with Mrs. Appleby. I want to nail them – Ellie's sustained severe injuries."

"Sir," DS Hocking said. Although he was the only one who responded at that moment, Rowan could feel the energy and urgency from all those around him.

Rowan continued: "Ellie's stated that Nathan Waters told her about his part in Martin's murder. He admitted to her he used the fungus to poison Martin. That was his part."

"The tox results on Martin's blood fits," DC Mann said.

"Yes. Nathan also said there were two others involved – one definitely male. He didn't give names because one of them threatened to kill Ellie if he talked."

"A real threat?" Mann asked.

"Apparently. Nathan's all over the place, scared, so yes, let's treat it as genuine. We know Nathan's lost his jacket and pliers, we know he's got the knowledge and technical skill to create the psychoactive compound. And we've got Ellie's statement. Hocking take a team and bring Nathan in. Mann chase up the jacket and pliers with forensics, let's see if we can get something concrete before he gets here. My suspicion is that Nathan won't talk until he's got a solicitor. I'll get Jennings on it, pre-empt any hold-ups."

*

Nearly one-thirty. Rowan, needing to stretch his legs, went over to DC Mann's desk and peered over his shoulder. Mann had the latest update from the MIR open.

"Anything on the pliers?" DI Black asked – his eyes scanning over Mann's empty sandwich packet, yet to be eaten chocolate bar, and some kind of 'fresh' juice bottle.

"Still waiting on the pliers. But forensics submitted their report on the jacket a few minutes ago, and MIR have logged it. The fibre from Martin's body is a direct match to the dumped jacket. That's the confirmation we were expecting. They're certain. And it's Martin's blood on both."

"Good. So, whoever wore that jacket, walked down Pier Road, murdered Martin in it, and dumped it in Wraith Forest."

"Yes, sir. Also," DC Mann said, tapping his keyboard, "forensics lifted two separate DNA profiles from the jacket. But neither's on the database – they're unknowns."

"Okay. One's Nathan, but the other – we need to find out. Keep chasing the lab on the pliers. Find me the second you get anything."

*

By the time Nathan arrived and then the duty solicitor – Emma Wright – a couple of hours later, Rowan still hadn't heard about the pliers. But he pressed on with the interview, deciding they had enough to be getting on with. Even though he knew Wright's MO – keeping her clients calm and quiet, talking only when absolutely necessary – Rowan had the upper hand because Nathan looked a wreck. Pulling a confession out of him, assuming Ellie was right, wouldn't be difficult.

Once the formalities were done – caution, date, solicitor, recording – Rowan cast a glance at DS Hocking before turning to Nathan. "I want to check in first, Mr. Waters. How are you? When Sergeant Jennings and I saw you yesterday morning, you seemed out of sorts. Stressed."

Nathan glanced at Wright then back at Rowan. "I'm, I'm . . . I don't know. Terrible."

"Well, let's just take this one step at a time. It's been noted you didn't resist arrest – you came willingly. Okay, for starters, tell me how you knew Martin Howler."

"I've told you that already."

"For the benefit of the recording, Mr. Waters," DS Hocking said.

Nathan told them about his petitions, environmental meetings, his squabbles – as he put it – with Martin Howler; about his concern for the Wraith's Hollow ecosystem; and about how he hated how little Martin cared. It was evident that their ideals and objectives were about as far apart from each other as two people could possibly get.

"Thank you," DS Hocking said.

"What do you know about the fungus that's invading the island."

"I'm studying it. Making progress."

"What sort of progress?" Rowan asked.

"Like I told you before, I'm analysing its neuroactive compounds – toxicity, growth rates, how it behaves in different environments."

"Can we focus on the toxic aspects for a minute," DS Hocking said.

"What do you want to know," Nathan said, glancing at Wright.

"How toxic is it?"

"Depends."

"On?"

"Eaten raw, it's likely to cause adverse effects. Make the average person ill, possibly affect the normal functioning of the brain – perception, that kind of thing. I wouldn't recommend eating it."

"Is there a way to ramp up the intensity?" DI Black asked. "Make it more toxic?"

Nathan looked at Wright. Wright said: "You need to come to the point, Detective Inspector."

Rowan ignored Emma Wright and waited for Nathan.

"Yes. But it requires a strong extraction process. Repeated solvent pulls, reducing it down, concentrating it."

DS Hocking asked: "Do you know how to do this?"

Nathan nodded.

"For the benefit of the recording Nathan Waters nodded. Please confirm."

"Yes, I know how to make a psychoactive compound."

"From the fungus growing on the island?" Rowan wanted him to confirm.

"Yes. From the fungus on the island."

"Thank you," DS Hocking said. "And, because I don't know much about it, what form does a high concentration of this compound take?"

"Liquid."

"Clear liquid?"

"Yes, clear – once purified. It's murky before that." Nathan shifted uneasily in his seat.

"Again, you know how to do this?" Hocking asked.

"Yes."

"What about taste – say, if it was put in a drink?"

"A little bitter."

"But not overpowering?"

"Depends how much you put in – why're you asking me this?" Rowan saw Nathan's jaw clench.

Rowan took the lead. "We've reason to believe that you extracted the psychoactive compound from the fungus growing on the island and gave it to Martin Howler."

"Ellie! Did this come from her!?"

"I'm not disclosing that information. Please either confirm or deny."

"Don't answer," Wright said to Nathan. "On what evidence are you alleging my client's involvement?"

"We have a witness statement that your client confessed his involvement in Martin Howler's death. We have toxicology evidence proving that the psychoactive compound Mr. Waters works with was found in the victim's blood. We also know that Mr. Waters claimed he wasn't physically present on the night of Martin's murder and that two other people were involved."

In a flash, Wright said: "I would like some time to consult with my client, Inspector Black."

"Of course," Rowan said. "The time is 16:07. Interview is suspended for private consultation."

*

Rowan Black and DS Hocking allowed them fifteen minutes. Meanwhile, they checked their notes, discussed points still to be made, and both agreed that they now faced the part of the interview where Nathan would've been strictly advised to answer, 'no comment'.

*

"Interview commences 16:22," DS Hocking said.

"Did you know Martin introduced the fungus to Wraith's Hollow?" Rowan asked.

Nathan looked stunned. "Why would he do that? I don't think even he would stoop that low!"

"It's true. He wanted to devalue the land. Make it suitable only for building on. He had no time for conservation."

"You see, he was destroying everything!" Nathan burst out.

"Right in front of everyone – he really didn't care."

"No. He was a bastard," Nathan was stopped by Wright's hand on his shoulder.

"He angered you, didn't he," Rowan stated.

"Yes. We didn't see eye to eye. I don't care who knows that."

Emma Wright looked at her client, sharply.

"How did you feel knowing Martin Howler had raped Ellie Crick?" Rowan asked as he watched DS Hocking preparing the photos of the jacket and pliers.

"How is this relevant?" Wright cut in.

Rowan knew that Emma Wright knew full well why he was asking this – but she was trying her luck. He explained: "We're establishing motive." Rowan eyed her. Then to Nathan: "Please, answer my question."

"Hated him for it. Wouldn't you! Seeing the man who raped the woman you love – knowing he'd got away with it. Seeing him all the time. Smug, evil bastard."

"Yes, apparently you said you wanted to kill Martin when you found out."

"That's right. I did. I'm not ashamed to admit that."

"You did it for love, didn't you?" Rowan said – hoping to catch him out.

"Did what?"

"Yes, please make the meaning of your questions clear, Inspector Black."

Rowan nodded to DS Hocking, who slid two photographs across the table and said: "Have a good look at these. Do you recognise them?"

Nathan looked at Wright before saying, "Yes. It's my jacket and pliers. I recognise them both. Part of the label's missing on the jacket. I've lost them – we spoke about that."

"We did," Rowan agreed. "Can you tell me when you last had them? When you noticed they were missing?"

Nathan shrugged. "Not really. I've got no idea when they went missing."

"You don't notice when things are gone?" Rowan asked.

"Yes, but as to when they went missing – I've no idea. I thought they were still at home somewhere or at my lab."

"Do you know why your jacket's covered in blood?" DI Black asked.

"No. I don't."

"We found your pliers," DS Hocking said. "At Silver Cove Marina, on the seabed where Martin's boat was moored."

"So," Nathan said.

"How did they get there?"

"No idea."

"You haven't got much of an idea of anything have you, Mr. Waters?" Rowan cut in.

Wright said: "What is the relevance of this line of questioning? As far as I'm concerned, my client has answered every question, Detective Inspector. If you're not going to charge my client, I'll advise him to make no further comment."

Rowan said: "I'm not finished . . . You don't know about your jacket, or pliers – fine." DI Black nodded to DS Hocking to retrieve the next photograph. Hocking slid it next to the others. "Take a careful look at this photograph, Mr. Waters. It's an image of someone quite clearly wearing your jacket walking down Pier Road at one thirty-five in the morning heading towards the beach – where Martin was subsequently murdered. Is this you?"

"No, I swear it isn't. It's my jacket but it's not me."

"Are you sure?" DS Hocking asked.

"I believe my client's already answered that question."

"Yes, he has." Rowan didn't engage with Wright; he focused on Nathan. "I'm sitting here thinking, the only question you've not given me a straight answer to is whether the witness statement we put to you is true."

"No comment," Nathan said, abruptly.

"Mr. Waters, is it true that you extracted the psychoactive drug from the island fungus as part of a plan to murder Martin Howler?"

"No comment."

"Is it true that you confessed these details to someone?"

"No comment."

"Mr. Waters, is it true that you also stated in this confession that two more people are involved in Martin Howler's death – one of whom is male?"

"No comment."

"Nathan Waters, I am arresting you–"

"It wasn't me!"

"Nathan, I am arresting–"

"No! No! No! It wasn't just me. I didn't do it by myself."

Rowan continued. "Nathan Waters, I'm arresting you on suspicion of causing a noxious substance to be administered with intent, and conspiracy to commit murder.

You do not have to say anything, but it may harm your defence if you do not mention when questioned something which you later rely on in court. Anything you do say may be given in evidence."

"Bastard! It wasn't! It wasn't just me! They'll pay for this!" Nathan was up like a raging bull – but DS Hocking, broader and stronger, pinned him to the floor. "Get off me! I didn't give him the drug that was. . ." he stopped.

Rowan crouched down: "Who gave it to him! Who poisoned him, Nathan? Who?!"

DS Hocking dragged Nathan to his feet. Nathan looked at Rowan. "No comment," he said.

"Take him away DS Hocking. He can spend the night here. Perhaps when you've had time to think, Nathan, you'll consider telling me who else is involved."

Sophie Marlow

Those passing Drift Edge on Saltmere Way wouldn't have looked at it twice – it exuded an undisturbed, peaceful air. But Sophie, on the inside, was panicking. She'd heard about Nathan's arrest when she was in town. Over and over, she asked herself the question: what if he's talked, what if he's talked?

"Have you heard about Nathan?" she said on the phone.

"Yes."

"We're screwed!"

"Shut up! Listen to me. This is how we planned it. It's falling into place."

"But they've got my DNA."

"Don't worry. They're not going to find anything. If they match your blood to the DNA on the boat, it doesn't prove anything. Except you've been on the boat at some point."

"If I go down, I'm bringing you with me!" she said.

"Sophie, it's not going to happen. Anyway, fuck that! I did this for you. We did this for you."

"Don't put it all on me. We all had our reasons for wanting Martin dead."

"Stick to the plan. Nathan will go down for it, I promise. I've heard about Tim, too. . ."

Rowan Black

It was coming up for six p.m. The energy in the incident room was tangible. News about Tim, Ellie, and, most recently, Nathan had pushed his team full throttle into the evening. DI Black had sent PC Everett to catch up with Roger Stone because the fact that the alarm system was shut down at the marina twice nagged at him. Digital hadn't finished investigating the laptop yet but maybe Danny could bring something back. Despite this element not being anywhere near resolved, Rowan instinctively felt the case was progressing towards the end. He knew who'd trashed the house; he knew Nathan had created the psychoactive compound; he knew two others were still out there. Now it was only a matter of time: either Nathan would break and bring the whole show down on top of everyone, or the final pieces of evidence would pin them all down.

Rowan was standing arms folded in front of the whiteboard, scanning the salient points about everyone who they knew was involved. Jennings had told him earlier that Tim Thorn was out on bail with strict conditions: no contact with Ellie Crick, Mrs. Appleby or any other members of Hollow Kin. He was not to set foot near Hollowspire Church nor Martin Howler's place. Sergeant Jennings was forwarding Tim's file to the CPS – the next stop for him was court.

"Hocking," Rowan said. "Have we heard back on the blood Sandra Mead discovered on Martin's boat?"

"Not that I'm aware, sir."

"Go check on it," Rowan said, rubbing his chin absentmindedly as he scanned over the photos of the case thus far: bloody jacket, pliers, Martin's body, the carving in his chest, the symbols, the Pier Road footage, Martin's house. Sometimes, when dreaming at night, he would see a bizarre amalgamation of photos from different cases. The nightmare was always the same: he stood there, with the evidence in front of him, and no idea how to proceed.

It wasn't long until DS Hocking was at his side saying, "Sir, just spoke to the lab. The blood on the boat isn't Martin's. They're making comparisons now. Tomorrow will be the earliest we know."

"Thank you," he said exhaling heavily.

Rowan had been in his office for some time reviewing his own notes from the interviews he'd had on the island, mentally refreshing himself, trying to build connections where he might have previously missed them, when Danny Everett came in.

"Sir, I've spoken to Roger."

"Anything?"

"Nothing new as such. Just what he said before about the cameras being shut down at midnight – and being back on at six. That it happened both nights: when Martin's boat was damaged and when Martin was murdered."

"Okay. Worth a shot."

"Yes," PC Everett said. "Sorry wasn't much else. But he did say as I was leaving, he should've got Jax to look at the alarm and CCTV system as he's a bit of a computer whizz. Roger didn't say that before."

"Thanks, Danny," Rowan said, making a note in his book. "Get yourself home. Get some rest – I've a feeling the next couple of days are going to be full-on."

Nathan Waters

Nathan felt like a fungus. One trapped in a jar.

He had no idea what the time was. There was no window, and he'd lost all track of where he was in the cottage station. His anchor, the sea – usually heard so clearly, so beautifully from his lighthouse – was silent. It wasn't cold on Wraith's Hollow, but he shivered; and there was a metallic smell in the air that he couldn't get used to.

What the hell was going to happen? How did he even end up here?

Why did he do it? Didn't he want it just as much as the others? At times, arguably more so. Ellie was in his mind, but she slipped away as he heard the door outside of his holding cell open. Footsteps approached. As Nathan got up from the bench, he saw Rowan's face through the small window. The sound of his cell door unlocking and the mechanism clunking followed.

"Thank you, Frank," Rowan said. "Nathan, take a seat." Nathan obeyed. "I wanted to call in before I left the station and wandered home."

Left the station! Wandered home!

"Long evening?" DI Black asked.

Answer nothing, say nothing unless I'm there – that's what Wright had said to him. "I don't know what I'm doing here."

"You do. You're here for your part in Martin's murder. Remember?"

"Not literally. I just meant, I don't know *why* I'm here. I'm trying to piece it together."

"Meaning?"

"I don't know. I'm so confused."

"Say what you're thinking."

"If I, if I – look, I want to know, if I give you names, will it help me?"

Rowan shook his head. "That's not how it's going to work for you, Nathan. I don't need to bargain with you. You see, I'm convinced we've enough evidence to send you down for a very long time. CPS will see it that way too . . . but," Rowan let that one word linger.

"But what? But what?" Nathan pleaded.

"But if you cooperate, I'll make sure the CPS knows. You'll need to discuss this with your solicitor, but if you plead guilty early, you could get a reduction in your sentence. Something to think about," Rowan said, casually leaning against the door frame.

Nathan thought about it. It would be so easy to tell him, just let the names slip out. How would they sound? How would he sound saying them? Would it be so hideous? Would he despise himself even more?

"Rowan," he said. "Rowan," but he couldn't say any more.

Rowan Black

Rowan's phone rang, waking him. It was Sergeant Jennings. "Frank, everything okay?"

"Sir, Nathan's cracked. He's told us who else is involved."

Rowan sat up in bed as Jennings relayed the information. "Shit. I'm on my way."

*

Wednesday morning. The station buzzed. Rowan Black felt it as he headed into the incident room. PC Everett had arrived just before him and was conferring with a pair of mainland officers. More would be along presently. DC Mann and DS Hocking were en route. By the time Jennings had finished telling Rowan that it was on a welfare check that Nathan suddenly opened up, Mann and Hocking were stepping through the door.

"One night and he's choked," Jennings had said.

"He's got plenty more nights where he's going," Rowan replied.

Before briefing his team, Rowan interviewed Nathan. He not only wanted to hear Nathan's reasons for his part in Martin's murder, but he also wanted to hear him say those names; look into his eyes. You could learn a lot from someone's eyes when they spoke. More than they realised.

"Jennings has arranged for two more duty solicitors. They're on their way. I don't want our suspects conferring. Now, I want two teams. Two coordinated arrests. Hocking, you'll lead Team A, you're taking Sophie Marlow. I'll lead Team B; we're going after Jasper Flint. Jax is a potential flight risk. He's got access to boats, and he knows the water. Sophie's likely at home; she works from there. We'll start there. Jax, on the other hand, could be anywhere: Silver Cove Marina repairing boats, Havenmoore Port on his own boat, the *Hollow Rose*, or at home. I want teams positioned at all those locations. Let's just hope he's not out at sea. We move simultaneously at fourteen-hundred. That will give us time to finalise warrants and get the remaining forensics back. On arrest, seize phones and laptops immediately. No chances for them to wipe anything. According to Roger Stone, Jax is a bit of a computer whizz, so we need to stay sharp."

"Shall we get a couple of plainclothes officers on Jax – keep eyes on him in case he moves?" DC Mann put forward.

"Good call. We'll get them out straight away. I want constant updates from them. This is a non-firearms operation – I don't suspect them of possessing weapons – but stay sharp and focused. Post-arrest, in custody, keep them separate. Sophie will be interviewed first."

Chapter Ten

Two O'clock

DS Hocking

DS Hocking led a team of four up to Sophie's cottage. He instructed the two mainland officers to secure the back. He and PC Everett knocked the front door.

"I can't believe something like this is happening," Everett said.

DS Hocking told him to be quiet – he was listening for Sophie inside. There wasn't an answer, so he knocked louder.

PC Everett slipped around the side to a window. "She's in. Headphones on. She's painting."

"Bang the window," DS Hocking told him. "Make sure she hears it."

"Open the door, Sophie," Everett shouted.

There was movement inside. Sophie's muffled voice: "Danny, what the hell!"

She swung the door open.

Before she had the chance to say anything more DS Hocking said: "Sophie Marlow, I'm arresting you on suspicion of the murder of Martin Howler. You do not have to say anything, but it may harm your defence if you do not mention when questioned something which you later rely on in court. Anything you do say may be given in evidence."

She didn't speak. She didn't look surprised. But the colour drained from her face, and there was an acceptance in her eyes.

Rowan Black

Rowan Black shoved his phone in his pocket. They had no idea where Jax was. Reg Harris had seen Jax out on the water that morning when he was going back and forth to the mainland. But on his last journey back, he hadn't seen him – Reg assumed he'd gone to drop his catch at Moira's.

But Jax wasn't at Moira's – and she didn't plan on seeing him that day. He wasn't at Havenmoore Port either – where Rowan now stood – and he wasn't at home. Silver Cove Marina was locked up. Rowan and his team had searched the port, but it was obvious Jax wasn't there.

He called DCI Hargrave. "I need more uniforms out here. Jax's disappeared. We need to search the whole island . . . No, I don't know how he knew. But he knew."

*

Rowan instructed Sergeant Jennings and DC Mann to coordinate the search for Jax. Jennings knew the island better than anyone: the pathways, the beaches, the forest, the cliffs – he'd been walking around them for years. If anyone was going to find him, it would be Jennings. Drones and more officers from the mainland would be with them by four o'clock.

The interview began at three thirty-seven. Sophie Marlow and her solicitor – Rose Woods – sat opposite Rowan and DS Hocking. Rowan delivered the caution, then opened the file.

"Now, Miss Marlow, before we begin," Rowan started. "Is there anything from our last interview on Saturday that you wish to reconsider: anything you want to change or add?"

"Like what?" Sophie said.

"You stated the reason you phoned Martin on the night of his murder was to tell him that you didn't want him to build you an art studio – you didn't want him in your life anymore. This call was at nine twenty-three p.m., and it lasted for five minutes. Is this still correct?"

"Yes."

"Thank you. Please confirm if that was the only communication you had with Martin that night."

"It was."

"You didn't see him?" Rowan asked.

"No."

"Have you ever been on Martin Howler's boat?" DS Hocking asked.

"Not for a long time. I can't remember when the last time was."

"You need to take a moment, Miss Marlow. Think about what DS Hocking's just asked you."

"My client's already answered your question," Rose Woods said.

"Miss Marlow?" Rowan prompted.

"Not for a long time. I can't remember when I last went on his boat."

"According to Nathan Waters' account, you were on his boat right up until Martin was murdered. Why would he tell us that?"

"No comment," Sophie Marlow said.

Rowan knew this was coming, he knew too that DS Hocking would've been expecting it. He pressed on. "Nathan also said that you were the one who gave Martin the psychoactive compound he created." Rowan flicked through some notes. "You told Nathan, when he visited you at home on Thursday afternoon, just hours after Martin was found dead, that once you slipped the drug in Martin's drink, he went nuts. Within twenty minutes, he was completely nuts. You described how Martin was hallucinating and how you were so scared: you thought he was going to kill you. Please confirm or deny that you said this to Nathan."

"No comment."

"Miss Marlow, you can play the no comment card all you like. But silence is not always the best option," DS Hocking said. "This is your chance to tell us what you know."

Rowan leant forward, ignoring the solicitor entirely. "You see, Sophie, you've told us already that you had no contact with Martin that night other than when you called to tell him you didn't want him in your life any longer. You know this is a lie. I know it's a lie–"

"My client has already given you an account of the events around this phone call."

"DS Hocking knows you're lying. Would you like to know how we know?"

Sophie was silent.

"Because we found your DNA, your blood, on Martin's boat."

"No comment."

"There was also evidence of tampering," Hocking added. "Someone tried to clean up the blood – but they missed some."

"And you already know that we know who that is, don't you, Sophie?" Rowan said.

"No comment." She folded her arms. Some vague attempt, Rowan thought, to protect herself from their questioning.

"Nathan Waters. He saw the boat early Thursday morning up on the rocks, checked it out because, as he says, it wasn't part of the plan. You were supposed to go back to Martin's house. And when Nathan climbed aboard, checking for Martin's dead body, he saw your blood." Rowan folded his arms. "Nathan confirmed that you cut your leg when Martin crashed the boat. You showed him, didn't you?"

Sophie glanced at Woods. Her jaw tensed. She took in a breath.

"Please confirm or deny whether you showed Nathan your injured leg," DS Hocking said.

"I didn't. It wasn't. No comment."

"Sophie," Rowan spoke softly. "We need to see your injured leg . . . Your left shin, I believe."

"You're not under any obligation to show them," Woods said.

"If you refuse, it will be noted," Hocking said.

"If you provide us with your consent, two female officers would accompany you. This is your chance to discredit Nathan's account of your actions. Your refusal will do you no favours in the long run. I'll just seek authorisation under PACE, and we'll get to it soon enough."

Sophie, not looking at Woods, pulled up the left leg of her jeans, revealing the cut across her shin.

Jasper Flint

Jax was certain he could hear them looking for him – but it was just the ocean carrying ghostly voices. The waves crashed harder and harder as time slipped on . . . slipping away from him.

The sea air was salty, it was damp. Once it had been the only tonic strong enough to revitalise him; but now, as he paused, dragging a hand through his hair, knees burning, it suffocated him.

He was alone, the light receded the further he crawled, but Martin's face, his bloody face never left him.

Sophie Marlow

It was the wrong thing. It was the wrong thing to do. But she couldn't *undo* it. They were all looking at her leg – it felt like an eternity. She could feel the tension in her ankle, spreading into her knee, climbing her back, burning behind her eyes, and tightening across her brow.

"Thank you, Miss Marlow. We'll need to have that documented and photographed," Rowan said, noting the injury in his book.

"Before we get your account of your involvement–"

Woods interrupted DS Hocking. "My client is under no obligation to offer you any information. It is for you to prove her involvement."

Hocking continued: "In his statement, Nathan Waters says you contacted Jasper Flint when you were out with Martin – you needed to change the plan. Is that true?"

Sophie was so angry. She felt stupid. Why did she do it? Why did she let Jax talk her into it . . . Yes! It was Jax! "Jax got me to do this. It's his fault!"

Having made a brief note, Rowan said: "Miss Marlow. That kind of deflection may work in your head, but it won't here. Not when we have Martin dead. And your blood on his boat."

"I didn't know it would go that far – that Jax would kill him!" Sophie slammed the table.

"You're saying you were coerced – that Jasper Flint made you take part in killing Martin?"

"Yes! You don't know him like I do. He's nasty, Rowan. Please, you've got to believe me!"

"If you were so frightened, why did you tell Nathan he was either part of the solution or part of the problem?" Rowan said. "That doesn't sound like someone who felt threatened. It sounds like someone making a threat – unless, of course, you meant something different?"

"I didn't say that. It's my word against Nathan's."

"Inspector Black, with respect, that is circumstantial at best, and open to interpretation. It's not fact," Woods intervened.

"I'll move on," Rowan said. "You admit you played a part in Martin's murder?"

Sophie didn't know what to do; she just nodded.

"Please answer yes or no," DS Hocking said.

"Yes."

"If you're alleging coercion, that's a serious claim. You need to be clear about what Jasper Flint did to you," Rowan said. Then: "We have your phone, Miss Marlow. Soon forensics will analyse your messages, emails, call history – and when we have that, it will be obvious, not just to us, but to the court, whether Jasper Flint coerced you or whether you acted of your own accord." Rowan flicked through the file. "We also have evidence that Jax hacked the security system at Silver Cove Marina. He did that to protect you, didn't he – keep you off camera when you went to Martin's boat?"

The feeling of loss crashing down upon her took her back to how she felt when Cynthia died. Why did she murder Martin? It was all so confusing. She wanted to shout at Rowan for what happened to Cynthia, but she had no fight left. And after all it wasn't Rowan who'd kept hurting them. It was Martin who'd run roughshod all over their lives – had done for years: trampling over the little peace they had.

She hated him. The world allowed him to live when her beautiful sister was taken.

Sophie hated Martin. Nathan hated him. Jax hated him. They each had their view of the island without Martin Howler around; when combined, their vision grew into some beautiful but, she could see now, seriously flawed idea of Wraith's Hollow. It was never going to be a utopia without him around. Cynthia was still dead. And with powerful but damning and painful clarity, Sophie realised she'd made the biggest mistake of her life.

"I thought without him around, I would feel better."

"By him, you mean Martin Howler," DS Hocking clarified.

"Yes."

"How could it, Sophie? Cynthia's gone. What happened was tragic. But she's never coming back," Rowan said.

"I truly hated Martin. But I'm sorry for what's happened. I don't know what we've done," she said with a slow, futile sigh. "It was me who gave Jax the symbols to put on Martin's body."

"Why?" DS Hocking asked.

"To make it look like Hollow Kin were responsible."

"You're involved with them, aren't you?" Rowan Black asked.

"Rowan, you have to be around here."

"Well. Not for much longer – Hollow Kin won't even be a thing soon."

"You don't know Wraith's Hollow anymore. You really are an outsider," Sophie said.

Sergeant Jennings

Although Jax thrust the knife into his left side in one fast, calculated movement, Jennings felt the blade go in by stages. With each stage, the pain increased exponentially. First, the outer skin tearing; then the knife grinding against bone; then the puncturing of an organ.

Everything preceding this moment – the chase from the cave; the argument on Tide Fall Beach; Jax's confession that he beat Martin to death, disabled the alarm system at Silver Cove Marina, planted the jacket and pliers; their fight; all of it slipped away from Jennings as the intensity of his injury peaked. Even the distant voices behind him – was it Danny? Was it Rowan? – drifted into silence.

On his back, unable to lift his head, he knew he was bleeding out on the sand.

It was Danny's voice he heard next – it flew past him. Around Jennings was a medley of movement and shouting. Nothing made sense until:

"Frank! It's me, Frank. Rowan. We've got him. Got Jax."

Jennings opened his eyes: he took in Rowan's blurry outline. "It was him," Jennings managed with an intensity he'd dragged up from the bottom of his soul.

"You're going to be okay. Ambulance is on its way. Helicopter."

Jennings gently swayed his head. No – he tried but it didn't come out. The word died in his throat.

"Hang in there, Frank. I've got you," Rowan said. Jennings watched Rowan shouting at Danny, shouting at other officers. Jennings couldn't see who, but he was in safe hands. Rowan was a good police officer. The thought that he'd known Rowan since he was a young lad nearly carried him into the darkness.

But this wasn't his last thought. As the noise faded, as the pressure of Rowan's hands on his wound eased, as the voices no longer registered, as the blue sky was lost to darkness, the last image that Jennings saw was of his daughter: Penny.

She was as beautiful now as the day she was born.

Rowan Black

Three days had passed since Jennings' death. Rowan stood at the back of Reg Harris' boat with the sea breeze gently brushing his face, travelling towards the mainland. His eyes were on Wraith's Hollow and, even as it diminished into the distance, its impact on him grew.

The sea was perfectly smooth, but he gripped the railing tightly as the mystery of the letter entered his mind. Rowan still didn't know why Martin had sent it to him. It wasn't in Martin's character to be spooked by anything or anyone, but he had been. Who was it? Tim? Hollow Kin? Sophie? Nathan? Jax?

He sighed, easing his grip on the railing. Not everything in a murder case was always neatly solved, and it would play on Rowan's mind for some time: beyond Frank's funeral; beyond Tim's sentencing for burglary and his joint assault on Ellie Crick with Mrs. Appleby; beyond the trials of Nathan, Sophie, and Jax for Martin Howler's murder; beyond Jax's trial for killing Frank Jennings.

Wraith's Hollow. A case unlike any other. But the same dark emotions were present: revenge, love, anger, jealousy – that's what people killed for. He turned his back on the island and walked to the bow. He thought of Frank. Thought, too, about reporting him – even just to safeguard himself if Tim ever raised it again.

To hell with it. He'd cross that bridge if it came to it.

The sea ahead was as still as it was blue. It was peaceful. Quiet. Welcoming. He was going to make the most of it, let the faces of the guilty sink beneath the surface. Rowan Black breathed in deeply. Before he could let out that relaxing, restful breath, his phone rang.

It was DCI Hargrave.

"I'm on my way."

Thank you for reading Wraith's Hollow.

Printed in Dunstable, United Kingdom

79466097R00211